THOR'S SERPENTS

THE BLACKWELL PAGES

THE BLACKWELL PAGES
BOOK 3

K. L. ARMSTRONG
MELISSA MARR

Ⓛ Ⓑ
Little, Brown and Company
New York Boston

Copyright © 2015 by K.L.A. Fricke Inc. and Melissa Marr
Interior illustrations copyright © 2015 by Vivienne To
Shield and logo by Eamon O'Donoghue based on the work of Lisseth Kay

Little, Brown and Company

Hachette Book Group
1290 Avenue of the Americas, New York, NY 10104
Visit us at lb-kids.com

Little, Brown and Company is a division of Hachette Book Group, Inc.
The Little, Brown name and logo are trademarks of Hachette Book Group, Inc.

The publisher is not responsible for websites (or their content)
that are not owned by the publisher.

First Paperback Edition: June 2016
First published in hardcover in May 2015 by Little, Brown and Company

The Library of Congress has cataloged the hardcover edition as follows:

Armstrong, Kelley.
  Thor's serpents / K. L. Armstrong ; M. A. Marr.—First edition.
    pages cm.—(The Blackwell pages ; book 3)
    Summary: "As Ragnarok—the apocalypse—approaches, the thirteen-year-old descendants of the gods realize they can't take every step of their journey together, as Matt must fight the Midgard Serpent alone, and Fen and Laurie are pulled in different directions"—Provided by publisher.
    ISBN 978-0-316-20495-8 (hardcover)—ISBN 978-0-316-33698-7 (ebook)—
ISBN 978-0-316-33700-7 (ebook library edition)   [1. Adventure and adventurers—
Fiction. 2. Supernatural—Fiction. 3. Shapeshifting—Fiction. 4. Gods—Fiction.
5. Monsters—Fiction. 6. Mythology, Norse—Fiction.] I. Marr, Melissa. II. Title.
    PZ7.A76638Tho 2015
    [Fic]—dc23

                                                                            2014031317

Paperback ISBN 978-0-316-20493-4

10 9 8 7 6 5

LSC-C

Printed in the United States of America

MM: To Dylan and Asia Alsgaard, since I learned
Norse myth to be better at being *your* mother,
the series is obviously for you.

KA: For my sons, Alex and Marcus, this trilogy
was for you. And for my nephew, Marshall,
I promise they don't all die in the end.

ONE

MATT

"WOLVES AT THE DOOR"

It was hard for Matt to pretend he didn't know two wolves had followed them from the campsite. Reyna seemed to have no such problem. Maybe she thought he was imagining the Raider Scouts. More likely she just wasn't about to let something as inconsequential as imminent death distract her from detailing every mistake he'd made yesterday, fighting the Viking zombie warriors known as the draugr.

"And then, when you made it to the king's throne, I noted a few tactical errors."

"I'm sure you did."

"I'm just trying to help you improve. You do want to

improve, don't you?" She smiled when she said it, not bothering to pretend she didn't enjoy needling him.

"I have a suggestion for the next battle," he said. "You could join me on the front lines."

"I'm the descendant of Freya. Unlike Thor's champion, I'm not supposed to be on the front line." She moved aside a branch. "However, I could be persuaded to join you, if I had a proper weapon. I'd like a sword. The draugr king's looked good."

He shook his head and cast a sidelong glance into the surrounding forest, trying to catch a glimpse of the wolves. After the draugr fight, where Matt had recovered Mjölnir—Thor's legendary hammer—he'd retreated to the forest with the other descendants of the North: Reyna and her twin brother, Ray, along with Laurie, Fen, Baldwin, and Owen. There, they planned to regroup before their next mission, but after the adrenaline-pumping fight, no one really wanted to rest. Fen had wandered off first. Matt had gone next, with Reyna following him.

Matt hadn't planned to walk far, but after about twenty paces, he'd realized two of the Raider Scouts—*wulfenkind*—were following them, so he was leading them away from the others.

"We could take them hostage," Reyna said. "Question them."

He mouthed, *They're wolves*, and she shrugged, as if to say

So? While he'd agree it would be great to question Raiders, he wasn't sure he should risk it when they had fangs and claws. Also...

"Questioning means getting them talking," he said. "That could be tough if they're in wolf form."

"Oh, I could make them talk."

He shook his head. He was getting used to Reyna. She wasn't what he'd expected—in a lot of ways. He'd figured the descendant of Freya would be, well, more...blond. Reyna's hair *was* blond, but she'd just dyed it black. When he'd first met her, she had her nails colored black, too, and had worn makeup in the same harsh shade. By now the makeup was gone, the nail polish was chipping off, and she'd traded in her black clothes for faded jeans and a T-shirt advertising some band he'd never heard of.

The wolves seemed content to follow, but Matt knew better. He might not be much of a football player—boxing and wrestling were more his thing—but a guy couldn't grow up in Blackwell without playing the game. These two were flanking him. Waiting for him to fumble the ball, so they could swoop in.

The question was: what was the ball? He had his shield, which he'd taken back from the Raiders. He had his amulet, too, but its "Hammer power" only worked for a descendant of Thor. They could take the amulet, but it wasn't unique and he could easily get another. The bigger prize, of course, was

Mjölnir, but even the draugr king had barely been able to lift that.

The *wulfenkind* might want Reyna. If that was the case, though, he'd be tempted to hand her over because they'd discover their mistake soon enough—she'd probably drag them back, slung over her shoulder like a brace of wild turkeys.

Taking Matt out of the game would be more useful, since Freya didn't play a major role at Ragnarök, the Norse apocalypse. But while the Raiders might have the advantage of wolf forms, Reyna had magic and he had both Mjölnir and his amulet's power. So how did they expect to capture—?

Matt stopped short. Reyna kept going, still talking, for a few feet before she realized he wasn't beside her. She stopped and mouthed, *What's wrong?*

"I just remembered there's a stream with a waterfall. I wanted to take a closer look. I think it's over here...."

He began walking left. Reyna apparently trusted he didn't really want to check out a waterfall and fell in step beside him. Ahead, he could make out the wolves' brown fur through the bushes. They regrouped, ready to block his path.

"They were herding us," Reyna whispered.

He nodded. The Raiders must be camped along the path they'd been walking. As long as he and Reyna had kept going that way, the wolves had been happy to follow in the shadows. Now that Matt veered off the route, they'd strike and drive them to their camp.

"Showtime?" Reyna asked. When he hesitated, she whispered, "Don't worry. I'll help you."

"That's not—" He caught her teasing grin and shook his head. "I'm not sure it's safe."

"It never is. So...?"

As Thor's champion, Matt was the group leader, which was way more responsibility than he liked. It also meant he couldn't afford unnecessary risks. But his only alternative was to lead them back to the others, which he'd never do.

They *could* use a hostage....

"Okay," he said. "Follow my lead."

"Yes, sir."

Onward it was, then. Play dumb and wait for the attack.

"If you want a logistical problem to solve," he said to Reyna, "figure out how I'm supposed to carry this hammer around."

"That's boring. I like battle strategy better."

"All the strategy in the world won't help if I strain my wrist carrying this thing."

"Whine, whine. You've got a magical hammer, a magical necklace, a magical shield, magical battle-goats...and now you want a magical hammer holder, too? You're so spoiled. You know what—"

She swung around midsentence, her hands going out, lips moving in a spell.

Matt lunged at the charging wolf. Reyna hit it with a jet of fog, which startled the first wolf, and it fell back, leaving Matt with the second, still barreling toward him.

Matt swung Mjölnir. Then he realized he was aiming a solid metal hammer at a kid's head. Yes, it was a Raider, but that didn't change the fact this "wolf" wasn't a draugr or a troll or any other kind of Norse monster. One blow to the skull with Mjölnir, and this kid-in-wolf's-clothing would be dead.

Matt couldn't stop the swing. The momentum was too much. All he could do was divert the strike. It still hit the wolf in the front leg, and there was a sickening crack as the bone broke.

The wolf yowled in agony and collapsed onto its side. Matt wheeled on the other one, now recovered from the surprise of the fog blast and racing toward him. He quickly switched Mjölnir to his left hand, but that threw his balance off too much for a good punch. He launched his other Hammer instead—the invisible blow from his amulet.

There was a flash of light and a boom, announcing the invisible punch, but it came too late for the wolf to veer off course. The Hammer blow knocked the beast backward into a tree. Matt ran to tackle it, but Reyna was closer and leaped in first. She knocked the wolf down and then pinned it in a choke hold.

"Umm..." Matt began.

"Did I mention I know self-defense? Aikido and karate. When your dad owns a casino, you need to know how to take care of yourself. You aren't the only fighter in this little god-gang, Matt."

"Okay, but what I was going to say is that you're using a hold meant for a person. That's not a—"

The wolf bucked and slipped right out of her grasp. The beast twisted around, snapping. Matt managed to yank her away in time. Then he jumped the wolf . . . as the one behind them began yowling in fresh pain.

No, not yowling. It was howling.

Wolf. Howl. That was how they communicated with pack members. . . .

Matt leaped up, cursing. Reyna looked as shocked at the oath as if he'd changed into a wolf himself. He tore past her, saying "Use the fog. Confuse the other one" as he lunged for the wounded wolf. He grabbed it by the muzzle, managing to avoid inch-long fangs. He snapped the beast's jaws shut and cut off its howl midnote.

"It's calling the others," Reyna said. "I'm sorry."

Reyna cast her fog spell. When the wolf ran through it, she landed a surprisingly accurate kick to the underside of its jaw. It fell back with a yelp. Then, lost in the fog, the beast started to howl. And in the distance, other wolves replied, their howls growing closer until Matt could hear the pounding of paws.

"We need to go," he said quickly. "We can't fight them all—"

Reyna delivered one more kick to the second wolf while Matt released the injured one. They started to run. Behind them, he caught the sound of voices. Human voices. That wasn't unusual—not all Raiders changed to wolves for a fight. But what slowed Matt was one of the voices. The loudest of them. Shouting. He couldn't make out the words, but they sounded angry.

He knew that voice. Knew it in a heartbeat.

He's been captured. He's in trouble. I need to help him.

Matt turned back. The fog had cleared, and he could see a few wolves in the distance. Behind them were two figures. Hattie, one of the leaders of this pack of Raiders. And standing beside her, shouting orders at the wolves?

Fen.

TWO

FEN

"LEADING THE ENEMY"

Fen lost his footing as he saw Thorsen stare at him in shock. Fen couldn't tell Matt that he'd fought Skull and won control of the very pack of Raiders that he and the descendants of the North had been fighting only yesterday. Fen wanted to tell Matt what had happened, to explain that he was trapped, that he wanted to walk away from the Raiders and rejoin Laurie and Matt. Unfortunately, what he *wanted* didn't matter anymore. Fen was bound by magic far older than any of them. He had to stay with his pack; they were as much a part of him as his lungs now.

Even more powerful than the need to stay with them was the absolute compulsion to do right by them. If he had the ability to make the pack of *wulfenkind* join the side he wanted to be on, his new position wouldn't be all bad, but he had to do what was in the pack's "best interest." Helping Matt stop Ragnarök and save the world would endanger all of the *wulfenkind* because Matt's side—which included Fen's cousin and friends—wasn't likely to win. Ragnarök was fated. Even the death of the gods hadn't stopped the prophesized battle from coming. The Raiders believed that the end of the world was better for them, and that the new world order would give them freedom and security. Since Fen was bound by magic to do what was best for his pack, Fen was stuck on the wrong side of the coming fight. He was Matt's enemy now.

Worse yet, he was his cousin Laurie's enemy.

Fen muttered a word he wouldn't have said around Laurie. He wasn't a big thinker, so figuring out how to fix the mess he was in seemed impossible. Laurie was the one who thought things out. Laurie was the one with plans. He was the one who threw himself into danger to keep her safe.

But Laurie was impossibly out of reach.

Fen's only comfort was that she wasn't alongside Matt and Reyna as they tried to vanish into the woods. Laurie wasn't there to see that Fen was leading the enemy. *Yet.* He snarled another word, and the girl who was now at his side laughed.

"Feeling guilty?" Hattie asked. "That will pass, you know. We will win the great battle, and you'll be glad you're with us."

"Shut it, Hattie," Fen said. He glared at her, and she ducked her head obediently instead of punching him. It was an odd feeling. Hattie was a wolf like him, second in command of this small group of Raiders until this morning. He'd spent more than a few hours nursing bruises he got when she enforced the former pack alpha's rules. Hattie was scarier than most boys he knew, and that was when she was being nice.

She stepped closer. "We can take them. Thorsen and the witch are alone."

"No."

"They're not your friends anymore. They're *our* enemies," she pointed out.

"I said no," he repeated.

"It's a great chance...or we can follow them to camp," she continued. She was supposed to offer him ideas. Once Skull, the pack's former leader, recovered from the fight, that would be his role, but right now, Hattie was his advisor, and she was doing her job.

The small group of Raiders who had come with him to collect the scouting party were whooping and hollering as if they had achieved something remarkable by finding Thorsen. They hadn't. All they'd done was reveal that Fen was with the Raiders—and earn one of the Raiders a broken leg.

"Pull back!" Fen ordered.

He stopped walking, and the three Raiders with him—all in human form—stopped, too. The two kids who were wolves came to stand in front of him.

"What are you thinking yelling like that? Head back to camp before you get us all captured!"

"They're running away. We could go to their camp and capture them all," Hattie argued.

"Really? There are a lot of Berserkers and more gods' representatives in that camp. There are *six* of us and one's injured already." He looked at them, meeting wolf and human eyes, before asking, "Who do you think would win that fight?"

All the Raiders, both humans and wolves, looked down. For a flicker of a moment, Fen wished he could tell the Raiders to pursue Thorsen and Reyna; then Fen could let them know why he was gone, why he was on the enemy's side, and maybe they'd have a plan to get him out of this mess. Unfortunately, as much as that was what *Fen the person* wanted, it wouldn't be in the best interests of the pack—and that was what Fen the Alpha had to do. He *had to* protect the pack by leading them on a path that would be best for them, not best for him.

The forest around them was silent except for the sounds of birds and small animals. There were no signs yet that the Berserkers or anyone else was coming after the Raiders. That didn't make Fen relax: he'd been with the heroes long enough to know that they could move silently. Thorsen could have already retrieved the others. They could be ready to attack at any moment.

"Move it," Fen snarled at the Raiders. "And you two"—he pointed at two of the Raiders whose names he didn't know—"carry him. He can't hop all the way back to camp on a busted leg." He gestured at Hattie. "You lead. I'll take the back."

In some ways, it was just like being with Matt and Laurie: someone had to take first and last position, the vulnerable needed help, and danger was everywhere. The difference was that the danger was now *because* of his friends instead of to them, and Fen had to protect those who were in his pack instead of protecting his friends. Fen huffed in frustration, but he kept his words to himself.

After the other Raiders started toward camp, Fen shot one last look in the direction that would lead to his cousin. As he walked away from the heroes' camp, he tried not to think about the look of betrayal he saw on Matt's face. He and Matt hadn't always been close, but going to Hel, escaping a river of dead people, and fighting monsters created a sort of friendship. Now they'd all hate Fen. He couldn't explain, and they'd all remember his earlier mistakes: keeping his ties to the Raiders a secret *and* stealing the shield *and* lying about it.

They'll probably believe I was a traitor all along.

Fen really didn't want the world to end, but he wasn't sure if Matt and the others would believe that now. They'd already discovered that some of the myths seemed impossible to avoid. In the myths, Loki led the enemy. He was the one who freed monsters and brought them into battle against the gods. Since this whole crazy descendants-of-dead-gods business had started, Fen had feared turning evil because he was the representative of Loki.

When he'd found out that Laurie was the god's champion instead of him, Fen had been relieved and disappointed. He figured he would go into the upcoming battle to help the *real* Loki's champion and keep Thor's champion safer. He'd thought he would fight at Laurie's and Matt's side, but now...now he was confused.

Loki's champion was fighting on the side of good, where Fen wanted to be, and he was tricked and trapped on the other side. Was it because the myths said Loki led the monsters and Loki's *real* representative wasn't going to do that? Were there two champions, one for each side? Or was Fen just supremely unlucky? Trying to figure out the line between what could and couldn't be changed from the old myths was the sort of thing that he counted on Laurie and Matt to explain.

He led the Raiders to their camp, still thinking about everything that had changed literally overnight and how much he'd lost as a result.

"He was right there," one of the Raiders said as he transformed into human shape. "We had a chance, and the boss said—"

"Exactly. I'm the boss now," Fen growled at the boy. "And any advantage we had to my being here was lost when they saw me."

"You're our alpha, but you're not the big boss," a girl interjected in a strong voice.

Fen took a calming breath. "Right. Mayor Thorsen gives us orders. A *Thorsen* is telling Brekkes what to do, and no one has an issue with that?"

"You didn't have a problem with obeying a Thorsen until right now." Hattie folded her arms and glared at him.

"Yeah, well, *that* Thorsen wasn't suggesting that we end the world, so I think my choice made a bit more sense. Matt wants to do the right thing, to save the world, and his grandfather...." Fen tried to sound calm, but he was failing. "Look, I don't see how ending the world is such a great idea."

"And I don't see why you're even here," Hattie muttered.

"I'd be happy to go," Fen snapped. "It's not my choice to be here."

Hattie glared at him, but unlike in the past, today Fen met her angry eyes and stared until she looked down. He might be new to the alpha position, but he'd spent his whole life around wolves. He wasn't going to let her challenge him and get away with it. If he did, the rest would follow, and then he'd have an even worse time of it.

The other Raiders who had been out in the forest shuffled their feet and waited. He could sense their feelings as deeply as his own—they felt his anger radiating out at them, and they weren't sure what to do about it. It was confusing for them—and him.

He closed his eyes for a moment to try to separate his feelings from theirs. He didn't want his pack to be unhappy. That was instinct. He also didn't want to fight his friends or lead his pack against his friends. No matter who won in any fight between the two sides right now, Fen would be miserable.

"Look. You don't want me here, and I don't want to be here," he started. They all looked back at him then. Their expressions were a mix of confusion, shock, and sadness. It didn't make anything easier. "I like the world. Yeah, it would be fun if there were less rules about running in wolf form, and it would be great to not be constantly worried about Thorsens getting us in trouble for things we do."

They nodded.

"I just don't think the end of the world, millions of people dying, and monsters roaming free is *better* than what we have now." He didn't know what else to say, but he wasn't going to fail at protecting them if he could help it. Instincts made that impossible. Cautiously, he said, "I know that the

Raiders are bonded to working for old man Thorsen, so I'm not going to try to force everyone in *our pack* to break a bond bigger than us."

"So what are you going to do with us?" a Raider named Paul asked.

That was a good question, and if he were someone else—Matt or Laurie—he'd probably know. Fen wasn't like them. He didn't have a clever idea or a stupidly brave plan. All he had was the hope that there was a solution and he'd muddle through until he found it. Maybe it wasn't a great idea to admit that, but he didn't have a better answer yet.

"I don't know. Keep you safe? Try to figure out how to keep you from getting beat up again by Matt and the others?" Fen shrugged. "It hasn't even been a whole day since I got here, so I'm still figuring this out. At least give me a day or two."

He *had* been thinking about it, and he wasn't sure what he was supposed to do with them all. The only thing he was certain of right now was that he was still going to protect his cousin. Fen looked around at the assembled *wulfenkind* and met each one's eyes as he said, "The one thing I *do* know is that if anyone touches my cousin, I'll beat them myself and feed them to the Midgard Serpent. Laurie is a Brekke and not to be touched."

Maybe it was the seriousness in his voice or maybe it was just because he was defending his family, but they all smiled or nodded at him. *Wulfenkind* put family first. He hadn't tried to, but he'd proved that he was one of them after all.

"Break down camp. We're moving out tonight," he ordered, and then he walked away.

He didn't need to watch to know that the *wulfenkind* had started to tear down tents and gather their supplies the moment he turned away. Raider packs were well trained. Everyone knew his or her role, and there was no shirking work. Although he knew that the whole thievery thing that packs lived by wasn't okay, and he didn't like camping enough to want to live the way they did, he could still respect their skills.

While the rest of them were getting ready to leave, Fen walked into the tent where Skull was now recovering. The soft *whump* of the tent flap falling shut seemed ominous. Being closed in with Skull wasn't something that had ever gone well for Fen. He ignored the twinge of fear, reminding himself that things were different now.

"You could have taken more of the pack with you," Skull said.

"Why?" Fen asked, trying not to cringe at the sight of the bruises all over Skull. He didn't like the older boy, never had, never would, but he still felt a flash of guilt at the ugly red and purple marks. He'd done that, beat Skull up. It had been in a fight that Skull started and Fen couldn't escape, but he still felt bad at seeing the proof of his anger.

"If the others were with you, you could all have followed Thorsen to camp," Skull said.

"I already know where the camp is. I was staying there until you forced me into this mess." Fen smothered another ugly word at the realization that his stuff was still at the camp with Laurie and the rest of the descendants of the North. It wasn't like he had a lot of things, but his Aunt Helen—the god who ruled Hel, the land of the dead— had given him a great bag that seemed to offer whatever he needed. Food, clothes, toothbrush: they just magically appeared when he opened the bag. All of the kids who'd been to Hel got one, and his was in camp with them. He hadn't carried it when he'd left them, not expecting that he'd never return.

He shoved that thought away quickly. He'd lost too much. Matt had never been someone he'd even tried to tolerate, but after fighting monsters together, they'd become friends. Baldwin, on the other hand, who was the god Balder's representative, was someone Fen liked from the moment they'd met. The worst, though, was Laurie. She was his best friend, his partner in so many ridiculous adventures, and now she was completely forbidden to him. Instead, Fen was left with the Raiders, none of whom he liked at all, especially the one glaring at him.

"Well, if you knew where their camp was, you should've taken the advantage!" Skull snapped, and then immediately frowned and added, "That's my advice. As your second, that's my advice."

Clearly, Skull wasn't adjusting to being second in command any better than Fen was adjusting to being alpha. They both hated it. They were also both stuck. Fen had to make the best of it.

"We . . . the kids in that camp, I mean, just defeated a host of draugrs," he said. "A small group of Raiders wouldn't be able to take them, especially since Matt has his hammer. He smashed someone's leg with it already. Retreating was the right plan today." Fen flopped to the ground and stared at the bruised boy. "I hate you, by the way. I was happy there. This alpha business is no good."

Skull looked confused. "You're in charge here. How is that bad?"

"Seriously? I'm in charge of a bunch of kids who obey Mayor Thorsen in his crazy quest to end the world."

"But after the great fight, we'll be rulers of a new world." Skull grinned, which looked pretty disturbing with his swollen eye and bloodied lip.

Fen couldn't understand how anyone believed the mayor would treat them fairly. Aside from the centuries of bad blood between Brekkes and Thorsens, there was the fact that he was okay sentencing his own grandson to die. Nothing about the man made Fen think he could be trusted, but

Skull and the others obviously bought all his lies about their role in the future.

That meant that Fen had to be careful in trying to explain things to Skull. What he needed was an ally, someone to help him plan. Even if Skull couldn't see that willingly letting billions of people die was the *wrong* thing to do, he might be able to grasp that trusting the mayor was a bad idea.

"We won't rule anything," Fen said. "We'll be the ones who enforce the laws that old man Thorsen wants us to. It's like in chess where you have a bunch of pieces you throw away to position the king and queen. Those pieces are us."

"Those are called pawns."

"Right, pawns," Fen agreed. He knew that, but he needed Skull to make the connection. He didn't have a proper plan yet, but he was working on the start of one. Step one: get the Raiders with influence on his side. Hattie did whatever Skull said, and the rest of the pack was used to following Skull, so if *Skull* sided with Fen, maybe there was a chance to get out of the hurtle-toward-doom plan the Raiders were on right now.

"Maybe at the end, we'll beat Thorsen, too." Skull folded his arms over his chest and promptly grimaced in pain. He kept them folded as he added, "We're not pawns, man. You just don't understand."

"Right. It's *me* that doesn't understand," Fen muttered. He decided to try to channel Matt Thorsen for a minute. Maybe

Skull would do better with a different tactic. *What would Matt say?* Fen figured it would be something about teamwork, so he suggested, "Just think about it, okay? If we're going to work together, we need to trust each other and stuff."

"I don't trust you, and I know you don't trust me." Skull grinned again. "You'll see, though. It'll be awesome when we win. The sky will go dark, the serpent will rise, the monsters will come from Hel to fight on our side, and the new world will begin. We'll be like kings, protected by the Midgard Serpent."

Fen decided not to point out that Aunt Helen had already thrown her lot in with Laurie, so *her* monsters weren't going to be fighting on the side of the Raiders. He also didn't point out to Skull that Matt already had the hammer and shield he'd need to defeat the serpent. There was no way he could trust that Skull wouldn't find a way to let that information slip to the mayor. Fen might be bound by magic to do the right thing for his pack, but that didn't mean he was under any obligation to help Mayor Thorsen.

"Just think about it," Fen repeated. "Working for the mayor and trying to end the world doesn't seem like it'll go well for *us* ... and since you trapped me here, I need to think about what that means. Dying isn't cool. Trust me on that. I was just in Hel. It's not where we want to be."

Skull didn't say anything, but there was no disguising the curiosity on his face.

"Giants, river of acid, a cave bear…" Fen started, watching Skull's expression of interest grow. "And that was just part of it. Hel is intense."

"Sounds like more fun than here," Skull said.

Fen laughed. "It wasn't boring. Weird, but not boring. Oh, and the rooster. There was this giant chicken that is some sort of omen of the start."

Skull nodded this time. "There are two others yet to crow." He stared up at Fen. "I thought you went to school still. Don't they teach that stuff?"

Fen shrugged. "I don't know. I'm not always big on paying attention to the myth stuff. How was I to know Ragnarök would really happen?"

They were silent for a few moments, and then Skull said, "Maybe the others would like to hear about Hel, too."

There it was: the opening Fen needed. Skull might not trust him, but he was curious. There weren't a lot of libraries that were out in the middle of the forest, and there certainly weren't any televisions or movie theaters. That meant that Raiders told stories around the campfires.

"Sounds good," Fen said. "I'll tell you what happened, and you can tell me the myths."

Skull nodded, and Fen hoped that this was the start of enough trust that they could eventually work together to get out of Mayor Thorsen's pro-Ragnarök plan.

THREE

LAURIE

"SACRIFICING FEN"

L aurie was a mess. The only thing keeping her from falling apart right now was knowing Fen as well as she did. Her cousin was moody, so disappearing wasn't entirely unusual for him. He hadn't done it on their trip so far—other than when Baldwin died. Maybe this was like that, a grief thing. Maybe something had happened during the battle that upset him. Maybe he realized that he *was* upset about not being the champion after all. That didn't mean that he should've stayed away from camp all night. She'd be angry with him when he came back...right after she hugged him.

"You better be safe, Fenrir Brekke!" she muttered as she

stared out into the trees that surrounded the campground where they were staying. "Please," she added in a small, whispered prayer to anyone who might be out there listening or watching.

That was the weird thing about myths being true-ish. Sometimes there *were* people out there paying attention to them. Okay, not people, really. There were Valkyries, warrior women straight out of the myths; her Aunt Helen, a daughter of a long-dead god and ruler of Hel; and probably a bunch of other beings. There were Norns, who were like some sort of Fate beings, and monsters . . . far, far too many monsters were out there and real.

When Laurie heard the wolves' howls in the forest, she'd shivered. She wasn't sure how to tell Fen's howl from others, so she wasn't sure if he was one of the wolves, but she could tell that there were *multiple* wolves. That meant that even if one of the howls was Fen's, the others were either Raiders' or natural wolves'. South Dakota didn't have so many wolves that they were a common sight, but they were wild and free in the state. Some people thought of them as predators that should be killed, but Laurie didn't. She *really* didn't agree with that now that she knew that her father, her cousin, and a lot of her family could transform into wolves. The idea of anyone hunting her family was horrible.

"Where are you, Fen?" she muttered as she hopped to her feet and started pacing.

She was trying to stay inside the campground where they'd settled temporarily. It wasn't a bad spot. The seemingly deserted campground still had running water, but there were no RVs or tents in sight. The only people there were the ones she'd fought alongside.

But right now they weren't at her side. Both Fen and Matt had taken off. According to Ray, Reyna had taken a walk with Matt. No one knew where Fen was. He'd come back to camp with everyone after their fight with the draugrs, but he'd vanished right after that. Laurie was already worried—and that was before she'd heard the howls this morning. Now she was *beyond* worried.

"This is ridiculous. I'm going after them," she announced again.

"I think you should stay here," Owen said, just as he had said several minutes ago when she made the same suggestion.

"Fen's out there! Matt and Reyna were together at least. Fen's by himself, and now there are wolves howling." Laurie grabbed her bow. She didn't need to grab arrows, because the weapon, a gift from Helen, fired ghost arrows. She never needed to find more, never needed to nock an arrow. They simply appeared when she fired.

Baldwin walked over to join her. "I'm coming, too."

Owen pressed his lips together and glanced at the forest. "I don't know the possibilities. Not seeing the future now that I'm involved in it is...confusing. I'm not sure what to do. I don't know if things changed from what was to happen next or—"

"What things?" Laurie asked. "Things with Fen? You *knew* he was in danger and didn't tell me?"

"Some things have to happen," Owen said gently. "There are so many possible ways that the future will unravel. Most of them lead to Ragnarök crushing us, so we have to make sacrifices now to have a better then. Fen has a role to play. We all do."

"Fen isn't the Champion of Loki."

"I know. You are, and heroes must make sacrifices." Owen touched the edge of the eye patch he now wore. He'd lost an eye, as the god Odin had in the myths.

"I'm not sacrificing Fen." She shook her head at Owen. She liked him; sometimes she thought she might *like* like him, but his seeing-the-future thing made her as angry as Fen's and Matt's insistence that she stay out of the battles when possible. As calmly as she could, she said, "Owen, you and the Berserkers can stay here. I'm going to find my cousin." She turned to Baldwin and added, "Let's go."

They hadn't gone far from the camp, just barely walking into the shadows of the trees, when Matt and Reyna came running out of the woods. Laurie raised her bow and looked for the threat, but they didn't seem to have pursuers.

"Camp." Reyna grabbed Laurie's arm. "Come on."

Laurie started to object. "But—"

"We need to get out of here," Matt interrupted.

Laurie froze. There was something in his voice that scared her. It was the sound that she recognized from their battles with trolls, mara, and assorted monsters. She looked to the woods again. There weren't any more wolves howling, and she still saw no threats. Still, a look at Matt erased any doubt she'd had that the earlier howls were from Raiders. There were enemies near camp, enemies who were hidden among the trees somewhere, and her cousin was out there alone.

"Fine, but I need to find Fen first," Laurie objected. "I'm not leaving him to face Raiders alone."

"No. We need to go." Matt motioned Baldwin toward him.

Baldwin obeyed. His movement put the two boys between the woods and the girls.

"Fen is in no danger from the Raiders," Matt added.

"We are, though," Reyna said. "We *really* are."

"Trust me, Laurie," Matt said softly.

She did trust Matt. She had to trust him if they were going to stop Ragnarök. Right now, though, she didn't like the results of trusting Matt. Reluctantly, Laurie turned and walked the short distance back to camp.

As the four of them reentered the campsite, Owen and Ray came toward them instantly. The Berserkers were still being their usual selves, flipping and leaping about like hyper acrobats, but they were all very aware of Owen, too. A word from him was all they needed to switch from bored gymnasts to his attentive soldiers.

Laurie saw Reyna and Ray exchange a look that was similar to ones she and Fen had shared for years; it was a look that said *I'm okay, and I'll tell you everything soon.* It made her miss her cousin even more than she already did.

"Raiders," Matt said, but he looked pained. "We need to move out. They can find our camp."

"How would they find us?" Laurie asked. "Did they follow you?"

Matt glanced at her but didn't reply. Her twinge of worry grew into a full-out panic as she saw a flash of sympathy on his face. Over the past week, they'd fought the dead, trolls, mara—and the nightmares the mara caused—as well as towering, two-headed, flaming Jotunn. They'd faced the police and were captured by a tracker. They'd escaped stampeding buffalo, dead Vikings, and an actual cave bear. The Raiders simply weren't as scary as they had been on the first day the kids had left Blackwell. So why did Matt look so upset *now*? Laurie looked at his hand. Mjölnir was there; he hadn't lost the hammer.

"Laurie, can I talk to you alone for a minute?" Matt finally said.

Briefly, Reyna met Laurie's eyes and then offered a sad smile. That was worse still. Whatever had happened with the Raiders must have had to do with Fen. Matt had said he wasn't in danger from the Raiders, but whatever had happened to Fen was the only reason why Matt would want to talk to her alone while Reyna looked so sympathetic.

Laurie nodded. She couldn't speak. Her throat felt like it was closed off. Visions of Fen being killed—as Baldwin had been—made her shiver. He'd almost been choked by a troll last week. Matt had nearly drowned a few days ago. Saving the world was dangerous.

Owen came to stand beside her and whispered, "I'm sorry."

"Is he . . . dead?" Laurie blurted, her voice cracking as she spoke. "Did they kill Fen or get him arrested or—"

"He's fine," Matt interrupted.

"He's not here, though. If he were *fine*, he'd be here." She glanced past Matt toward the forest. No wolf or boy came running into camp. "He's not hurt, and he's not here, and you look like it's bad news, and—"

"Everyone, give us a minute." Matt walked toward Laurie and motioned to one of the battered picnic tables at the campground.

Laurie felt like she might be sick. He wanted to sit down to talk. That was what grown-ups did when they wanted to tell you something awful. Every time her father was going to leave again, her parents sat her and her little brother down to tell them. It was stupid. Sitting down to talk didn't make the news less horrible.

Matt sat and stared at her, but he didn't say anything. He looked as upset as she felt. It wasn't helping her *at all*.

"Just tell me."

"Fen was with the Raiders," he said.

"So we need to figure out a rescue? Okay. We can do that." She laughed. "You scared me. I thought it was something really b—"

"It *is* bad," Matt interrupted. "He isn't a prisoner."

Laurie shook her head, not understanding. "So he's hiding from them, and we need to get to him before they see—?"

"No." Matt rubbed his face. "Reyna and I were being followed by two of them, and then Fen showed up with more."

"That doesn't make sense. If they saw him, they'd take him prisoner or something."

Matt looked sad as he said, "Fen was the one giving them orders. They were *obeying* Fen, Laurie."

"No." She stood and folded her arms. "Maybe it was one of our cousins you saw. A lot of Brekkes look alike, and—"

"It was Fen." Matt stood and stepped closer to her. "I saw his face, and...it's Fen, Laurie. Fen is working with the Raiders. I can't believe he was a spy all along, so maybe not being the Champ—"

"No. That doesn't make any sense." She shook her head. "He's my cousin. He's *Fen*. I'm going after him. He'll explain."

"You can't." Matt moved in front of her, blocking her path. "The woods are full of Raiders. Fen ordered them to retreat to him, and they *obeyed* him. Maybe we can talk to the Valkyries or something. We can't go after him, though, and"—he took a deep breath—"and you can't go on your own. We have to focus on stopping Ragnarök. Fen's not the Champion of Loki. *You* are, and you need to stay with us."

After a moment, Laurie turned her back on Matt and walked away. There was nothing else she could think of to do. What Matt said didn't make sense, but he wasn't lying. She knew he wouldn't lie to her. She trusted him as much as she trusted Fen.

And that was the problem. She trusted Fen. He was impulsive and did things that were bad ideas on a regular basis, but he was a good person. She knew that as surely as she knew that Matt was determined to stop the world from ending.

Matt had to be wrong somehow. He *had* to be.

She shoved Fen's pack into her own, and as the magical bags did with everything—including larger items like sleeping bags—her bag sucked his inside as if a powerful vacuum were hidden in there. Laurie paused. Fen wouldn't have left this behind if he'd been planning on leaving. It was one more small thing that made her sure Matt was somehow wrong.

She knew Fen better than anyone. This whole business of him being on the dark side was a mistake, and she was going to figure out how and why. The only other possibility was that he'd been on the enemy's side the whole time, been a spy for them, and she couldn't accept that. If he had, he would've told her.

"Sorry," Baldwin murmured as they left the camp.

Laurie didn't reply.

The group walked through the woods in a kind of quiet that reminded her of what it'd felt like when Baldwin had died. Everything felt hopeless right now—at least to her it did. Maybe that wasn't what everyone else was feeling, but Fen was the one person in her life she'd counted on for as long as she could remember. He'd never let her down. He'd never broken his promises to her. It wasn't what Fen did.

"It has to be a mistake," she said after several quiet minutes.

"I saw him, Laurie. He was the one giving them orders," Matt repeated.

"It doesn't make sense, though. He fought against them yesterday. He's been at our side through several fights. Your grandfather almost had him arrested. Why would he be ordering Raiders around? Why would they *listen*?"

"Raiders only listen to their alpha or to someone their alpha tells them to obey," Owen interjected.

She didn't want to hear anything Owen said right now. He hadn't even wanted her to go after Fen. As far as Laurie was concerned, he could keep his mouth closed and stay away from her. Laurie shot him a quick glare and said, "Unless you want to tell me what sacrifice you were talking about earlier, you can keep out of it."

Silently, Owen walked back to keep pace with one of the Berserkers. His two ravens swooped in and landed on his shoulders. They cawed in his ears, probably telling him more things he wouldn't share. She glared at him and his birds.

"Skull," Matt said, interrupting the tense silence. "I didn't see him there. He's their alpha."

"Maybe it's a different group of Raiders," Baldwin offered.

Matt was quiet for a minute, and then he shook his head. "No. That girl was there, and the kid we held prisoner before was there, too. They're usually with Skull."

Tears blurred Laurie's eyes. This was wrong. She wasn't sure how or why, but it didn't make any sense that Fen would turn against her. He didn't want the world to end any more than the rest of them did, and he hated Mayor Thorsen.

"Maybe he didn't like not being the real Champion of Loki," Ray offered.

"Or maybe he was their spy all along," Reyna said.

The glare Laurie turned on her had Ray stepping closer to his twin and Baldwin patting Laurie's shoulder. "You don't know him," Laurie snapped. "He's not like that."

Reyna tilted her chin up and said, "He was in the forest with the same Raiders who fought us."

"If he was a traitor or a spy, he would've taken me with him." Laurie smiled, pleased that she had irrefutable proof to back up her instincts. Of course she trusted him, but now she *knew* he wasn't a traitor. Her cousin was foolish, and he had a lousy temper, and yeah, he seemed a bit down about not being Loki's champion, but she was his whole family. If he'd meant to join the other side all along, he'd have at *least* invited her to go with him. She wouldn't have gone, but Fen had talked her into so many bad ideas throughout their lives that she knew he would've tried to persuade her to join the enemy team with him. Fen was in trouble somehow. This was proof.

Laurie waved a hand between Reyna and Ray. "Do you trust your brother? If he did something that seemed really stupid, would you forget everything you knew about him?"

"Well, no, but—" Reyna started.

"That's me and Fen. He's like my brother. There's an explanation. I don't know what it is, but I know he wasn't a spy for them *or* a traitor."

"He was supposed to deliver Matt to them," Baldwin said quietly. At Laurie's glare, he held up his hands and added, "I'm just reminding you."

Laurie's shoulders slumped. "I know."

Owen came up to stand at her side again and announced, "We need to go to Rapid City." His ravens were still perched on his shoulders. One of them was watching her, and the other was leaning close to Owen's ear, cawing quietly. Owen nodded. "We are needed there, and answers will be waiting."

"Answers?" Laurie prompted. "About Fen?"

The ravens both took flight at her words, and Owen shook

his head. "Answers. The battle will come soon, Laurie. Fen's defection is one of many steps leading to Ragnarök. He went where he needed to be."

"Bull!" She turned her back on him and wiped away tears of anger.

The others said nothing.

"Let's move out," Matt said after a moment.

In silence, they walked in the general direction of Rapid City. Everyone seemed lost in their own thoughts. Matt and Reyna spoke quietly, and Baldwin made occasional observations.

They had reached a clearing in the woods, when Baldwin's voice drew everyone's attention. "Hey, guys?"

"What now?" Ray asked.

"It's still the middle of the day, right?" Baldwin asked in a weird voice. "We weren't walking for hours or anything?"

"Right," Matt said in a voice that sounded as strained as Baldwin's.

"So why is the sky like that?" Baldwin pointed to where they were all already staring. It was like an ink spill spreading slowing over the sky toward them.

Owen announced solemnly, "The wolves have eaten the sun and moon."

Laurie and Baldwin both turned to stare at Owen. The twins did the same. Only Matt looked unsurprised by Owen's words.

"Wolves can't eat solar objects," Ray said, his gaze already returning to the growing darkness. "That's not physically possible."

The Berserkers, who had been following the kids and keeping a perimeter of sorts, moved closer to the descendants of the North. Most of the Berserkers were staring at the sky, but some were scanning the area for any threats. Owen's troupe of acrobatic fighters wasn't speaking or doing anything. They simply guarded the group, following along like a traveling circus in search of trouble.

Laurie opened her bag and pulled out flashlights for everyone. She passed them out, and then she stepped closer to Matt and whispered, "We're losing, aren't we? No matter what we do, we're not stopping Ragnarök."

"Wrong!" Matt said firmly. "We are *not* losing. We'll find a way."

She nodded. She'd lost her best friend, and the sky was turning black. It wasn't looking very hopeful at all.

"Come on," Matt said. "To Rapid City."

And they followed him. No one voiced doubts, but Laurie suspected that her own fears were matched by other uncertainties in the rest of the descendants of the North. No matter what they did, Ragnarök was coming. They were fighting fate, trying to stop a cataclysmic event that had been foretold for millennia. It was absurd to think they could actually succeed.

FOUR

MATT

"BLACKOUT"

They'd been walking through the Black Hills for hours, hopefully heading toward Rapid City. Finally, as they crested a ridge, Matt saw the glow of a town below. He squinted into the darkness and spotted the landmark he'd been searching for.

He pointed. "There's—"

"Ooh! I see it!" Baldwin said. "The floating face."

It was indeed a face, carved in the side of a mountain. The Crazy Horse Memorial. It was supposed to be a huge monument, carved into Thunderhead Mountain, showing Crazy Horse on his steed. Seventy years after construction began, it was still just a face in a mountainside. There was lots of controversy surrounding the memorial, but what mattered now was that it told him exactly where they were.

"Rapid City," he said with a flourish at the lights below.

"We always stopped there on the way home from camping," Baldwin said. "There's this great ice-cream stand just off the highway. But I guess we aren't going for ice cream, are we?"

"Probably not," Ray said. "Unless it's being served by monsters."

"That could be cool," Baldwin said. "An ice-cream fight. Like a snowball fight, with fifty flavors of snow. Good, safe fun. No one ever died from ice cream."

"Unless they drowned you in a giant vat of it," Reyna said. "Or forced you to eat it until you choked. Or—"

"You're no fun at all, you know that?" Baldwin said.

"Depends on your definition of *fun*. Besides, unless there's mistletoe in the ice cream, you'd be perfectly fine." Baldwin was a descendant of Balder, so the only thing that could kill him was mistletoe. And it had, until they rescued him from Hel.

Reyna and Baldwin went on bantering like that as they walked, with Ray chiming in when he could keep up. Matt stayed quiet and kept them moving toward Rapid City.

Even without seeing the Crazy Horse Memorial, Matt would have known where they were as soon as they crested the next rise. Rapid City had around seventy thousand people, making it the second-biggest city in the state. He looked at the sprawling glow stretching from—

The lights went out. All the lights. Like someone hit a switch. Matt blinked hard, rubbing his eyes.

"Did that city just...?" Ray began.

"Go poof?" Reyna said. "Looks like it. Massive power failure. Meaning we've lost our compass, so get your bearings now."

She said it so calmly. The lights are off. No big deal. But she was right. There *must be* a logical explanation. The city hadn't been swallowed into a giant sinkhole as the Midgard Serpent broke through the crust. If that had happened, they'd hear the collapsing buildings and the screaming victims and—

Matt swallowed and tightened his grip on Mjölnir. It was just a power failure. As Reyna had said, they should carry on and not lose sight of their destination.

But when they drew closer to Rapid City, they *did* hear screams.

"Something's happening," Baldwin said.

"Um, yeah," Reyna said. "The sun and the moon have been devoured by giant wolves."

True. Still, Matt noticed that, like him, Reyna kept scouring for monsters as they passed the edges of the city. He could hear people inside the homes, shouting and arguing as they tried to figure out what to do. Ahead, the roads were filled with cars of those who'd tried to escape the city. Angry people, yelling at one another because the cars weren't moving. They weren't jammed too tight or stuck behind a collision. They'd just stopped.

"Um…" Baldwin said. "Does anyone see a problem here?" He looked at Reyna. "And don't tell me the lights are off."

"The power's out," she said.

Baldwin rolled his eyes. "Same difference."

"Actually, no," Matt said. "She means *all* the power is out. The cars have stopped. The batteries are dead. Which isn't simple electrical failure."

He looked out at the road, packed with cars and trucks and people shouting, bickering, crying. It was like something out of a movie. The start of the apocalypse.

Because that's exactly what it is.

His gut clenched.

"What could cause it?" Baldwin asked.

"Maybe an electromagnetic pulse?" Ray offered.

"Sounds good to me," Baldwin said. "Well, it wouldn't be *good*…"

"Does it matter what the technical explanation is?" It was Laurie. The first words she'd said since they started their walk. "It's Ragnarök. It doesn't need an explanation."

As they continued forward, a figure ran from the darkness, and Matt swung up his shield and Mjölnir but it was just a teenage guy. He raced past, wild-eyed, as if he didn't even see them. Matt watched him tear down the empty road, running toward more empty road, not going anywhere, just running.

"Monsters chasing him?" Baldwin whispered.

"Panic, I think." Matt wrapped his hand around his amulet and closed his eyes as he tried to pick up the vibration that suggested otherwise. The amulet lay in his hand, cold and still. "No monsters detected."

Even as he said it, he felt a tickle at the back of his neck, like a little voice saying *Are you sure?* As they kept walking into the city, he clutched his amulet in his free hand, and listened for real screams or shrieks or any sounds of absolute terror or pain. All he heard were the same shouts of anger and confusion. Which meant no monsters.

Does it?

He rubbed the back of his neck.

Owen fell in step beside him. "Trust your instincts, Matt."

Matt looked over.

Owen gave a slight smile. "I know you wish I'd do more, but you're handling this just fine. You came to Rapid City for a reason. Now you need to find that reason. Keep following your gut."

Matt nodded. He tried to focus on whatever he was feeling, but as soon as he did, that weird tingling vanished. When they reached an intersection, instead of continuing on, he stopped and looked at all three options, mentally searching for a sign. He stepped one way. Then another. They felt exactly the same.

"As soon as you tell someone to follow his gut, he can't," Reyna said to Owen. "At least not if he already overthinks every step and agonizes over his choices."

"I do not," Matt said.

Ray nodded slowly, as if reluctant to be quite so blunt about it. Matt looked at Baldwin, who said, "Maybe a little, sometimes. But that's a good thing. Otherwise, you'd be like the myth Thor, thundering into battle and getting us all killed. Well, getting everyone other than me killed."

"Matt," Laurie said, getting his attention.

He turned to her and she walked over, lowering her voice.

"You were walking straight, right? So just keep doing that until your amulet buzzes or you really feel like you're going the wrong way." She turned to Owen with a mock-stern look. "And advice is good, but it needs to be more concrete than 'follow your gut.'"

Owen looked confused, but he murmured something like agreement.

Matt resumed walking. At some point, he turned—he didn't even consider his choices, just followed his feet as they went down one street and then another. None of the locals paid any mind, which seemed perfectly rational, given the circumstances...until he realized he was striding down the road with a wooden shield on his back, a hammer in his hand, and a gang of kids following him.

He slowed and looked around. They were on a quieter street, narrow and lined with homes. He could hear arguing in one house. At another, a couple of younger kids bickered on their lawn. Matt walked toward them. Behind him, the others stayed on the road, all except Reyna, who dogged his steps, whispering, "What are you doing?" He ignored her and walked up to the kids.

"—and you read my diary," the girl was saying. "I know you did!"

She was about twelve, the boy a few years younger. They looked like brother and sister.

"Hey, guys," Matt said. "Can you tell me—?"

"Why would I read your stupid diary? It's all about boys and *feels* and TV shows."

Matt cleared his throat. "Um, guys?"

"How would you know what's in it if you haven't read it?"

"Yo!" Reyna said, stepping between them. "Time out, kiddies. We need to talk to you."

"I don't need to read it to know what's in it," the boy said. "All the same stupid stuff you talk about with your friends when you're supposed to be babysitting me."

The boy didn't lean around Reyna to yell at his sister. He just kept talking, as if there weren't someone standing between them.

"They don't see us," Matt said. "We're invisible."

Reyna took the girl's hand, lifted it, and then dropped it. The girl kept arguing. Reyna tweaked the boy's nose. No reaction.

"We aren't just invisible, Matt. They can't see *or* feel us. And they're fighting about everyday stuff…in the middle of a freaking apocalypse."

Matt clutched his amulet. It still gave him no clues, and he let out a hiss of frustration.

"You were walking," she said. "Did you *decide* to come talk to these kids or feel *compelled* to do it?"

"I was wondering why no one was reacting to us."

"Okay, so your *gut* was still telling you to keep moving. Ignore this and do that."

He started to turn away when he noticed an old man in the window, watching the kids. Matt thought of his grandfather. He didn't want to—he'd been trying so hard not to for the last day—but seeing an old man brought it all back.

Granddad betrayed me. He betrayed us. Our family. Our town.

His grandfather was leading the monsters. His grandfather expected Ragnarök to happen, exactly as it did in the old stories. He expected Matt to die.

Reyna swirled her hand, fog billowing over the children. "Whoops, they're gone. Too bad, so sad. Guess you'll have to just keep walking, Matt."

48

"I wasn't thinking about them. I was thinking—"

"Don't. You need all your energy for fighting or you'll do something stupid like use an aikido pin on a wolf."

"Um, pretty sure *you're* the one who—"

"Nope, you did." She winked at him. "I've rewritten the scene. You pinned the wolf. I saved your butt. It was epic. Now, back to the road, or I'll call the Berserkers to carry you."

When Matt's amulet began vibrating—signaling the presence of actual monsters in Rapid City—it came almost as a relief. He felt guilty thinking that, but in a weird way, it settled his nerves. These days, monsters made sense, far more than anything else.

The buzzing amulet lit his trail in neon. It let him know when he was getting closer. Like a little voice saying *Hot, hotter, cold, hot again . . .*

It led him to the Journey Museum. He'd been here on a field trip last year. He'd thought it was fascinating. Cody and his other friends had nearly died of boredom. They'd ended up touring maybe a quarter of it, at Matt's insistence, just enough to complete their assignment. Then he'd led them on a very different kind of tour, one exploring the areas clearly marked DO NOT ENTER.

"The monsters are inside?" Reyna said as they stopped outside the front doors.

Matt started to say *I think so*, then changed to a simple "Yes." His amulet and his gut told him they were inside. Qualifying that made him look indecisive.

"I don't hear screaming," Ray said. "If it's anything like that creature at the water park, there should be screaming."

"Maybe there's no one left to scream," Reyna said.

Matt gave her a look.

"What?" she said. "It's true. Although, I suppose, if the monsters killed everyone, they wouldn't still be in there. Unless they're busy eating—" She stopped herself then, and her pale face turned even whiter. "Sorry. There, uh, aren't any Norse monsters that...do that, right?"

Matt thought of Nidhogg—a giant serpent that gnawed at the roots of the world tree. When Ragnarök came, it would finally break through into the world and...Well, it was called "the corpse eater" for a reason.

"Maybe the monsters are locked inside alone," Baldwin said. "Without any people to eat."

"The doors *are* locked," Ray said. "But I do hear people inside. While they aren't screaming, they don't exactly sound happy."

Matt could hear a girl pleading. Like she was begging for her life.

"If you guys are going in, someone should stay out here," Ray said. "I'll do it."

"What?" Reyna said. "Absolutely not."

Matt heaved on the door as hard as he could. It wouldn't budge.

"Spread out," Laurie said. "Find another entrance—"

Matt pulled Mjölnir back and swung it at the glass door. It shattered on impact.

"Or we could do that," Laurie said.

Ray glanced over at him. "Next time, could you give us some warning? So we don't get sliced and diced?"

"Glass shatters in the opposite direction of the force applied," Matt said as he stepped through. "So the shards all land inside."

Reyna looked over at him. "Have some experience with breaking windows?"

"No, I learned it in science class. Now, watch your step."

He jumped over the glass, then raced past the abandoned ticket booths and into the main hall. The girl was there. She was about his brother Josh's age and wore a museum employee uniform.

"Please," she said. "Please, please, please. I didn't mean it. I was just a little kid. It was a mistake. I never meant for anything to happen to you."

"Um, where's the monster?" Baldwin whispered.

The girl was pleading with thin air. Tears streamed down her face and she wobbled, as if her knees were about to give way. Before Matt could grab her, she screamed and tumbled onto the floor. He lunged to catch her and told her it was okay, but she crab-scuttled away, her eyes wide with terror as she stared at something—or someone—he couldn't see.

"It was a mistake," she sobbed. "Please believe me. I never meant to hurt you. I never meant to hurt anyone."

"It's mara," Matt said to the others.

He looked around sharply, searching for the ugly old crones who were the personification of nightmares. The bringers of nightmares, too. They'd encountered mara before at Baldwin's house, soon after they'd first met him.

That was why the lights had gone out. So the mara could come and infect everyone with nightmares. Some people had fled, while others argued with their families or neighbors. But those weren't really nightmares, just irrational fear and anger. Real nightmares were like this—the girl trapped in the darkest corners of her mind, imagining someone she'd hurt had returned for revenge.

"The mara are here in the museum," he said. "This is the epicenter. Their power broadcasts, so it's not as bad outside."

"I didn't really like the mara," Reyna said. "I'd prefer trolls."

Matt agreed. Trolls were real. Big chunks of rock, nearly impossible to fight, but still solid. Nightmares were a whole other thing.

"We've done it before," he said. "We can handle it. Owen?"

The older boy looked over.

"Can you send your Berserkers out to hunt for mara and people in trouble?"

"I can."

Once Owen had stepped out to speak to his troops, Matt said, "Let's stick together, see what we can do to make sure no one gets affected."

As Matt walked through an exhibit hall, he marveled at how much more difficult everything was in a near-total lack of light. For one thing, you couldn't see the dinosaurs until you smacked into their leg bones and the skeletons nearly toppled onto your head. For another, plans to "stick together" really didn't work out so well.

They'd lost Laurie, Baldwin, and Owen back in the lobby. When they started out, he'd considered asking everyone to hold the shirt of the person in front of them. But they'd feel as if he were treating them like little kids. Now he wished he'd done it, no matter what they thought, because at some point before they left the lobby, half their "train" derailed. Once they reached the paleontology area, he'd called a question back to Laurie and hadn't gotten an answer. That was when he realized she was gone. Along with Owen and Baldwin.

He couldn't blame Reyna and Ray, either. They might have been walking in front of Laurie, but they'd been wrapped up in their magic, trying to weaken the mara when they took manifested form, changing from smoke into hideous old women with black pits for eyes.

Now, as Matt headed back toward the lobby, he whispered Laurie's name. He didn't dare call it, for fear it would bring the mara. He could hear the crones' handiwork deeper in the museum—people jabbering and begging and crying.

"We need to get to them, Matt," Ray said.

"I know." Matt squinted about, looking for any sign of the others. "You guys keep going. I'll catch up as soon as—"

"Uh-uh," Reyna said. "We've seen how the mara operate. No one goes anywhere alone. But Ray's right. I think we're actually weakening them this time, and the longer we're hunting for the others, the longer we aren't stopping the mara and helping those people. Laurie can handle it. You know she can."

He hesitated and then whispered, "Okay. Fall in line behind me. And hold my shirt. I'm not losing anyone else."

They weakened a few of the mara and freed the people they'd been terrorizing. Well, *freed* might not be exactly the right word. They'd had to leave the people where they were, dazed and bewildered, still shaking from their nightmares as Matt, Ray, and Reyna raced off to help the next victims.

Matt kept hoping they'd bump into the others. When he caught sight of a blond girl up ahead, he took off so fast Reyna and Ray had to shout at him to slow down. As he neared the girl, he knew it wasn't Laurie. She was too short. She looked younger than them, maybe seven, with pale hair and bright blue eyes. She wore a blue sundress and no shoes, exactly as she had in Blackwell, when she led Matt into the community center to overhear his grandfather's true plans.

"Matthew Thorsen," she said. "You are here."

"Friend of yours?" Reyna whispered.

"This is one of the Norns," Matt said. "It's Present. I don't know..." He looked at the little girl. "Do you have a name?"

She smiled beatifically, in that slightly unfocused, surreal way of hers, like someone perfectly happy in the moment, with no worries about the past or cares for the future. Which made perfect sense, all things considered.

"Do I need one?" she asked.

"I guess not." He looked around. "Are your sisters here?"

"Not now."

"You mean they're coming?" Reyna said. "Or they were just here?"

"Don't ask that," Matt whispered. "She only knows the present."

"Seriously?"

"That could make conversation tough," Ray said.

"Tell me about it," Matt muttered. He turned to the Norn. "I'm hoping you're here looking for me. That you have something to tell me. Maybe a clue about what I'm to do next."

"That would be Future's domain."

He winced. "Right. Okay, um…"

"Let me try," Ray whispered. "Are you here looking for Matt?"

The girl smiled. "For all of you. But especially Matt. He is confused about his path. We have come to guide him."

"Good," Matt said, exhaling.

"Can you tell him what he's supposed to do?" Ray asked. "I mean *be* doing. Now."

"He ought to be speaking to Future."

"Okay," Ray said. "Where is she?"

"Behind you."

He turned to see a girl who looked around his brothers' age, sixteen or seventeen. She wore a rough skirt, like a Viking woman, and her blond hair was done in tiny braids, piled on her head. She turned around and, seeing him, she smiled.

"Perfect," Ray said. He turned quickly to Present. "Now, don't go anywhere. At this moment, do not move and continue not moving while we speak to both of you. Can you do that?"

"I can, Raymond," Present said.

Ray turned to Future. "Matt needs to know what to do next. Obviously, we're heading to Ragnarök, but we don't know where that is or what we need to find before we get there."

Present answered with, "You have all that you need."

"Then what *will* we need? In the future. For the battle."

"Nothing more," Future said. "Except to know where to go."

"The battleground," Matt said. "So...it's that close? I haven't heard Gullinkambi crow."

"When will the rooster crow?" Ray asked, rephrasing it as a question for Future.

"Soon," she said. "When you are ready, you will hear the cock crow and you must get to the battlefield."

"Perfect," Matt said. "Now where is the battlefield?"

The two Norns looked at each other. "We do not know," they said in unison.

"Because that's in the past?" Matt said. "No, it can't be." He glanced at Ray.

"You should know," Ray said, turning to the older girl. "The battle comes in the future, so you must know where it will be held."

"I do not."

Panic nestled in Matt's gut. "Does that mean there is no battle? We don't make it that far?"

"You will," Future said.

"Wait, does that mean there's no battle because we avert it?"

"It cannot be averted. To find the battlefield, you must find the one who knows the rules of engagement."

"And that's not you. Okay, so who's in charge of the battle? The, uh, referee or whatever."

"That would be us," the Norns said in unison.

Matt groaned. He glanced at Reyna.

"Don't look at me," she said. "I'm more lost than you are. Ray?"

Her brother shook his head. "Sorry, I don't get it, either. Let me try, though." He turned to Future. "You and your sisters are in charge of the battle to come. Is that correct?"

"Yes and no. The rules have been set since the dawn of time. Past knows what they are, but she cannot tell you, because that could give you an advantage, and that is not our place. Our place is simply to enforce the rules as they are set for both sides."

"So who knows these rules?" Matt asked.

Ray said to Present, "Who currently knows the rules?" Then to Future, "And will she explain them? Can you tell us that?"

Future nodded. "We can tell you this much—look to your family for answers, Matthew."

"And by family..." Matt said slowly. "You don't mean my grandfather, right? Because he's not going to help me."

"He may, and he may not. The future has yet to be set, so we cannot tell you what is to come."

"But the person who knows, it's a family member, but not my grandfather. Right?"

"Your grandfather knows," Present said. "Yet he does not know. He understands the rules, but does not know the location of the battle."

"Anyone got an aspirin?" Reyna muttered.

Matt tried again, as patiently as he could. "At present, though, a Thorsen family member other than my grandfather knows and I may ask him—or her."

"Yes."

"Is it my—?"

"That is all we may say," the Norns said in unison. And they disappeared.

FIVE

LAURIE

"FACING FEARS"

L osing track of the rest of their group didn't frighten Laurie quite the way it would have before their trip to Hel. She didn't like being split up, but this wasn't the first time she'd faced the mara, so she knew that everything should be okay. They'd fought these monsters before, at Baldwin's house the night before he'd died. Unfortunately, it was scarier without Fen at her side. *Everything* was scarier without Fen.

She hadn't realized how much she counted on the way that Fen and Matt were both there for her. They'd become a team, and she wasn't sure how to fight the monsters alone—not that she was truly alone. The Berserkers, Matt, and the twins were somewhere in the museum, and Owen and Baldwin were still at her side. It was only Fen who was truly gone.

"This way," Owen muttered as he grabbed her arm and started pulling her through the lobby deeper into the Journey Museum. "Watch for wolves. They're everywhere."

"Wolves?" She looked at him and saw that he had the glassy eyes of someone trying not to be swept up in the *unreal* things he was seeing. "They're fake, Owen. Whatever you see is fake. These are mara."

He nodded. "The Berserkers are protecting people. I need to protect you."

His words weren't wrong, but they weren't exactly *right*, either. He'd helped her learn how to use her bow, and he'd rescued the twins. He wasn't usually the sort of person to hover at her side like this. Not seeing the future any longer appeared to have left the representative of Odin a little lost. Around Matt and the others, Owen still seemed to be trying to sound like himself. With her, he was more... vulnerable.

"They'll take my other eye," he whispered. "They might take your eyes, too. We need to hide from the wolves."

"Focus." She lightly slapped his cheek. "Focus on me, Owen. There are no wolves. There are only mara here. They're creating nightmares from your fears."

"Shhh! The twins are with Matt, so it's just us with no

magic to help." Baldwin was beside her then, standing on her left, so she was between the two boys. Walking three across wasn't a good plan, though. It made them too much of a target. It also made them more likely to run into obstacles and meant that she didn't have a free hand.

Laurie linked hands with Baldwin, and then ordered, "We'll walk in a row. Grab Owen, and don't let go of him."

"Got him," Baldwin whispered. "Lead on."

She kept her flashlight tucked under her shirt to dim the light. She wanted to keep them from being seen, but she couldn't totally go without it. When there is no power at all, the world gets *very* dark—especially when the sun and moon aren't anywhere to be found in the sky. The sky was black, and the lights were out. There was nothing but darkness inside and outside.

I can do this.

It might be a lie, but Fen wasn't there. Matt was somewhere else. She didn't have a lot of options. She would have to lead them.

As if the dark weren't already terrifying enough, monsters waited in the blackness all around them. Laurie wasn't certain of it, but it seemed pretty likely that mara could see better without light than the humans could. They were creatures of nightmares, and nightmares happened at night. It only made sense that they were stronger in the dark. So Laurie would get them to a safer place than out here in the lobby, and they'd figure out what to do from there. Hope-fully they could reconnect with Matt and the twins.

Laurie led Baldwin and Owen farther into the museum, but they didn't find any of the others. What they found were monsters. She heard growling only a moment before Baldwin jerked her to a stop.

"Fen?" Baldwin asked.

"Raiders!" Owen stepped forward so the three of them were standing in a small cluster.

And there, in front of her, was Fen. He had a lantern of some sort, and he was only a few steps away. She was relieved. He was here! They'd all been wrong. She knew it! But even as she smiled, she noticed that something was wrong. Fen wasn't coming to help her. He wasn't explaining what Matt had seen in the forest. Instead, he stood there with Skull and Hattie at his side. Hattie held his hand in hers, and Skull smirked at them.

"How does it feel?" Skull asked.

"What?" Laurie croaked.

"To know that Fen was working for us for almost two years," Hattie said. "We knew that Ragnarök was coming. He's been our spy. He left you."

"I would've saved you, but you aren't worth saving." Fen flashed his teeth at Laurie. "You didn't think I'd care about you after you lied to me, did you?"

"I didn't lie." She tried to step forward, but someone held

on to her arm. She dropped her flashlight trying to pull away from the person who had her arm.

"You didn't tell me about Owen. You kept secrets from me." Fen watched her.

"I'm sorry I didn't tell you everything, but that doesn't mean you should help *them*." Laurie tried to reach the flashlight, but it had vanished. The light was still shining at Fen, who was walking toward her now. As he got closer, she could see that there were teeth marks in his arm. Someone—probably one of the wolves—had attacked him. His arms were bleeding now.

"You don't understand. You're not like me." Fen shook his head. "I hoped you would be a wolf, too, but you're not. That's really why I had to leave. You won't survive the fight, so I'm not going to bother trying to help you anymore. If you were a wolf, you could join me, but only the *wulfenkind* will survive Ragnarök. You'll die." He inclined his head toward Baldwin and Owen. "Them too. It was a waste to worry about trying to rescue either of them when they're going to die soon anyhow. You were weak, and you were trying to make *me* weak, too."

"No," she insisted. "You listen to me, Fenrir Brekke. I didn't lie, and the world isn't ending. We can win. You can come back with me, and we'll win."

Hattie and Skull laughed. They were laughing so hard that they seemed to be shaking like they were ready to fall over. Laurie realized that she was shaking, too. It wasn't from laughter, but because the floor was vibrating.

"Something's wrong," she told them all. "Something is very wrong."

No one listened, though, and the vibrations from the floor were making it hard to stand. Earthquakes weren't typical in South Dakota. Tornadoes were, but that wouldn't explain why the floor in the museum was rattling.

"Pay attention!" she yelled.

Skull and Hattie kept laughing, and Fen was staring at her in anger. Laurie looked around the surprisingly bright room. It seemed strange that she could see when everything had been so dark only a few moments ago.

Before she could figure out why, Laurie saw the trolls running toward them. Giant trolls, a whole army of them, were running so fast that it would only be a moment until they trampled the Raiders.

"Fen!" she screamed. "Look out!"

But the troll grabbed him in a hand that was already turning to stone—even though it was obviously *not* dawn— and Fen was swept up into the air. His legs were dangling, kicking at nothing, and the two Raiders were laughing. He was being choked by a troll, and the Raiders were *laughing*.

"It's your fault," Hattie said. "You lied to him, and now he's dying."

"No!" Laurie started running toward her cousin, but in

66

a moment, she was jerked back by both arms. Fen, the troll, and the two Raiders all vanished. Everything went dark again, as if the light she'd seen all around them had been turned off. Suddenly, she was standing outside the Lakota tipi in the center of the room with Baldwin and Owen at her sides.

"How…Where…What happened to Fen? And the troll?" She looked around the room. The light that she had seen by just a moment ago was gone. "The light went away—"

"Mara," Baldwin said quietly. "Remember? Whatever you saw wasn't real. No Fen. No light. No trolls."

"It was like you were asleep but standing." Owen nudged her toward the tipi, and as much as she didn't want to move away from where she thought she'd just seen Fen, she knew that she had to. Fen wasn't really here. Those were her fears. It had seemed so real, but her cousin wasn't here. The whole thing was a waking nightmare caused by monsters.

"I should've known that," she whispered.

Baldwin hugged her. "You're worried about him. The mara took advantage of that."

Owen handed her the flashlight, and the three kids went inside the tipi. It was one of her favorite spots in the museum. Last year, she and Fen had been here to listen to a Lakota storyteller. They'd listened to a story about *Inktomi*, the spider. He was a trickster and could take the shape of a man or a wolf. Laurie didn't know then that Fen was able to change his shape—or that her father could, too. *Inktomi* seemed a lot like Loki, their dead ancestor, so it was no surprise that Fen loved that story. After the storyteller was done, Fen was happy and laughing, and he agreed with Laurie that the Journey was an awesome museum.

"I hope you're safe wherever you are," she whispered, letting her hand graze the tipi. Then she took a deep breath and looked at the descendants of the North who were still with her. "Okay. We can move through the next rooms. If we see any crazy nightmares, we shake each other free. Once we find Matt, we get out of here. The three of us can't vanquish the mara, so we're just here to get any humans free. If there aren't any, we portal out."

The boys nodded, and the trio went through the museum, looking for any people who were trapped inside the building with the monsters. In one corner of the pioneer exhibit, next to a creepy-looking old doll in a case, they found a family, curled up together and shaking. Laurie didn't want to know if that doll was a part of their nightmare, but from the way they were staring at it, she wouldn't be surprised. Baldwin and Owen pulled the three people to their feet, shook them free of their nightmares, and then the small group kept moving.

After a few minutes, they found a museum employee fighting invisible intruders and rescued him, too. He'd broken free several rocks from the geology exhibit and was using them to beat invisible enemies. Once he was free of his nightmares, he looked around with wide eyes.

"You're okay," Laurie promised. "They're gone now."

The man nodded but didn't speak. She suspected that was what the descendants had all looked like the first time they fought creatures that shouldn't exist. She knew it was what she had felt like the first time she'd seen a troll.

"We're here to help," Owen said calmly.

"What he said," Baldwin added.

It wasn't much, saving only a couple people when the world outside was in chaos, but it felt good. It felt like they were doing something right, and that helped. At least, it made Laurie feel better.

When they came across the Berserkers, they handed the people over to them to escort them out of the building, and they kept going in search of their missing friends or more trapped people.

"We're keeping them all in the lobby," one of the acrobatic fighters said. "And we're guarding them."

Owen murmured something approving, and then he and Baldwin continued following Laurie. There weren't any other museum visitors in the next few rooms, so she supposed that the Berserkers had done their part in rescuing them all. That only left Matt and the twins.

"Maybe they're in the lobby, too," Baldwin suggested when she commented on their absence.

"The Berserkers would've told us," Owen pointed out.

The three of them kept moving until they came across a theater. Inside, the twins were finishing some sort of spell. The two kids had their hands clasped together, and Matt stood at their side—hammer and shield at the ready—as if he were their bodyguard.

As the mara snapped out of existence, back to wherever nightmare creatures should rightly exist, the twins slumped to the floor, looking like they were ready to pass out in exhaustion.

"Are you all okay?" Matt asked.

Laurie nodded. "We gathered up a few people, and the Berserkers took them to the lobby. You?"

"Tired," Reyna said.

Ray smiled. "But safe."

They stood silently for a moment before Matt said, "The building's clear now. It'll be a safe place for those who need it."

"But not us," Baldwin added quickly. "We're not staying here, right?"

Laurie almost laughed at the look on his face. Baldwin was all for adventure, and even the scariest monsters didn't seem to make him pause for long. His attitude reminded her of Fen. Quickly, she shoved that thought away. She wasn't giving up on her cousin, but she had to concentrate on right now.

"Matt?" Laurie prompted. "What's the plan?"

"We need to go back to Blackwell," Matt said. He quickly summarized his conversation with the Norns, and added, "If I'm looking for family to talk to, I need to start there."

"I want to check in with my family to see if they've heard from Fen," Laurie said.

"Right," Matt said. "Laurie and I will go to Blackwell, then."

"Ray and I should come, too," Reyna said. "I'll watch Matt's back and Ray can watch Laurie's."

The truth was that Ray was the last person Laurie would've picked for reinforcement. It was easier when Fen was with them. Then, there was never any doubt as to who had her back. Ray wasn't a bad guy, but he wasn't a fighter. He seemed nice but content to stay in the background. In essence, Laurie would be on her own.

"Owen and Baldwin, you can handle whatever chaos is left here," Matt said.

"Sure thing," Baldwin said.

"Actually, the Berserkers can handle this," Owen pointed out diplomatically. "Baldwin and I can go with you."

"Sure thing," Baldwin repeated.

Laurie flashed a grateful smile at Owen and told Matt, "That would work. Ray and Reyna can stay together with you, Matt, and Baldwin, and Owen can come with me."

"Fine," Matt said. "Laurie, can you get us a portal to Blackwell?"

"On it," Laurie said. She turned to Owen and whispered, "Thank you."

He nodded, but said nothing.

Then she took a few calming breaths, trying to find the peace that she needed in order to open a portal. It was like pulling taffy out of the middle of her body when she started to open a doorway. There was a weird, stretching feeling that started the moment she located the energy inside her that would then become an opening in the air. She clasped her hands, and then she slowly and steadily pulled them away from each other. The taffy feeling from inside her body was between her fingers, too, then. In the space between her hands, the air shimmered like there was something almost liquid and shivering in the air. It widened as she spread her hands farther apart and then stepped to the side.

The feeling of opening a doorway was still uncomfortable even though it was floating there now. She knew what to expect, so the weird feeling of being turned inside out each time she did this was easier. She still didn't *like* it, but it was the quickest way to get from the middle of the darkened museum to their hometown.

"Go on," she urged the four boys and Reyna.

Baldwin dived through without pause. The twins held hands and stepped in with the sort of grace that made them seem more supernatural than she ever felt—even when she had just opened up a magical doorway. Owen followed. Then, as soon as Matt went through, Laurie stepped into the portal.

"Meet up back at the longship in no more than two hours," Matt said once they were all together in Blackwell, and then he and the twins left.

Laurie was standing with Baldwin and Owen outside the Thorsen Community and Recreation Center. The sky was dark here, too, and all she could hope was that Raiders or trolls wouldn't be any better at seeing in the dark than she was.

"Follow me," she told Baldwin and Owen, and together they set out through the pitch-black streets of the town.

SIX

MATT

"BROTHERLY LOVE"

Back to Blackwell. The last place on earth Matt wanted to be. In some ways, fighting the final battle of Ragnarök seemed easier than facing his parents.

"So what's the deal with your folks?" Reyna asked as they skirted the edges of town, heading toward his neighborhood.

He shrugged and said nothing.

"Are they *okay* with the apocalypse thing?"

Another shrug.

"She's not prying, Matt," Ray said. "It'll help if we know what we're up against here."

"We're not up *against* anything," he said. "It's my family.

I'll handle it. You guys are just standing watch in case of trouble."

"And if the trouble comes from them?" Reyna said.

"My family would never—"

He stopped. He'd thought the same thing about Granddad once.

"I'll handle it," he said. "Whatever happens."

"We'll be right outside," Ray said. "If there's any trouble, shout."

After a few more steps, Reyna came up beside him, her voice lowered as she said, "You don't need to handle this alone, Matt."

"Yep," he said. "I do."

Returning to Blackwell was much easier in the dark. There was electricity here. Whatever the monsters' plan, they clearly weren't going to attack the town run by the guy leading them.

There were still only a few lights. All the Thorsens knew what was happening, and they wouldn't panic and throw on every light to fend off the darkness. That was a blessing as they crept through yards, Matt making his way home.

Home.

He could see it ahead. Just an ordinary house on a street of ordinary houses. Inside was his room. With a bed and clean clothing and an iPod and a laptop, and all the things he'd taken for granted. A week ago, he'd have longed to sneak in, to sleep on a real mattress and take a hot shower and put on clean clothes. He'd have fantasized about going back to school. Yes, school. Where he understood what was expected of him. Where he knew he could succeed, with the right effort. Where he was normal, like a million other kids. Not the smartest thirteen-year-old boy. Not the most athletic or the most popular. But smart enough, athletic enough, and popular enough that no one picked on him and some looked up to him. A good life for a kid. A really, really good life.

Now, looking at his house, he couldn't imagine that life. He couldn't foresee a time when he'd be back in his bedroom, trying to sleep and worrying about the next science fair project.

If he defeated the Midgard Serpent, would things just go back to normal? Would *he* go back to normal? *Could* he?

"Is this it?" Reyna asked, and he realized he was in his neighbor's yard, perched on the top of the fence, and staring at his house.

"Yep. Not quite like yours, huh?" He'd seen Ray and Reyna's house. You could fit five of his inside it.

"It's very..." she began.

"Small?" he said.

"I was going to say normal."

He choked back a laugh, and she glanced over, not getting the joke. He shook his head and jumped over the fence. As soon as his feet touched ground, he heard Reyna shout and suddenly he wasn't touching ground anymore. He was whipping through the air.

Mjölnir fell from his hand and struck the ground with a thump. Matt hit the ground next, flat on his face. He tried to scramble up, but a foot stomped the small of his back.

The air whooshed from his lungs. Ray shouted. Matt twisted to see the twins running toward him. Then whoever had him pinned caught Ray by the arm, throwing him aside. Reyna had been running to Matt's aid, but when she saw her brother go flying, she tore after him instead.

"Tell your new friends to back off, Matt," said a voice above him. *"Now."*

It was a voice Matt knew very well. Jake. His brother.

Before all this started, Matt would have said the person he got along best with in his family was Josh, his other brother. Matt had a decent enough relationship with his parents. They were disappointed by him—always had been—but they loved him. Jake, though? Jake barely tolerated him. To him, Matt was a screwup. An embarrassment.

"It's okay, guys," Matt said. "It's my brother."

"I guessed that," Reyna said. "And I don't care. Either he lets you up by the count of five or—"

Jake grabbed Matt by the collar and lifted him into the air. "Better?"

"Can I hit him now?" Reyna asked.

"You really think you can hurt me, little girl?" Jake pulled himself up to his full height, towering head and shoulders above Reyna.

"Depends on where I hit you. Now let him—"

Jake threw Matt to the ground, his chin hitting hard enough for him to nip his tongue. He winced, his eyes tearing up with pain. Then he slowly rose, keeping his back to everyone so Jake wouldn't think he was crying.

"Matt?" Reyna said. "Remember what I said about you needing to be less nice? If this is what you'd be like, forget I mentioned it. Nice is good."

She walked over to him as he brushed himself off, his back still to Jake. Then his brother grabbed the shield, yanking it off so fast Matt nearly fell again.

"Hey!" Reyna said, wheeling on Jake. "Can you stop being a jerk for two seconds? I don't know what your problem is, but Matt came to—"

"Came to what? Steal something else?"

Matt turned to see Jake holding out the shield.

"I shouldn't be surprised you stole this," Jake said, "after everything you've done, but I still thought you were better than this, Matt."

"No," Matt said, as evenly as he could. "Whatever you think I've done, I'm pretty sure it's exactly what you expect. In fact, I'm sure you're kind of happy about the whole thing. Now everyone else can see what a loser I am."

Jake's face screwed up. "What?"

"Never mind. I don't know what Granddad has told you—"

"Granddad hasn't told me anything. No, strike that. He's told us that this isn't what it looks like. That you haven't ditched your responsibilities as Thor's champion, run away to hide, and left the rest of us watching the end of the world come without any way to stop it."

"Is that what you think?" Reyna said. "Seriously?"

"It's what they expect," Matt said.

"Then they don't know you at all."

Jake turned to her, shield still in hand. "I don't know who you are, but stay out of this." He glanced at Matt. "And I don't know what you mean about what I *expect*, but I *expected* you to man up and face this."

"Man up?" Reyna said. "Did you really just say that?"

Jake ignored her. "I expected better of you, Matt. We all did. You might have been scared by what Granddad said, but it was your responsibility to fight. I'd take your place if I could, but I can't, so you needed to let us help you and train you, not sneak off in the night like a scared little boy, hook up with these street kids—"

"Street kids?" Reyna said.

"They're the descendants of Frey and Freya," Matt said. "I didn't run away. I left to do what I was supposed to do—gather the champions."

Jake peered over at Ray and Reyna. "If someone told you those are the descendants of the gods of love and beauty, then you've been tricked. Or you need glasses."

"*Excuse* me?" the twins said in unison.

"The Brekkes got you into this mess, didn't they," Jake continued. "I heard you might have joined up with them. They're the other *side*, Matt. Loki leads the monsters. Maybe you thought you could...I don't know, flip them to our team? Avert Ragnarök? You're just a kid—you don't understand these things. The Brekkes were playing you all along. Then they dumped you with these two fake—"

"Does this look fake?" Reyna cut in, swirling fog from her fingertips.

"No, and it doesn't look like the work of a goddess, either. You're a witch."

"I've heard that before." She pulled the feathered cloak out of her bag. "Your baby brother—who you think is too *dumb* to spot fake-god kids—knew what this is. Do you?"

It took a moment, and Matt could see Jake struggling, mentally thumbing through the myths. Then he said, "It looks like Freya's cloak, but it's clearly a fake."

Reyna put it on and disappeared. "Does it *look* fake?" As

Jake stood there, staring, she took it off, stuffed the cloak back into her pack, and strode over to Mjölnir. "How about you come and pick this up? See if it's fake, too."

Jake stood there, staring at the hammer, past scoffing but uncertain and confused.

Matt walked over and carefully lifted Mjölnir, trying not to be too confident about it. He knew why Jake doubted him. Matt was just a kid, and he always messed up, always got into trouble, always made mistakes. Even if Matt had come to realize he didn't actually mess up more than the average thirteen-year-old—that's what Jake thought of him. Of course Jake would believe he'd run off or been tricked.

So he lifted Mjölnir, then threw it, and everyone watched in silence as it returned to his hand.

"See?" Reyna said. "Matt—"

Matt quieted her with a look. He appreciated that she'd defended him, but it wasn't necessary now as his brother stood there, staring.

"I..." Jake said. "That's... You have..."

"Mjölnir," Matt said quietly. "I took Mjölnir from the tomb. I took the shield back from the Raiders. I even have Tanngrisnir and Tanngnjóstr, Thor's goats. I've met the Valkyries. I've fought trolls and mara and draugrs and jötnar. I *am* with Laurie Brekke. She's Loki's champion, and she's on my side. We've found the twins and Baldwin—Balder's descendant. Baldwin died, just like in the myths, but it was one of the monsters who did it, not the Brekkes. We got Baldwin back, though. From Hel. I even fell in the river of the dead, swallowed some of it, and survived. We've changed the myth, but Ragnarök is still coming. I've seen the Midgard Serpent. We can't stop it. We can only prepare."

Jake stared at him. "You..."

"Yes," Reyna said. "He did all of that. He's the real Champion of Thor. Your *loser* little brother."

Jake blinked. "I never said..." He looked at Matt. "*You* said that. I've never..." He trailed off, studying Matt's expression. "Is that what you think? Sure, you make mistakes. But you're just a kid. I expect you to mess up."

"I'm not *just* a kid," Matt said. "And I don't mess up nearly as often as you think I do."

Jake's mouth worked. Then he stepped toward Matt, his voice lowering. "Sure, I might have been hard on you sometimes. You're my little brother. But..." He looked at Ray and Reyna, and straightened. "Anyway, enough of that. You're obviously in trouble, and you need our help. You never should have left." He lifted his hands. "I know, you don't want me giving you crap, but in this case, I think you deserve it."

"Actually, he doesn't," Reyna said. "There's more to the story."

Matt asked the twins to scout for a few minutes. Then he told Jake about their grandfather, about what he'd heard at the meeting and, later, that Granddad admitted to everything.

When Matt finished, Jake looked like he was going to be sick. He kept shaking his head, saying, "No, that's not right. You've made a mistake. There's no way Granddad would ever—"

"It's true," Ray said, walking over. "Reyna and I weren't there, but others were with Matt when your grandpa admitted it. Lots of others. There was no question of a misunderstanding. Whatever his reasons, your grandpa is leading the monsters' side."

"He expected Matt to lose," Reyna said as she joined them. "He wanted him to lose." Her voice shook, as if with anger. "He says it's for the best, a new world order, but he expected Matt to *die*. That's what we're up against. That's why Matt took off and why he couldn't come back. For all he knows, you guys—his family—are on your grandfather's side."

"What?" Jake's eyes went wide. He wheeled on Matt. "You didn't seriously think I'd do that."

"Not you or Josh. But maybe Mom and Dad—"

"—would be okay with you dying? Really?"

"If Granddad's fine with it..." He shrugged. "I couldn't rule out the possibility, could I? It's not like I thought Mom and Dad *wanted* me dead. But if it had to happen...well, at least it wasn't you or Josh."

Jake stared at him, mouth open. "You actually *did* think they'd be okay with you dying."

"That came out wrong. I'm not feeling sorry for myself. I'm just saying that it was a possibility. It had to be. It still is."

"No, it isn't."

Matt looked up, meeting his brother's gaze. "Yes. It is."

"Matt's right," Reyna said. "Sure, the chance your parents are involved seems tiny, but it's *still* a chance. Maybe they wouldn't be okay with it, but it's possible they know and they're trying to figure a way out of it, like Matt thought your grandfather was doing."

"I really, *really* don't think they know," Jake said. "They're a mess, Matt, and not because their champion has disappeared—because their *kid* is gone."

"But we have to—"

"Okay, I get it. We have to consider all the possibilities." He shook his head. "I can't believe my little brother is the one telling *me* to be careful. But I get it. Still, you need to let Mom and Dad know—"

"Are you even listening?" Reyna said.

Jake turned on her. "Look, you may be the descendant of Freya, but I don't know you, and you don't know my family."

"I know Matt. Not like you do, obviously, though I'm not sure how well you know him if you thought—"

Matt cut her short with a look. Then he turned to Jake.

"I came back because I need information. Something the Norns say my family knows."

"Norns? You've met…" Jake trailed off, shaking his head. "Sorry. Go on."

"They said someone in my family knows where the battleground is. For Ragnarök. I would have guessed Granddad, but obviously I can't ask him now, and anyway, the Norns say he doesn't—Never mind. That's just confusing. Typical Norns. Anyway, they say someone in my family knows, other than Granddad. I'm guessing Dad, but he's never exactly been into that stuff…."

"It's Uncle Pete."

"What?"

"You need to talk to Uncle Pete. In Mitchell."

Matt went quiet. "Uncle Pete? I haven't seen—"

"—him since you were practically in diapers. I know. He had a huge falling-out with Granddad. I was old enough to remember it. Not that it made much sense at the time— I was just a kid. But you've heard Dad say how much you remind him of his brother."

"Um, yeah, the screwup uncle that Granddad won't talk about and who we haven't seen in ten years."

Jake made a face. "Okay, I can see where that probably made things worse, but Dad didn't mean it like that. Uncle Pete didn't screw up. He disagreed with Granddad on some things and got kicked out of Blackwell. Dad isn't supposed

87

to talk to him, but he sees him whenever he has an excuse to go out that way. When he says you're like his brother, yeah, he means you're different, that you don't see things the way the other Thorsens do, but Uncle Pete is smart—super-smart. And no one knows the old stories like him. That's what Dad means. And that's why you need to go talk to him. The problem is getting to Mitchell."

"We have portals," Ray said.

"Por...? I won't ask. But if it means we can get there easily, that works." He took out his cell phone. "I'll text Mom, saying I'll be back late tonight and—"

"You can't come with me," Matt said.

"Why not?"

Because I'd rather you didn't. Because I'm finally feeling like a champion, and I can't have my big brother treating me like a kid. It's not about making me feel bad—it's about undermining my confidence when I need it most.

"You...you should stay here. Look after Mom and Dad."

Jake shook his head. "Not today. Today I'm going to be a real big brother. I'm going to look after *you*."

SEVEN

LAURIE

"SPILLING NOT-SO-SECRETS"

Laurie wasn't sure how she felt about being back in Blackwell. Mostly, it just felt wrong, or maybe it was just the idea of being here without Fen that felt wrong. She trusted Matt's instincts, and if he thought he needed to see his family, he did. That didn't mean she really wanted to see hers. The side of her family that knew what was really going on was the enemy. The Brekkes knew why the sky was dark now. They knew Ragnarök was coming. Her mother...well, she probably just thought Laurie was being stupid, following Fen and getting into trouble.

She wasn't actually wrong. That was the worst part. Laurie *had* followed her cousin, and they had gotten into a bunch of trouble, but it was for a good reason. She knew her mother could never understand that, though.

With Baldwin and Owen at her sides, Laurie walked through Blackwell. There were a few lights on in some houses, but people were being cautious. She realized that was the Thorsens' doing. The mayor, despite being insane enough to want the world to end, had at least found some way of explaining to the town that they had to be cautious with their resources.

"Creepy, but not as bad as Rapid City," Baldwin said.

"Yeah," she agreed in a low voice. "But this town is also run by the leader of the enemies, so . . . there's that."

"Okay. I take it back: Blackwell is just as creepy as Rapid, but in a different way."

Owen stayed silent. His ravens had appeared when the kids entered Blackwell and were now perched on his shoulders. They didn't disturb her as they had initially, but she still wasn't a fan of the birds. Sharp beaks and wicked talons didn't invite cuddling in her book.

She hoped that if the birds had no news, Owen could see where Fen was. That was how his seeing worked: he couldn't foresee things when he was involved, but Fen was away from them now. Surely that should mean that Owen could see something that could be useful. The others didn't seem to get how it worked, and Laurie thought that they respected his silence and listened to him a little more when he did speak because they thought he could still see things—or maybe he *did* still see things that helped him to know.

"I want to know if you see anything about Fen," Laurie told him. It wasn't quite an *order*, but it wasn't a question, either.

Owen simply nodded once... which could either mean that he heard her or that he was agreeing with her. His two ravens chattered into his ears, speaking to him in words no one else understood.

Laurie took her bow in hand and turned her attention to the potential threats in Blackwell. With the mayor being the head of the enemy side, there were plenty of reasons to suspect that there would be wolves in town. Maybe he wouldn't have trolls or mara or anything so obviously monstrous, but a few wolves wouldn't be noticed.

And that's why we need to see our families, Laurie thought. *I need to warn Mom.*

"So my mother doesn't know about any of this," Laurie told Baldwin and Owen. "My dad's the... umm, wolf. He's a Brekke, and my mom's just normal or whatever."

"My parents both seem normal." Baldwin frowned. "Not that *we* aren't normal. We're just kids, so that's normal. Superpowers and all aren't really common, though. Just us. Okay, and the enemy has superpowers.... Oh! I wonder if there are other people with god- or monster-powers, but we don't know them."

Laurie smiled at the babbling that had become as familiar to her as Fen's bad attitude and Matt's optimism. She looked at Baldwin and told him, "I missed you when you were dead."

"Oh, I know. Fen said..." Baldwin's words quickly faded. "Sorry."

"It's okay to say his name. I know he's not a traitor or spy. You'll all see it, too."

Owen sighed. "He is where he must be. Like you, he has a role in the final battle. He *will* be with the monsters, Laurie, not us."

Laurie ignored him and pointed toward her building. "This is it. Home."

"I hope you're right," Baldwin said. "I mean, about Fen. I'm sure you're right about your building."

She shook her head. "I am right... about *both*."

The boys stopped beside her. Owen's ravens flew away after pausing to swoop close enough to her that her hair blew around in the breeze from their wings.

As they walked to her apartment, Laurie considered her options. There were really only two choices now. She could take the boys inside with her, or she could leave them alone outside to wait while she talked to her mother and little brother. Dividing into an even smaller group seemed like a bad idea... especially if they needed to flee.

She put a hand on Owen's arm as they reached her door.

He still had a faraway look in his eye, and she needed to be sure he was listening. Once he met her eyes, she told the two boys, "If Mom tries to make me stay, I'll portal us to the longship."

"Right," Baldwin said. "Escape parents with your super god-powers. That's Plan B, I guess. What's the plan that doesn't require us to escape?"

Laurie shrugged. "Talk to her. Make sure they're safe. Maybe tell them about Ragnarök."

"Plan A, complete craziness. Got it." Baldwin gestured to her door. "Let's do it."

She laughed and opened the door. "Mom? It's me."

"Laurie?" Her mother came running to her. "Oh my goodness! *Laurie!*" Her mother grabbed her and hugged her. "I've been so worried. What were you thinking? And you, Fe—you're not Fen."

"Baldwin." He held out his hand like he wanted to shake. "That's Owen. He's not very talkative."

Laurie's mother stared at Baldwin, barely sparing a glance for the blue-haired boy wearing an eye patch like some otherworldly pirate.

"You're the boy who's supposed to be dead," her mom said. "The mayor came, and he told me that F—"

"The mayor lied," Laurie interrupted, pointing at Baldwin. "Baldwin's fine, and Fen did *nothing* wrong. The mayor isn't someone you can trust."

"Oh, sweetie, is this that Brekke-Thorsen thing your father goes on about?" Her mother sighed. "I know they don't get along, but that doesn't mean—"

"Did the mayor say Fen killed Baldwin?"

"Yes, but—"

"So you can see that he *lied*. You can see that with your own eyes, Mom." Laurie was about to say more, when her brother, Jordie, came running into the room.

"I *did* hear you!" he yelled as he tackled her. "I thought you were gone forever."

Laurie felt her eyes burn with tears as she stumbled at the fierceness of his hug. She held on tightly to her brother. "No, not forever." She lowered her voice and added, "But I'll be gone for a while longer."

He didn't say anything, but she felt him shake his head.

"I came to see if you were both okay," Laurie said as she straightened, releasing her brother. "We wanted to check on you."

"The mayor did, too, and the sheriff," Jordie said. "*And* your cousin Kris, the one who lives with Fen."

"Oh." She looked at her mother.

"Why don't we sit down," her mom suggested.

Baldwin and Owen followed Laurie and Jordie into the living room. Jordie was still clinging to her like he was afraid she'd vanish the moment he let go. She felt a wave of guilt because she was going to leave again. She *had* to.

"Ragnarök is coming," she blurted out as they sat down on the sofa.

Instead of being shocked, her mother simply said, "I figured."

"I know it seems crazy but…wait, *what* did you say?" Laurie glanced at Baldwin and Owen, silently asking if they heard the same thing she had.

Baldwin's eyes widened, but Owen nodded.

"Ragnarök," her mom said calmly. "Sky darkened, wolves, Brekkes and Thorsens at odds because of their ancestry."

Baldwin exchanged another look with Laurie. Then Baldwin prompted, "And do you know about the *wulfenkind*?"

"Laurie's father, probably Fen, and" she folded her hands tightly together—"are you…a wolf, too, Laurie?"

"Umm, no." Laurie swallowed and stared at her mother and then at her brother. "You know? You both know?"

Her mom nodded. "Your father explained it years ago. Why else would I forgive him for coming and going like he does? It's because he doesn't want to join the crazier part of his family. I figured Fen would join them, though, and I was afraid he'd talk you into it, too. I worried about his influence."

"You thought Fen was a bad influence because he'd persuade me to join one of the family wolf packs?" Laurie asked. "It wasn't because we got into trouble?"

Her mother smiled. "Well, there was that, too."

Laurie closed her eyes for a moment, pinched her wrist, and then opened her eyes. She was awake. "This is real."

Owen nodded.

"No mara as far as I can tell," Baldwin murmured. "Plus, this isn't really a *nightmare*. It's good, right?" He looked at her mom. "You aren't going to say Laurie should join the bad guys or something, are you?"

"No." Her mother sighed. "I hoped you were making peace with the Thorsens. It is that youngest Thorsen you ran away with, according to the mayor."

"It is," Laurie said quietly. "Him and Fen."

Her mother nodded. "Jordie, go get that picture I had you hide."

Laurie's brother squeezed her quickly, and then he ran toward his room. Laurie watched him go. She wasn't in shock. After everything that she'd experienced lately, shock wasn't likely. She was, however, more than a bit surprised. "You knew."

"I hoped you wouldn't get swept up in it, but then you turned into a fish—"

"That was a dream." She remembered it more like a nightmare, though. She'd woken up to find that she was a salmon and had been terrified that she would suffocate. A few days later, she'd been on the run with Fen, who could become a wolf, and Matt, who could throw people backward with some invisible power. "I overreacted, but—"

"No, dear, you really were a fish." Her mother patted her hand. "I thought maybe we could ignore it. I told your father, of course, but he said that fish were rare in the family. There hasn't been a salmon in generations, apparently. I figured it was better than a wolf, though. Maybe it would mean you wouldn't get mixed up with that Brekke bunch."

"You're a fish?" Baldwin asked. "How come you've never turned into a fish around us?"

Laurie opened her mouth, realized she had no answer, and closed her mouth.

Owen looked at her and smiled. Then he walked away to stare out the window.

Jordie came back carrying a picture and a bag with fish scales. He'd obviously heard the end of the conversation, though, because he said, "I took a picture of it the next night when it happened. She didn't wake up when it happened; it was just *poof*, my sister was a fish. Maybe she can be both a wolf and a fish someday. Dad says it happens." He looked at Baldwin hopefully and asked, "No wolf signs when she's been sleeping?"

"No, not so far," Baldwin said very seriously. "She's always been a girl, no scales or fur, but she does have a bow that shoots invisible arrows."

"Cool!" Jordie yelled. He flopped down next to Laurie and asked, "Can I see it?"

"Not right now."

Baldwin started to add, "She can also make—"

"Stop." Laurie cut him off. She looked at her mother. "Okay, so you already know most of the stuff I didn't know how to tell you."

Her mother nodded.

"Here's the rest: don't trust any of the Thorsens or the Brekkes. Don't go anywhere with any of them, and . . . I don't know. Can you get to where Dad is?" She felt better knowing that her family wasn't as vulnerable as she'd feared, but she felt worse because this meant they realized how dangerous things were in the world—but had no way to stay safe.

"Your father is on his way to us. Last I heard he'd reached Canada, but he's traveling by foot or by bus when he can. He doesn't want to get caught sneaking into town."

Laurie nodded. "Good. Good. So . . . okay, then. He'll keep you safe while I'm away."

"Away?" Her mother's smile vanished then. "You're home now. We'll be here together when he arrives."

That's when Laurie realized that her mother didn't know the big part. "Mom, I can't stay. I'm Loki's champion. I have to fight in the final battle, alongside Matt and Baldwin."

Her mom opened and closed her mouth, but no words came out.

"Matt is Thor's champion, Owen is Odin's, and Baldwin is Balder's, and then the others are waiting for us, too. Frey and Freya's representatives are with Matt. We've got the hammer and the shield, and we're going to fight the great serpent, the Thorsens, and the Raiders...who are mostly Brekkes."

"No," her mother said. "You can't go fighting anything."

"I have to. I'm *Loki's champion*." Laurie stood up and started pacing. "We fought a bunch of monsters already, but the battle is coming. I can't stay here."

"No."

"The world will end if we don't stop them."

"Someone else can do it." Her mother stood, too. "You and your friends will stay here, and when your father gets home, we'll deal with all of us getting somewhere safe."

Baldwin came to his feet. Owen left his post at the window and walked back to Laurie.

"I'm sorry, Mom."

Laurie grabbed Jordie and hugged him tightly. "Be careful," she whispered.

"I mean it, young lady. You are not walking out that door." Her mother gave her the sort of stern look that used to make her quake.

"Okay." Laurie looked at the boys and nodded once. Then she closed her eyes for a moment. She put her hands together in front of her. When she opened her eyes, she spread her hands apart and opened a portal. "I'm sorry, Mom. I'll be as safe as I can. I love you. Tell Dad...I love him, too." She glanced at her brother. "Be good for Mom. Love you."

Her brother and mother were staring at the glowing portal in the living room, but Laurie knew that their shock would fade.

Owen finally spoke. "She's brave, and we'll be with her to help." Then he stepped into the portal.

"Baldwin, *now*," she ordered.

"Nice meeting you. See you after the battle!" he called, and then he jumped through the portal.

"I love you. I'll be careful," Laurie promised, and then she went through the portal, too, just as her mother's shock was fading enough for her to reach for Laurie's arm. Her mother was too late, and Laurie was gone.

EIGHT

MATT

"SMOKE DAMAGE"

Laurie was obviously upset, but she didn't want to talk about it. Matt introduced Jake and explained the plan to go to Mitchell. Then, as Laurie talked to Baldwin and the twins, he asked Owen to take Jake aside and persuade him not to join them, in hopes that his brother would listen to a guy closer to his age.

"It's not happening," Reyna said as they watched Owen unsuccessfully trying to dissuade Jake. "How about we make sure your brother brings up the rear—to guard us, of course. And then, whoops, the portal shuts before he gets through?"

"That wouldn't be right," Matt said, with some regret.

"Doesn't matter," Reyna said. "Even if he's not a Grade A

jerk—and the jury's still out on that—he's going to second-guess your every move because you're his kid brother. He's not Thor's champion. You are."

Laurie nodded. "Reyna's right. It might sound cowardly, but if it's possible to 'accidentally' leave him behind, let's do that. I'll ask him to bring up the rear in case of trouble. You go first as Thor's champion and he goes last as another Thor descendant. I'm pretty sure the portal will close after I go through. It's like a part of me—that's why I always go last, but he doesn't know that."

Matt hesitated. "I'm not sure he'll buy that."

"I'll go second-to-last," Ray said. "That way it won't look suspicious. Laurie goes in. The portal starts to close. I leap through."

"No," Reyna said. "I'll do it. You—"

"I've got this, sis. Now, let's get moving."

As they moved away, Ray caught Matt's arm and led him to the side.

"I'm going to make sure Jake doesn't follow you guys," he said.

"Okay. Thanks."

Ray kept hold of Matt's sleeve. "I mean I'm going to do it by not following you myself. I'll stall him as the portal closes."

"You don't need to do that."

"I want to." Ray met Matt's eyes. "I'll be there for the battle, but I . . . I'm not cut out for this. Reyna is. As long as I'm with her, though, she's torn between protecting you and protecting me. Like at your place with your brother. It's your back she needs to watch. Not mine."

"I don't need—"

"Everyone needs someone to watch his back, Matt. Even Thor's champion. I have to let her do that. I'm better off here anyway. Your family has all those books you read. I can look through them for stuff about the battlefield, in case your uncle doesn't have it. I'm good at that—reading and research." A wry smile. "Better than I am at fighting."

"That's not true."

"Yes, it is. Reyna's powers might work better with me there, but when she's trying to help you, I hold her back more than I help. I get that. So I'm staying behind."

"Okay, we'll talk to her."

Ray shook his head. "There's no time. She'll fight us on this and I'll end up going, and that's not the right move."

But she'll kill me. That's what Matt wanted to say. When Reyna found out what he'd agreed to, she'd be furious. With good reason.

And that couldn't matter because Ray was right.

"Guys?" Baldwin called. "Opening a portal over here . . ."

"You've got this," Ray said. "I'll be there for the big battle and hopefully I'll find something useful in your books. Until then, look after my sister." He leaned over and whispered, "Try not to let her drive you crazy."

They exited the portal into a dust storm. Or that's what Matt thought, seeing the gray floating around them, feeling it burn and chafe as he sucked it into his lungs. He braced himself, peering about wildly for stampeding bison. That's what had happened the last time—he'd come through to see this grayish fog and nearly gotten trampled. It took about five seconds for his brain to remind him that bison in the middle of a city was highly unlikely. Then he smelled the acrid stink of smoke.

"Ray?"

Matt turned and saw Reyna's dim outline through the smoke. Between that and the darkness, it was impossible to see more than a few inches.

"Ray?" Reyna called as she disappeared into the smoke. "Does anyone see Ray?" Her voice started rising in panic.

Matt's gut clenched. He had to tell her, but not until he was sure everyone was safe.

"Roll call!" he said. "Everyone check in."

Voices sounded in the smoke. "Baldwin!"

"Laurie over here, with Owen."

A hand grabbed his elbow. It was Laurie, Owen beside her. Baldwin stumbled to them, coughing and rubbing his eyes.

"Where's Ray?" Reyna said, still lost in the smoke. "Where's my brother?"

"He decided—" Matt began.

Baldwin coughed again, Owen echoing it.

"Um, guys?" Baldwin said. "Smoke might not kill *me*, but..."

"He's right," Matt said. "Everyone, grab someone else, and let's find a safe place."

"I'm not leaving my—" Reyna began.

"No one's leaving anyone." Matt lunged in the direction of her voice and caught her shirttail. He started hacking. "We just need to get out of this smoke."

They stumbled about for a few minutes, Reyna calling after her brother until she began wheezing and Matt made her stop. Baldwin spotted a door—a real door, attached to a building—and they staggered over, yanked it open, and tumbled inside. The first gasp of clean air seemed worse than the smoke, and Matt doubled over, hacking and gagging, feeling like he was going to throw up. Behind him, someone did, and he looked over to see Reyna puking against the wall. Matt tried to steady her, but she brushed him off, looking embarrassed.

"I almost did the same," Matt said. "It's the smoke. I can

still—" He coughed and realized his eyes were streaming, his face wet. "I swear I can still feel it in my lungs."

Reyna stumbled toward the door. He lurched and grabbed her arm.

"I'm fine," she said, shaking him off.

He kept his grip. "You won't be if you go back out. Ray's not there. He...he decided to stay behind."

Reyna brushed her hair back and stared at him. "What?"

"That's what he was telling me. He thought it was best if he stayed and helped Jake look through the old books in case my uncle doesn't have what we need. Ray said he was good at research. He's obviously smart—he handled those Norns way better than I could."

"You left my brother—"

"He *stayed* behind," Laurie said. "I overheard it. He wanted to for...various reasons. Good reasons. Matt still argued, and Matt wanted him to tell you. He could have gone along with Ray's story—that he was planning to jump through, but the portal closed. That's the easy way out. Matt told you the truth."

Reyna shook her head and walked away. Matt watched her go and then pulled his attention back to the others.

"Baldwin and I will go outside and take a look," he said. "Walk around a bit and see what's happening. Obviously a fire, but there's nothing in the myth about fire. Just..." He thought of something and trailed off.

"Matt?" Laurie said.

"We'll go take a look. Baldwin?"

"Right behind you."

The building they'd entered was some kind of office. Empty, it seemed—certainly no one came running to kick out the kids hacking and puking in their front hall. There was a restroom a few steps away. The door was locked—one of those you-need-a-key-from-the-office types. But Matt broke in easily enough, feeling little more than a twinge of guilt. Saving the world means breaking some rules...and some doors.

Matt took a spare shirt from his pack, soaked it with water, and tied it around his face before they went out again. Baldwin seemed impressed. It would be even more impressive if Matt could actually breathe freely with the thing on. But he *could* breathe—smoke free—and that was what mattered.

Shielding his eyes was tougher. He walked outside with his hand in front of his face, trying to wave the smoke back. He looked ridiculous, but there was no one in sight. No one he could hear, either—he realized that when he strained for voices, hoping to find someone he could ask about the fire.

Smoke. Darkness. Silence.

Whatever was happening, this was the creepiest thing

he'd ever experienced. Even creepier than the bone beach in Hel. All he could see was smoke, and it was like he was all alone on the street moving through fog, lost in the swirling.

Where were the fire truck sirens? The alarms?

As if conjuring one up, he heard the faint wail of a siren. It grew louder and louder and then...

Silence.

Matt stopped short. Baldwin did, too, whispering, "What just happened?"

I don't want to know.

But I have to know, don't I? That's why I'm out here. Thor's champion and all that.

He took a deep breath and turned in the direction he'd heard the siren. As they walked, a shape swerved in front of them so fast that Matt barely had time to lift Mjölnir. He saw the thing coming for them, huge and dark, whining as it bore down on them, and he threw Mjölnir the second he was certain it was too big to be a person. As soon as the hammer left his hand, he saw his mistake. It was a truck. Mjölnir slammed into the grille, metal crunching, the front end crumpling inward as the hammer seemed to drive right through the engine. The truck stopped dead...and Mjölnir flew back into his hand.

For a moment, the truck just sat there, smoke wrapping around it, the headlights glowing and then dimming as the smoke whirled past.

"It looks like there's no one driving," Baldwin whispered. "Maybe it's a ghost truck."

The door opened, and Baldwin jumped back. Matt had to steel himself not to do the same. They couldn't see anything. Then a woman stepped through the smoke, squinting, with her forearm over her mouth. Spotting them, she gasped.

"What are you—?" Her gaze dropped to Mjölnir. "Where did you get that? Did you steal—" She took a slow step back. "I don't have anything. I had to leave my purse at the office when we evacuated. All I had were my keys."

It took a moment for Matt to realize she thought they were going to rob her. That they'd wrecked her truck on purpose and now wanted her wallet.

"Um, we're here to help," Baldwin said. "We're trying to save—"

The woman turned and ran. Baldwin raced past Matt, calling after her, but Matt grabbed his shirt and held him back.

"Grown-ups," Baldwin said. "I'm not even a teenager yet, and they already think the worst of me. Do I *look* suspicious?"

Matt could not imagine any kid who looked less suspicious than Baldwin. But it was true. You hit a certain age and grown-ups started looking at you funny, like you were two seconds from slashing their tires for kicks.

When another car zoomed up, they heard it coming and

got to the side of the road in time. Baldwin waved his arms and hollered for the car to stop, but it sped past. The next one honked. The pickup behind it slowed just enough to yell at them to get off the streets, but roared away before they could ask what was happening.

"At least there are people," Baldwin said. "I was starting to wonder."

There were still no sirens, though. Not since that one that had been cut short. As they walked in that direction, they passed through the pocket of fleeing people and went right back into the silent gray emptiness. Except it wasn't completely silent. Matt could hear an odd scraping noise, like a fan with one blade catching.

As Matt followed the sound, the smoke got thicker, until his eyes were streaming tears again and he had to blink nonstop to see, though he wasn't sure why he bothered. All he could see was smoke. He could hear that weird scraping sound, like it was right in front of them and then—

He bashed into something huge and red.

"Is that...?" Baldwin whispered.

Matt ran his hands over the thing—a massive red metal box that disappeared into the smoke. When he walked farther, something tapped against his head. He reached up and felt a thick rope of canvas. He pulled it down to get a better look.

A metal nozzle hit him in the face.

As he staggered back, his hands flew up and his Hammer power launched in a rush of wind that scattered the smoke.

"It's a fire truck," Baldwin whispered.

It was indeed a fire truck. Upside-down in the middle of the road. That sound he'd heard was one of the tires still turning, catching on the crumpled fender.

Matt walked along the truck, casting his Hammer power, surprised that it was actually working. Fear was what fueled it. And that's what he felt, however hard he tried to hide it for Baldwin's sake.

He kept using the Hammer to clear the smoke as he ran to the driver's door. The safety glass was smashed out and it crunched under his sneakers, but when he looked inside, the seats were empty. He exhaled in relief.

Baldwin swallowed. "What could do this? I mean, it's flipped right over, as if…"

Matt looked at the truck again. There were huge dents in the side. Dents where the metal almost seemed melted, the red paint dripping like blood.

What could do this? Oh, Matt had a pretty good idea, and as soon as he thought it, his amulet vibrated.

"Better late than never," he muttered as he gripped it.

"Monster alert?" Baldwin whispered.

"Yeah. I think I know what—"

The ground shook. Someone screamed. Then came a

roar, like the roar of fire itself, but so loud that Matt slapped his hands over his ears, wincing.

"Matt...?" Baldwin tapped his shoulder with a trembling finger.

Before Matt could turn, a wave of heat hit him. He gasped, and it was like sucking in fire, scorching his lungs and sending him reeling back. Baldwin grabbed and steadied him, and they both turned toward the source of the heat. Turned...and looked up.

It was a fire giant. A Jotunn, like they'd met in Hel. Except this one didn't have two heads, which would be a relief except...well, that other Jotunn had breathed smoke and carried a flaming sword and its hair had been on fire. This one? It *was* fire. A fifty-foot-tall human-shaped torch.

"That..." Baldwin whispered, his eyes round. "That's what you guys fought when you came for me?"

No, that's what we escaped from. We hadn't dared fight it. And it was nothing like this....

"There was...less fire," Matt said.

Understatement of the century.

NINE

FEN

"VISITS FROM THE WRONG THORSEN"

As Fen watched the Raiders set up their new campsite at the edge of the Badlands, he felt almost like things hadn't changed. He was living rough, traveling with kids with unusual powers, and he wasn't sure he was ready to face whatever fight would inevitably come next. The difference was that these kids were watching him—not Matt or Owen—for instruction. The Raiders were counting on him...and instead of liking it, he wished he had Matt there for advice on how to handle it, especially when he saw Matt's grandfather Mayor Thorsen walking through the Raiders' camp toward him.

Fen never liked any of the Thorsens, not until he and Matt had fought against a few trolls and assorted monsters together. Liking *that* Thorsen didn't do a thing to change Fen's opinion of the rest of them. It went both ways. Neither family liked the other. They saw everything differently— except Ragnarök, apparently. Mayor Thorsen was commanding a bunch of Brekkes to do his dirty work, while Fen had been on the side of Matt Thorsen. This apocalypse business was confusing everything.

But Fen was still steadfast in his anti-Thorsen stance. He'd met another Thorsen, who shot Matt with a tranquilizer dart and threatened Laurie, and now he was standing in the woods with the chief of the redheaded clan. Mayor Thorsen was all the proof anyone would need that *most* Thorsens were not to be trusted.

"I'm glad you saw sense, young man," the mayor said. "Skull said he could talk to you so we could get you to your rightful place, and here you are."

"Skull cornered me, threatened my friends, and forced me to fight him." Fen glared at the old man. "That's not *talking* to me."

Around them, wolves patrolled and watched. Fen wasn't sure what the Raiders could hear, but he didn't care, either. Part of helping the pack was to let them understand that they were on the wrong side of the upcoming battle. They should already know that trusting Mayor Thorsen was a bad idea, but clearly that fact was somehow escaping them.

"Details don't matter," the mayor said magnanimously. "The point, son, is that you're here now. Loki's champion, ready to lead the monsters into the great battle."

"My cousin is Loki's champion," Fen argued, before he realized that he could be endangering her.

"No, son, you *both* are," the mayor said in a voice that sounded like he was talking to a small child. "The girl is on the other side. You lead the monsters. Loki was a trickster, a many-sided god, which means that for this fight, his descendants will fight on both sides."

Fen stared at the man, feeling like pieces were clicking into place. It wasn't that the Norns were pointing at him *or* Laurie when they directed Matt to Loki's champion. It was both of them. It made sense in a weird way, but it didn't help. He'd rather be no champion at all than be the champion for the *villains*.

"I won't hurt Laurie," Fen pointed out, staring directly at the mayor as he said it. "I'm bound to do what's best for the pack, but there's no way that hurting her *or* Matt is what the pack needs."

The mayor laughed. "Of course you won't! That's not your role. Matty fights the serpent, and she'll fight her own foes. You're not as familiar with the myths as you should be, are you?"

Fen stared at him, not understanding how he could be so calm discussing his grandson's probable death. "The myths aren't set in stone. If they were, we wouldn't have been able to bring Baldwin back," Fen pointed out.

"So you had an EpiPen? Gave him CPR? That doesn't mean—"

"No," Fen interrupted. "We went to Hel."

"Poppycock!"

Fen shrugged and continued, "We met my aunt there. You know, the one who rules the afterlife? We *rescued him from death*. We brought him back. Me, Laurie, and Matt."

The mayor stared at him for a minute. "What have you done?"

"Changed fate," Fen said firmly. "We can do it. Matt doesn't have to die. None of this has to happen."

For a brief moment he thought he'd reached the mayor. He thought he'd gotten through to the man, and he hoped that they'd finally have an adult on their side. It was scary trying to save the world. They'd been doing it, but it was frustrating that none of the adults understood. It was like they couldn't believe, couldn't hope. If that was what it meant to be a grown-up, Fen was glad he was still a kid.

"No," the mayor said. That was it, just *no*. He shook his head, and Fen could see that he wasn't going to listen.

He tried another approach. "But you want to save him,

right? Why would you help save Matt when the house fell into the ground if you want him to die? There are other choices. Maybe we can all sit down and t—"

"No," the mayor repeated. "My grandson needs to be strong and ready for his fight against the Midgard Serpent. I helped because he can't die before the final fight."

Any hope that Mayor Thorsen could be wavering on his path stopped then. He wouldn't alter his plan to sacrifice Matt. Fen filled with so much anger that his voice was shaky as he said, "So you want him strong before he...*dies?*"

"Yes," the mayor said.

"Did it ever occur to you that Matt might win?" Fen asked. "That maybe we could work together and stop the end of the world? You could help him. He's your *grandson*, and he's Thor's champion."

The mayor sighed. "Kids! You just don't understand. You can't stop fate. We can't avert Ragnarök!" He raised his voice and looked around at the Raiders. "This is the start of a new era. After the fight, we will be rulers of a new world. Wolves can roam free. We'll build a new world...one fit for gods. One fit for us."

The Raiders were obviously listening. They stopped whatever they had been doing and watched the old man. It was creepy the way they smiled at him and nodded as if he were sane. He wasn't. He might *look* sane, but he was spouting the kind of theories that only lunatics embraced.

"The blood of gods runs in our veins," the mayor continued. "We'll be the rulers of the new world."

"And sacrificing family members for this . . . perfect world
of yours is okay with you?" Fen asked quietly.

The mayor met Fen's gaze unflinchingly. "Of course I
don't *want* to sacrifice him, but Matt will die a hero's death
and go to Valhalla, the afterworld for the strong and brave.
He'll be happy there."

"Matt would be happier *alive*," Fen pointed out.

"That's not your concern, Fenrir. Your role is to lead our
monsters into the battle. These fine young wolves and the
creatures that will rise . . ." The mayor paused and grinned,
looking like he was talking about some parade or whatever
in Blackwell, not the *end of the world* and billions of deaths.
Then he met Fen's eyes again. "You'll be at the front of our
forces when the battle starts."

The Raiders were all watching them attentively, and for
a moment, Fen was okay being their alpha. Being in charge
meant putting their needs first. Regardless of what roles fate
had planned for any of them, Fen had a responsibility to the
wulfenkind watching him right now. He wasn't going to blindly
follow anyone's plans. It wasn't about whether or not he'd die.
He'd rushed into danger repeatedly, but he'd done it because
the younger Thorsen's plans were sane and logical. There were
things worth the risk—saving the world was one of them.

"You're going to need more than this to convince me that

supporting your plans is what's best for the Raiders," Fen said in a voice intended to carry.

The mayor folded his arms and looked at Fen from the bottom of his ragged shoes to the top of his shaggy hair before saying, "Fate, my boy. The Champion of Loki leads the monsters. If you don't do your job, I'll wipe out the lot of these ragamuffins and your cousin, too." He smiled in a friendly sort of way, as if he hadn't just threatened everyone Fen knew. He was—like most Thorsens—not concerned about the Brekkes. Fen had seen the flash of worry on the mayor's face when Matt's death was mentioned. He obviously cared about *his* family. That didn't mean he cared about Brekkes.

"Brekkes don't have a history of obeying Thorsens," Fen pointed out, thinking of all his family members who ended up in trouble. The Thorsens were the law, and the Brekkes broke the law. That was a fact.

The mayor merely said, "You will do your part, just as Matty will."

Without another word, the old man turned and walked away, leaving Fen with a crowd of *wulfenkind* who were watching him attentively. *Leadership is hard*, Fen thought. He looked around at the kids. Fear was obvious on more than a few faces. He knew only one thing to say that might help them understand his stance.

"Even if I weren't bound by *wulfenkind* law, I wouldn't let anyone hurt my cousin. You all know that I've paid Laurie's dues for years. I don't let down the people I'm sworn to protect. I'll do what I have to do to keep you safe just like I have with her. I'm going to find a way to protect *all* of us." He tried to keep from yelling at them for ever trusting a Thorsen.... Well, trusting one who wasn't Matt. As calmly as he was able, Fen added, "Following Thorsens isn't a great idea for Brekkes, and following *that* Thorsen really, *really* isn't."

He didn't wait to see what they all thought. Instead, he went straight to Skull's tent, which had been the first one Fen had ordered erected. He needed to see how his recovery was going, and if possible, learn some information from him. Skull had been the alpha since this pack was formed. He was the oldest and strongest kid there, and no one would have challenged him for leadership. That meant he knew everything about the pack—which meant that Fen needed to gain his trust if he was to rescue the pack from the mayor's crazy plans.

The older boy met his eyes expectantly when Fen stormed into the tent. "So..." Skull started.

"So, that lunatic is why you trapped me." Fen flopped to the floor of the tent.

"Yep."

"Do you believe in the whole better-to-end-the-world-and-rebuild-from-the-ashes thing?" Fen asked.

For a moment, Skull said nothing. He looked strangely normal in that instant, like he wasn't the same kid who'd tormented Fen for years. Then he ruined it all by saying, "Most of the time."

Fen snorted.

Skull grinned.

They sat, staring quietly at each other for an almost peaceful moment before Skull added, "It's not like it could be worse than now, you know?"

Fen's ears perked up like the wolf he sometimes was. There was a reason Skull was cooperating with the mayor, and maybe if Fen could figure that out, he could change things. Being a Brekke made him understand that people often make bad decisions not because *they're* bad, but because they're scared or angry.

"I need to think about my sister," Skull continued. "I need to think about what's best for the pack... well, I did before you took over. I have a little brother, too, you know? I never see him, and I don't want this life for him, too. Living like we do, always moving, camping, fighting. It gets hard. I have scars I don't even remember getting. My sister handles it, but she's an... unusual girl."

A bark of laughter escaped before Fen could smother it. Hattie was more wolf than girl. Over the years, Fen was pretty sure he'd grown more scared of her than of Skull.

Skull kept on like he hadn't heard it. "I know your dad is in the lockup. Mine is, too. So's my oldest brother. Wouldn't it be better if we didn't have to live like we do?"

There were a lot of answers Fen might've expected from Skull. What he didn't expect, though, was the hopefulness he heard in Skull's voice—and Fen got it. He *really* did. He hadn't seen either of his own parents in longer than he could begin to think about, and he'd been shuffled around between different relatives—from unwelcoming to semitolerant—for most of his life. His cousin Kris was one of the best, but that didn't mean Fen hadn't felt the sting of his fist a time or two. It was just the ways things were.

What if it doesn't have to be that way?

He wasn't sure life would be any better if Dad were out of jail. Fen had more than a few niggling doubts about that, but the hopes Skull had—for something better than the life they all lived now—were tempting.

Carefully, he said, "I understand. I want a different life, too. Was even trying to have one until you—" He cut himself off with a shake of his head, not able to think about his brief attempt to be on the right side of the coming fight. Dwelling on his thwarted attempt to be a hero would only lead to being angrier at Skull. Fen shoved those thoughts away and continued, "The point is that I don't think following a Thorsen on his crazy plan of world destruction is the way to get it."

Skull shrugged. "I'm not sure, but I don't have a better plan. The Raider packs I know of all support him." He stretched, winced, and added, "I'm not a thinker, Fen. I'm not the Champion of Loki, either. It's your pack now. You're the one who visited Hel. You're the one who's supposed to lead us and the monsters to victory. I'll follow you. We all will...just don't get us killed."

Fen stared at him. He wasn't sure if this glimpse of the older boy's fear and trust was better than listening to Skull spout lunacy or not. On one hand, it was easy to think of Skull and the rest of the Raiders as the enemy. On the other hand, Fen was just like them in some ways: Skull wanted a better life; he wanted to protect his family, and while Fen couldn't see even the first thing about *Hattie* that was worth protecting, he knew that he would do anything to keep Laurie safe.

They stayed like that, each boy silent, until they were interrupted by the arrival of a girl Fen would happily feed to the monsters if he could summon any—Astrid, the girl who had poisoned Baldwin with mistletoe and killed him. Fen would've been glad to never see her again.

"Fen," Astrid said.

That was all she got out before he lunged at her. He knew she wasn't a wolf, but she *was* a killer. That overruled the no-hitting-girls rule he used with non-*wulfenkind*.

She met his attack with her own. He landed his first punch, but she dodged enough that instead of connecting with her mouth, his fist glanced off the edge of her jaw. Her knee came up quickly, but he had already moved back and she didn't manage to bring him down with that dirty move.

"You killed Baldwin," Fen growled at her, and he tried to swipe her legs from under her.

"And you brought him back," she countered as she punched at him in a quick one-two of fists. "Fate."

Fen's next punch knocked her backward, but not as much as it should have. She was strong, far stronger than a human girl should be.

"I could've failed. He could've stayed dead," Fen yelled. "We could've *all* died in Hel."

"But you *didn't*." Astrid watched him with an attentiveness that seemed out of place. She punched him, snapping his head back with force.

He glared at her, both in anger and in planning. She fought surprisingly well, enough that he was surprised that Matt had fared okay in his fight with her after Baldwin's death. She'd apparently been hiding this from them, along with her allegiance to the enemy and murderous intentions toward Baldwin.

"Well?" She was waiting for him to figure something out, taunting him. Her eyes narrowed.

Astrid was in their camp, surrounded by wolves. Wolves didn't let non-wolves travel or stay with them. How had he not realized that she was *wulfenkind*? She'd tricked all of

them. That made sense for Laurie and Matt, but Fen could recognize others of their kind.

"You're a wolf?" he blurted, pausing in his shock, and in doing so, he lowered his guard long enough that Astrid landed a solid punch to his gut. "*Oof.*"

"Not a wolf." She grinned, lowering her fists and stepping back several paces, putting herself out of his reach. "I'm just a girl, Fen."

"No, you're not." He looked behind him at Skull, who was watching them with obvious amusement. "Is she usually here?"

Skull shook his head. "The boss said he'd be bringing her. Said she was to stay with us. I'm not sure who she is, but she's not a wolf. The mayor says she's going to be a part of the big fight, and we are to protect her, so you can't really do anything to her...unless she does something *new* to upset you. She's important to the old man."

Fen tried to think of what he could remember about the various stories he'd heard about Ragnarök. If she wasn't a wolf, what was she? Pink-tipped hair, bad attitude, strong, obviously on the monsters' side? He had nothing; no monsters matched that description.

Wish Thorsen were here with his book geeking. Bet he knows.

Astrid was watching Fen. Quietly, she said, "I'm not your enemy. I did what I had to.... Don't even try to pretend you can't understand *that*!"

Skull groaned as he sat up on his pallet. His face was damp with sweat, and Fen suddenly realized he was hurt worse than he'd admitted.

"Do you need anything?"

"I'm fine," Skull snapped, sounding like the boy Fen had known for years. "If the fight's over, get out."

Fen leveled a scowl at him.

"If you don't mind, Alpha," Skull added in a voice that was far from respectful.

It was enough of an attempt at politeness, though, for Fen to nod and motion Astrid toward the tent exit. "Out." He glanced back at Skull after Astrid was gone. "If you need serious help, we can get you to a hospital or something."

Skull rolled his eyes. "Raiders don't go to the hospital, Fen. We heal, scar, and fight some more. We're wolves. If we're too weak, we die."

"Not in *our* pack. Not now. If I'm alpha, I'll set my own rules. If you need the hospital, we'll go."

"With what money?"

Fen barked a laugh. "I didn't say we'd stop being Brekkes, just that we'd get help."

Skull grinned. "You make a good alpha."

At that, Fen realized that he *could* do this. If it weren't for Ragnarök, he might even enjoy being alpha. He didn't want to fight his friends, and he didn't want his packmates injured by his friends. Being alpha had effectively put him in a situation where he had to worry about people on *both* sides.

Unless I can find a way to get the pack to fight on the right side . . . which I can't, since that would endanger them more because the good guys—the descendants of the North—are likely to lose.

The enemy was stronger. They had monsters. They had a leader who had been manipulating everyone. The good guys were a bunch of kids . . . and some goats.

Fen stepped outside, where Astrid waited. He'd never liked the pink-haired girl. She was rude and pushy and— well, she was a lot like him, actually. *That doesn't matter,* he thought. *What matters is that she killed Baldwin.* Whether it was part of the whole fated events of Ragnarök or not, she poisoned Baldwin. She had killed the only boy with whom Fen had found an instant and true friendship. Sure, he had friends at school, but that was mostly because he was intimidating and they wanted to be on his good side. He wasn't stupid. He knew that they weren't the sort of friends who would stick by him no matter what. Matt was a friend, but they were still having to work at it . . . and that friendship might've just been destroyed when he'd seen Fen with the Raiders. No, there was no one quite like Baldwin, and Astrid had killed him.

"I don't have to be nice to you. If the pack is sworn to keep you safe, I can do that. That doesn't mean anything if you hurt any of them—or my cousin. I'm alpha, and I've already ordered them not to touch her. *You* will obey that, too, if you're traveling with us." He crossed his arms and glared at her.

"Understood."

It wasn't fair that he had to protect her, but he took some small joy in the fact that he'd at least landed a few hits on the girl who'd killed Baldwin—*and* framed Fen for it so he almost got arrested for murder.

"Is Matt, umm, okay?" she asked in a weird, soft voice.

Her question was so unexpected that Fen simply blinked at her. *"Seriously?"*

"Well, I mean, I know he's alive and stuff. He did okay in Hel, though, right?" she asked as she fidgeted. She looked down at her hands, which she'd clasped tightly together.

Carefully, Fen said, "I guess he's okay. He's out there somewhere with my cousin, fighting who knows what." He shook his head at the weirdness of his day and the whole situation he was in now, before adding, "And I'm left here trying to convince these fools that ending the world is a *bad* thing."

"You'll be a great alpha. I'm sure Matt taught you a lot." Astrid patted his shoulder awkwardly. "I'm glad he's okay, you know? I really don't want Matt to die."

Fen scowled at her.

"Or Laurie," she added quickly. "I know you worry about her. Maybe you and I should talk....We can't *stop* Ragnarök. It's already started, but maybe we can work together to save the people we, umm, want to protect."

Fen looked at Astrid. He was pretty sure he didn't trust her, but she was the only one in the camp who made even the slightest bit of sense. He shook his head again, trying not to think about the fact that she'd killed Baldwin once already.

"We've all had roles to play, Fenrir," Astrid said quietly. "Yours was to rescue Baldwin. Don't you think I knew you would cry for him? Trust me. I wouldn't have sent him to Hel if I thought you were going to let him stay dead."

Fen knew Astrid obviously wasn't a regular human if she was to be fighting with the monsters in the final battle. She was something else. He didn't know what yet, but he'd find out. "Why should I trust *you*?"

She frowned. "You're here with the pack who fought against you repeatedly. You're their leader now. Do you really think you're the *only* one who doesn't like what he has to do?"

Fen knew how tricky things could get with myths and fate. He had been the one to steal the shield and give it to Skull back before he knew about Ragnarök. It was hypocritical to act like other people couldn't get trapped, too.

"I don't like you," he said after a moment of their glaring at each other.

Astrid crossed her arms. "That's mutual."

They stood there scowling at each other for a few more moments, and then Fen said, "Fine. What do you have in mind?"

TEN

MATT

"LET IT SNOW"

So, the fire giant. Fifty feet tall. On fire. *Completely* on
fire, from head to foot. Carrying two swords. Flaming, of course. Matt barely had time to *think* before
the Jotunn turned his way. He would say it looked at him,
but for that, he'd need to see actual eyes. It had a mouth
apparently, though, which opened and breathed...yep, fire.

The tongue of flame shot right at them, like something
out of a fire-safety video they'd shown in school about
the dangers of back drafts, and Matt had this weird urge
to stop, drop, and roll. Luckily, the flame stopped short
of them, though he was pretty sure it still burned off half
his eyebrows. Then the Jotunn seemed to expand, as if it

were inhaling, filling its lungs with extra air to propel the flame—

Matt grabbed the window frame on the fire truck. It was still hot enough to make him wince, but he shoved Baldwin in. The younger boy scrambled through and Matt followed. They got inside just as the flames struck, licking through the window and hitting Matt's shield as he ducked behind it. Fire engulfed the wooden shield only to freeze in a spiky coat of ice. Yet he still felt the heat of the fire blast through the fire truck's cab. Even Baldwin gasped.

"Just hold on," Matt said. "It'll..."

The flames stopped then, seeming to only last as long as the giant had breath.

"You okay?" Matt asked, crouched behind the shield.

"I'm invulnerable, remember?"

True, but Matt wasn't sure if that meant Baldwin would be protected from the fire—or he'd burn to a crisp and come back to life. Baldwin might love pushing his limits, but Matt suspected that was one test he'd rather skip.

Another wave of flame hit the truck. This time, despite the icy shield, sweat streamed down Matt's face. He made the mistake of reaching to grab something and his fingers grasped hot metal. He yelped and jerked back.

"Hot in here, huh?" Baldwin said. "We'd better hope that big guy gets bored soon, because I feel like a Thanksgiving turkey."

When the Jotunn hit the truck with another blast, Matt realized that was exactly what the giant was trying to do—heat up the cab unbearably and drive them out.

"Head that way," Matt said, waving to the broken passenger window. "We need to get out of here."

They crawled out the other side and along the upside-down truck. When a dangling hose hit Matt, Baldwin whispered, "Too bad these things aren't working, huh?"

Too bad indeed. That might be the only way of stopping the Jotunn. Unfortunately, unless there happened to be a hydrant nearby, the hoses were useless.

"On my count, we're going to run," Matt said.

"Run where?"

"In the other direction."

Baldwin chuckled. "Sounds like a plan."

They got into sprinting position. Then they tore across the road and almost plowed into a building. The front door was locked. Behind them, the Jotunn roared, as if realizing it had lost its prey. Then Matt could see it coming, the flames shimmering through the smoke.

He wrenched on the door. The Jotunn roared again. Fire crackled and Matt swore his back heated as he kept yanking on the handle. The door was solid—no glass to break.

A blast of heat, and this time, fire really did lick him. Baldwin shouted a warning and smacked Matt's back.

"A couple more seconds, and you're going to be lit up like a birthday candle."

"I know. Hold on."

Matt slammed Mjölnir against the door handle. It cracked, and when he heaved again, the door opened. Baldwin shoved him through, the heat hitting again, enough for Matt to wince.

They ran along a dimly lit hall. When they were in far enough for Matt's eyes to adjust to the dark, he could see stuff on the floor. A jacket here. A laptop case there. A pair of sunglasses that he nearly crunched before snatching them up. A trail of belongings, as if the workers had grabbed what they could and ran, being shoved along in the crowd, abandoning whatever they dropped as they were jostled toward the door.

When they reached a stairwell, Matt threw open the door and they started up the stairs.

"Where are we going?" Baldwin asked.

"A higher vantage point."

"Vantage . . . ? Oh, so you can see the giant. From behind glass."

"Preferably fireproof glass."

Baldwin laughed. "No kidding, huh?"

They went up to the third floor and found the front of the building easily enough. Even from the hall, the open doorways to his left glowed red. He went through and saw the whole dim office space lit up by the fire giant's light.

"It looks kinda cool from in here," Baldwin said. "Less scary, too."

He was right. The third floor brought them close enough to see the Jotunn's head and now Matt *could* make out features. It was weird, like seeing flames twisting into a nose and a chin, dark pits for eyes and a mouth. As he watched, the features seemed to constantly rearrange themselves, ebbing and rising with the rolling flame. Fascinating to look at. More fascinating if he hadn't been well aware that an entire city had been put to flame by this creature.

"How are we going to stop it?" Baldwin asked as they stood by the window, staring out at the raging giant.

Matt didn't answer.

"That's what we're going to do, right?" Baldwin said. "Stop it?"

In Hel, all they'd needed to do was get past the Jotunn. Sure, Matt could argue that this wasn't actually a quest— they'd just stumbled on the fire giant like the mara in Rapid City and their real goal was finding that battlefield. It didn't matter. Everything to do with Ragnarök was their responsibility, and if they "stumbled on" a problem, they had to fix it.

"Yes," he said. "We're going to stop it."

"So . . . how?"

"I'm working on it. In the meantime, if you have any ideas . . ."

Baldwin stared at him. "Me?"

"Sure." He forced a smile. "Democracy and all that. I'm happy to listen to any ideas you might have."

"That's . . . not really my thing." Baldwin nibbled his lip. "If you want me to, I suppose I could try—"

"That's all I ask. We need all brains on deck for—"

The Jotunn stepped up to the window. They both stumbled back. Matt put a hand on Baldwin's shoulder and pushed them both down behind a desk. Matt peeked up just as the Jotunn lowered its face to their window, a few feet from where they'd been standing. Its mouth opened. Fire rushed out and engulfed the window, turning it into a huge rectangle of solid flame.

"Please let the glass hold," Baldwin whispered. "Please, please . . ."

It held. When the flames cleared, the Jotunn had its face pressed right up to the window and now Matt could really see eyes in that rolling flame. Black eyes peering through. Matt and Baldwin ducked again.

A roar of frustration reverberated through the glass, shaking the whole building. Matt waited. After a minute, he heard a *thump-thump*, and the crackle of flame started to fade. He peered over the desk to see the back of the Jotunn as it stalked off, still grumbling, the sound crackling like angry flames.

Matt cautiously moved toward the window. "I need to go after it."

"Uh..." Baldwin said.

"We had to make it give up on coming after *us* so I could go after *it*. Turning the tables. I can hunt it; I don't want to be hunted."

"Okay, I get that. But..."

"Can you find your way back to the others? Let them know what's going on?"

Baldwin squared his shoulders. "I'm not leaving you."

"I could really use them. This isn't a small job."

"It's not a small giant, either. They'll find it on their own. Laurie won't sit back and wait for you to handle this."

He had a point.

"They'll come," Baldwin said. "Now, let's go before *we* lose it."

It was easy to follow the Jotunn. Once Matt knew it was there, he could pick up its faint glow through the smoke. He could also hear the crackle of fire.

"Hey, I know where we are." Baldwin pointed at a storefront, barely visible through the smoke. "We came for a family trip. My aunt and uncle were visiting, and they wanted to see the Corn Palace."

"Corn Palace?"

"Sure, it's a big palace. Made of corn."

Matt knew what the Corn Palace was. Most kids in South Dakota did—and many had been there, including him, many years ago. It was, as Baldwin said, a palace made of corn. Well, *covered* in corn.

There was a fifty-foot-tall fire giant heading toward a city-block-sized square of dried corn.

Matt broke into a jog.

"Matt?"

"That's where it's going!" he called back.

"The Corn…?" Baldwin began as he jogged up beside Matt. "Sure, it'll burn, but no one will be in it. They'll all have cleared out by now."

"But it'll burn. That's the point." Matt waved around him. "It'll burn hot. Maybe hot enough to ignite everything else."

"So what are you going to do?"

"That's the question, isn't it?"

For a moment, Matt thought the words somehow came from him. It certainly was what he was thinking. But no matter how scared he might be, his voice wasn't pitched quite that high.

Figures appeared through the smoke. Reyna was in the lead, with Laurie and Owen following.

"Got a plan, Matt?" Reyna called. "I sure hope so, because if that Corn Palace goes up in smoke, the whole city does. No pressure."

She ran up beside him and tried for a teasing smile, but her face was too strained to pull it off.

"So how are you going to stop this thing?" she asked.

"I'm open to suggestions."

They all stared at Matt, and he was grateful he'd put on the sunglasses, so they couldn't see his own expression. He was absolutely stumped. Meanwhile, a fire Jotunn was about to set the city on fire.

"I'm thinking," he said. "Just . . . Let's keep moving."

Laurie ran up beside him. "Sorry to put this on you. Obviously it's a joint effort. It's just . . . well, I was really hoping you had an idea, because I sure don't. We saw that thing. It's fire. It's *entirely* fire."

"I know. Just throw ideas at me, however crazy they might sound."

That's what they did. They threw out ideas. Most of them were crazy, and the ones that weren't just plain wouldn't work.

"I hate suggesting this," Laurie said, "but we might need to call for help."

"I already tried," Matt said. "As we were running, I called the Valkyries. No one's answering."

They all skidded to a stop, so fast their sneakers squeaked

on the pavement. They were at the Corn Palace. As thick as the smoke was, there was no way to miss it. At least two stories tall and covering a whole block. There was even an arena inside. And the outside was decorated completely in dried corn, from the festival a few weeks ago.

"No giant," Baldwin said.

"What?"

The younger boy waved around. "Do you see it? Hear it?"

Baldwin was right. They'd been following the Jotunn, but after meeting up with the girls and Owen—and realizing where the giant seemed to be heading—they'd kept moving toward the Corn Palace. Now they were standing in front of it and there was no sign of the giant.

Laurie exhaled. "Okay, false alarm. That gives us time to come up with—"

The Jotunn's roar cut her off and they all snapped to attention, following the sound.

"Over there," Reyna said, pointing to the right. "It's heading that way. We're fine. Just—"

The giant roared again. They all turned to the left.

"That thing is faster than it looks," Baldwin said. "Now it's over—"

Another roar, from their right, where they'd first heard it. Then another one, from the left, answering it.

"Tell me that's an echo," Baldwin said.

"I would love to," Reyna said. "But..."

She pointed in both directions, and Matt followed her fingers to see two glowing shapes in the smoke, both closing in on the Corn Palace.

They'd split up again. Baldwin with Laurie and Owen now, and Matt with Reyna. One group going after each giant. Going after them to do what? Well, that was still the big question.

"There's got to be a body in there," Reyna said as they ran, her voice raised over the crackles and roars. "Inside the flames, I mean. It's a giant on fire. Which means there's still a giant we can injure, right?"

"Hypothetically."

"There has to be. So we'll get close enough and you'll throw Mjölnir at it."

"And do what?"

"It's a magic hammer, Matt. It'll know what to do, just like your shield does. You need to start trusting it."

"Okay."

"Try that again."

"Okay," he said, firmer.

"Better."

He looked over at her. "I'm sorry. About—"

"I'd rather not talk about it or I'll get mad again, and I can't watch your back if I'm mad at you." She ran a few more steps, then said, "I get why you did it, and I'm glad you were honest with me, and I know Ray put you in a bad position. So I'm mad at him and taking it out on you. Let's just figure out how to stop this thing."

They kept running. The smoke was actually clearer here. That didn't make sense, given how close they were to the Jotunn, but maybe the smoke—like breathing fire—was something it had to do on purpose to smoke people out, and now that there were no people around, it had stopped. While wisps still swirled about them, Matt could breathe and had pulled down the cloth from his nose.

The Jotunn was lumbering toward the Corn Palace. As they raced up behind, the crackle of fire drowned out the pound of their footfalls.

"How close do you need to be?" Reyna asked as they ran.

"I...I don't know. I should test that. Another time."

"We'll get as close as we can, then."

They picked up speed.

"Rope," Reyna said.

"What?" Matt had to raise his voice to be heard over the fire...while hoping it wasn't loud enough to be heard by the giant.

"If this doesn't work, we should get rope. Tie it on the hammer. Throw it around the legs. Bring it down like a roped steer."

Matt sputtered a laugh. "Sounds like you have some experience in that."

"Western South Dakota Junior Rodeo Girls Division Champ, 2010."

"Seriously?"

"I have phases. Most designed to drive my parents crazy. The only thing more embarrassing than a cowgirl for a daughter was a Goth girl. I liked the cowgirl phase better, though. Less moping. More roping. I might go back."

"Well, the roping is a good suggestion, if we need it. And if we can find rope. Until then, it gives me an idea. I'll aim for the back of the knee."

She grinned at him and said, "Good one," and he felt like he'd gotten an A-plus on an exam.

They were at the Corn Palace now, and he could make out the glow of the other Jotunn on the opposite side, also rambling toward its target. Matt clenched his fist around Mjölnir and sprinted as fast as he could. When he drew within about twenty feet, the giant slowed, as if sensing something coming. Matt swung Mjölnir. The hammer flew toward the giant with perfect aim. It hit on target, in the back of the Jotunn's right leg. It struck…and passed right through, then boomeranged back. Matt lifted his hand.

"No!" Reyna shouted.

She lunged and hit him in the shoulder, but the hammer knew where to go, and it struck his outstretched hand. He screamed.

He dropped the white-hot hammer. The pain was like nothing he'd ever felt before, so intense he had to bite his lip to keep from screaming again. Reyna caught his arm and something touched his burned hand, making him bite down hard enough to draw blood, a yelp still escaping. Then a wave of blessed cool, and he looked to see her wrapping on the wet cloths they'd used to breathe through.

"It's okay," she said. "It's okay. It's okay." She kept repeating the words, under her breath, as if reassuring herself as much as him. Lying to herself. It wasn't okay. His hand was the least of their worries, because . . .

"It's fire," he said. "The Jotunn. It's *completely* fire. We can't fight that."

"Yes, we can." She pulled the cloth too tight, as if in emphasis, and he sucked in a sharp breath. "We'll figure out—"

He grabbed Reyna by the shoulders and threw her aside. Then he swung up his shield just as a blast of fire hit it. The giant was lumbering straight for them. Matt grabbed Mjölnir with his bound hand and waved Reyna back, while holding the shield, ready to block the next blast.

The other Jotunn roared and theirs stopped. It turned. Matt told Reyna to keep going, just keep going. Then, as the giant seemed to consider what to do, Matt slid to a halt.

"Hey!" he shouted. "Hey, you! Do you know who I am?"

The Jotunn turned. Reyna had stopped, and when Matt

glanced over, he expected her to shout at him, tell him to get moving. But she stood there, confused but trusting he had a plan. Or maybe that look meant he'd *better* have a plan.

He did. Kind of.

"Yo! Jotunn!" he shouted at the giant.

"Yo?" Reyna choked on a laugh. "Please tell me that's an ancient Norse word, and you're not going to start rapping."

He may have made a rude gesture, but if ever called on it, he would claim he'd simply motioned for her to be quiet while he got the giant's attention. And get it he did. Tossing Mjölnir did the trick. He didn't aim for the Jotunn again—he wasn't an idiot—but he sent the hammer zooming past him. When it came flying back into his hand, he was pretty sure the giant's jaw dropped.

"Yeah, that's right!" Matt shouted, so loud his throat hurt. "I'm Thor's, uh, champ—"

"Again," Reyna said.

He coughed, pretending there was smoke caught in his lungs. "I'm the Champion of Thor and—"

"Stop messing around, Matt."

He lifted Mjölnir over his head. "I am *Thor. Vingthor! Battle Thor!*"

The giant went completely still. It stared down at Matt. Then one hand reached back...and sent a fistful of flame shooting toward him.

"Run!" Matt yelled at Reyna.

She did, and he did, and the giant let out a roar and thundered after them along the empty street.

"I'm really hoping there's a part two to this plan," Reyna said as they hid just inside the double doors of a restaurant. Outside, the Jotunn was stalking the street, crackling with frustration, while, in the distance, its partner roared for it.

Part one had, of course, been simply "Get the fire giant away from the highly flammable Corn Palace." Now that they'd lured the Jotunn away and found a place to hide, he needed to think up a plan for permanently dealing with it. That part was giving Matt more trouble.

"We can't physically fight it," he said.

"Actually, we can. Fight fire with fire. There's a service station down the road. Gasoline. If we could—"

"Fire *feeds* fire," Matt said.

Her cheeks flared red. "Right. I knew that. I'm just… I'm not thinking straight."

"Ray will be fine."

"It's not just that. Without Ray…" She exhaled. "I feel useless. My power feeds off his. I'm bugging you for solutions because, honestly, I don't have any. I'm not even sure what I could conjure up if I had the power."

"Ice cream?"

She managed a wan smile. Then she stopped. "Hey,

wait...ice. There's a rink in the Corn Palace." She caught his expression.

"Ice..." He fingered the shield. "My shield frosts over when fire hits it. If Mjölnir could do that, we could use it. But obviously it doesn't, and I can't just make it happen—"

"Yes, you can." She turned to him. "You're Thor. God of thunder and lightning. Baldwin said you made lightning strike with the bison."

"I don't think that was me."

"Of course it was. You can make it rain. That's the answer." She grabbed his arm. "Come on. Let's see the storm god in action."

They hadn't gone far—just outside the restaurant, so he didn't start a rainstorm indoors. Assuming he could start a rainstorm at all.

"You can," Reyna said, growing impatient now, perhaps because it was the tenth time he'd voiced his doubt. He was trying as hard as he could. Visualizing rain. Not lightning. He didn't want to make the situation even worse, but when he told Reyna that, she said, "That's what's blocking you. Stop worrying about what you *shouldn't* do. If lightning strikes, we'll deal with it."

Easy for her to say. After another minute, she skewered

him with a look. "You're still worrying about lightning, aren't you?"

"No, I'm—"

"You're a lousy liar, Matt. If rain makes you think of lightning, focus on hail. Close enough."

"Hail forms in thunderclouds, which are part of thunder—and lightning—storms. They're caused by updrafts, which can also trigger tornados."

"You know what I wish sometimes, Matt? I wish you weren't so smart. Fine. If you can't—"

The Jotunn turned toward them, as if finally catching the sound of their voices. Reyna noticed it before Matt could warn her, and they both ran for the restaurant doorway. The Jotunn pulled back one massive flaming arm and launched a fireball as big as a car.

"Duck!" Matt shouted.

Reyna dropped to the ground. Matt crouched over her, his shield raised to cover them. It was an imperfect cover, but the fireball wasn't coming their way. It flew past and exploded in the restaurant doorway, blocking their escape route.

"Run!" Matt said.

Reyna started for the next building . . . until a second fireball turned that doorway into a ring of flame. She veered between the two buildings. The giant tried to block their path, but they were too quick. The next ball struck the mouth of the alley and burst into a million embers. Matt held out his shield and threw his Hammer. He was only trying to use the Hammer's force to blow back the embers, but a fist of ice shot from his fingers and did the job twice as well.

"That!" Reyna said. "Can you do that?"

"Not reliably." He clenched his fist and felt the chill of his fingers.

Ice. That would work.

"Stay behind me," he said.

"Not arguing," she said. "I will try to help, though."

By helping, she meant casting a fog spell. It wasn't as good without Ray, but between the thin fog and the remaining smoke, it hid them in that alley while Matt closed his eyes and concentrated.

I know what I need. Just give it to me. Please give it to—

Wind howled down the alley, the gust knocking them back and scattering the smoke and fog.

"Uh, Matt?" Reyna said. "Not to question your judgment, but..."

He shushed her and, to his surprise, she shushed. Outside the alley, wind whined past. The Jotunn roared, but the wind whipped the sound away. Matt kept concentrating.

It's coming. I think—no, I know it's coming. I am Thor. God of wind and rain and thunder and—

The wind hit again. This time, Reyna gasped, and it wasn't the surprise of the gust, but what it brought—a blast of cold that hit their faces and stayed there, sliding down, wet and cold.

"Snow?" Reyna said. "You called for a blizzard?"

Matt turned toward her. "Uh, yeah. I thought—"

"You are a genius!" She threw her arms around his neck and hugged him. Then she pulled back and said, "Don't take that the wrong way."

"Uh . . . okay. I'm just temporarily a genius."

"Not what I meant, silly." She laughed, the sound ringing down the alley, and as he heard it, he realized he'd never heard her laugh before. Or seen her grinning like this, her face lit up.

"Stop blushing," she said, swatting his arm. "It was just a hug. Now, don't just stand there. Keep doing whatever you were doing. Let it snow."

"Yes, ma'am."

Reyna bounced there, humming "Let It Snow" under her breath, and as he turned his back on her, she broke into full song, her voice high and light, swirling down the alley, helping him find his focus.

Let it snow, let it snow, let it snow.

And it did. The snow fell and the wind howled, blasting it everywhere. He'd called up a blizzard.

"Good enough," Reyna said finally. "Let's go see if it worked."

She grabbed his hand—the one without the cloths. Her

fingers were warm against the falling snow. She tugged him, sliding down the alley, the pavement slick now with an inch of wet snow. The snow didn't stretch as far as they could see—the storm seemed to have been confined to this area—but it was enough. Snow, falling lightly as the wind died down.

Matt glanced at the two doorways that had been on fire. Both were charred black, but there wasn't so much as a spark smoldering. There was no sign of the Jotunn. Anywhere.

A snowball exploded against his shoulder.

"You did it!" Reyna called.

He looked to see her gather another snowball, grinning as she did it. He scooped up a handful and shattered hers midflight. She laughed and waved toward the Corn Palace.

"Looks like this is over, but we'd better make sure."

He nodded and followed her, running and sliding along the icy streets.

ELEVEN

LAURIE

"A PRESENT FOR AUNT HELEN"

ight a giant tower of fire, Laurie thought as she tried not to panic at the latest impossible task she had to complete. *Suuuure, no big deal.*

There was no way to fight fire when you were a normal human girl. Actually, she wasn't sure there was any way to fight it if she'd been a wolf like Fen or had a magic hammer like Matt. Mythic monsters weren't meant to be something that kids had to face. It was too big, too awful, too...everything to begin to figure out what to do. That didn't change the fact that she had to do that very thing.

She and Baldwin crept through the darkened streets of Mitchell toward the area where the Jotunn had seemed to be. They didn't see it just yet, but they'd heard the roar, so they knew they were heading toward it.

Despite the walking tower of fire, a sudden blast of freezing cold air rushed over them from somewhere. Laurie shivered. The last thing she wanted was to deal with a flaming Jotunn and something made of frost, too. This whole fighting-impossible-monsters business was *so* not covered in her school lessons.

"How does a giant flaming thing hide?" Baldwin whispered from her side, drawing her mind away from possible monsters to the one they had to face right then.

"I don't know."

"Maybe it can turn the flame on and off like a lightbulb," Baldwin mused.

Despite herself, Laurie snorted in laughter. No matter how messed up things seemed, Baldwin had no sense of doom. She, on the other hand, felt like it was right around the corner.

And she was right, sort of. She turned left in front of the next building, and there, lurking in the shadows, she saw three wolves. Obviously, there was a *slight* chance that they were real wolves, but she was pretty sure that they were like the rest of the wolves she'd seen the past few weeks: relatives of hers that shifted shapes and were foolish enough to want the world to end.

Before she had a chance to figure out what to do, a hand clamped down on her arm and jerked her backward. "Eeep!"

"Shh!" A hand covered her mouth, keeping her from saying anything else to draw the wolves' attention.

For a brief moment, she hoped it was Fen. It could happen. There were wolves; Matt said Fen was with the wolves now. Maybe he came to help them, and that was what he was really doing with the Raiders.

Her hope was dashed when she heard Owen whisper, "We have enough trouble without Raiders in the mix."

Baldwin stood shoulder to shoulder with her. He pointed into the darkness where a glowing shape was now visible. "*That* is our current problem."

The three stood quietly while the Jotunn walked through the darkness like a living torch.

"We could try to steer it toward Lake Mitchell," Laurie suggested.

"Like tag, but...painful if it catches us." Baldwin frowned a little.

It was a less-than-good plan, but she wasn't sure what else to do. She glanced down at her bow. A few invisible arrows didn't seem like much of a weapon against fire. She wasn't even sure if there was anything solid inside the Jotunn. It seemed like there should be. *Every living thing should be solid, right?* That seemed like a basic fact from science class, but she wasn't sure that science class—even in Blackwell—covered monster biology.

"Let's do it," she said.

The three of them walked toward the Jotunn, not bothering to try to hide from it. They needed the creature to see them in order for it to be willing to chase them. Unfortunately, by the time they reached it, they hadn't attracted its attention. It was ignoring them.

"Umm, Laurie? Plan B?" Baldwin nudged her with his elbow. "It's a blind monster or something."

"Jötnar aren't blind," Owen said.

Baldwin and Laurie exchanged a quick look, but neither of them asked why or how Owen knew that.

"Okay, the lake is…" She looked around. It was nearly impossible to get a good sense of direction in the pitch dark. "That way, I think?"

"So, we all run that way and…What? Hope it sees us and chases?" Baldwin asked.

"No," Owen said. "Extra running seems foolish. It needs to see us first."

"Right. Stay here." Laurie squared her shoulders and marched away from the boys. She walked into the street, feeling more like Fen than herself. That was the way she was going to handle this. She thought, *What would Fen do? Be brave like Fen.*

She didn't want to think about the fact that the sort of "brave" she was being was the exact sort of thing that would've made her yell and worry about her cousin. She was just going to do what needed to be done.

Once she was near enough to the Jotunn that she couldn't think of how it could possibly *not* see her, she yelled, "Hey, you!"

Nothing.

She tried again, "HEY! Flamey guy!"

Behind her, she heard Baldwin laugh.

Okay, it wasn't the best thing, but she didn't exactly know the creature's name.

"It's not working," Owen called.

Laurie rolled her eyes. He wasn't as helpful as he seemed to think he was lately. She tried one more time. "Hey, you!"

Still no reaction.

"Here goes nothing," she muttered. Then she raised her bow, aimed, drew back the sinew-string, and let loose an invisible arrow.

For a moment, she wasn't sure it would do anything. *Do ghost arrows burn up?* She drew again, and in short order, she let two more arrows fly.

Then she heard and felt a ground-shaking roar. At least one of her arrows had hit its target.

The Jotunn was scanning the ground, and although her plan was for it to see her so she could lead it to the lake, she quaked as it spotted her.

She was frozen in place as it stalked toward her.

"Move!" Owen called out.

The Jotunn was steadily approaching.

"I don't want to hurt you, but you can't stay here," she called.

It seemed to stare down at her.

"They watched your Aunt Helen the same way," Baldwin said.

Maybe it would listen to her! She was Loki's champion. In as stern of a voice as she could muster, Laurie said, "You need to go away. Go home or whatever."

It didn't move.

"Do you think it understands you?" Baldwin asked.

"Bow up," Owen suggested. "It understood that."

With a reluctant sigh, she did as he suggested.

"Fire," Owen ordered.

She let a volley of arrows fly.

The Jotunn roared again, and this time it took several steps toward them. It wasn't a full-out run, but it was charging toward them.

"Run!" Owen yelled.

The three of them ran toward the direction she'd thought the lake was. The Jotunn pursued them, letting out growls and roars as it did.

The angrier it got, the more it sounded like an inferno. There wasn't a forest nearby, but she could swear she smelled burning wood and heard the crackle of trees falling. She wanted to turn and look, but the heat behind her made it pretty clear that the Jotunn was closing the distance between them.

If it got too close, it would be a lot more than phantom trees that would be burning.

They ran until they reached Lake Mitchell and skidded to a stop.

"Now what?" Baldwin gasped.

This was the part of the plan they hadn't thought about: if they got into the water and it followed, they'd boil to death like vegetables in a soup. If they didn't keep moving, there was no reason for the Jotunn to get into the water.

"Get it in there." She gestured.

"How?"

"I don't know!"

They were only moments from being cornered by the tower of fire that they'd angered.

"Tell it to get in the water or something," Baldwin suggested.

"In the water!" she yelled, pointing at the lake, waving both arms toward it like she could shoo it in.

It didn't seem to understand or react. It didn't even look at her.

"I'll go in," Baldwin suggested. "It can't hurt me."

She hated that idea, but she didn't have a better one— and it didn't matter if she did: before she could say anything, Baldwin turned and jumped into the lake.

Quickly she jerked Owen with her and pulled him down behind a shrub.

Baldwin splashed and yelled, "Hey, you with the flames!" He smacked both arms on the water. "You're not nearly as intimidating as the ones in Hel, you know?"

The Jotunn charged toward the lake, and then all she could see was steam. The air was one giant white cloud as the fire hit water. The hiss was intense, like the largest snake in the world was hiding in that white cloud of steam.

The light of the Jotunn's fire dimmed.

"Baldwin?" Laurie called. "Are you okay?"

"I'm wet, but fine," he called back from somewhere she couldn't see.

"Owen."

"Soggy, but fine. I wasn't expecting a steam bath," Owen said from her side.

"Okay then..." She looked for Baldwin, but she couldn't see him without the light of the Jotunn—and with the blanket of steam all around them.

Then the steam seemed to start to glow. As she watched, the Jotunn's fire sparked back to life and the warm orange glow of the creature made everything look eerie.

Uncharacteristically, Owen bit off a curse word.

"What he said," Baldwin muttered. "I wish Helen were here. They listen to her."

"That's it!" Laurie whispered. She raised her voice and called, "Stay back."

The Jotunn pulled itself out of the lake and moved toward her.

The idea of the towering, flaming Jotunn going through her via the portal was scary, but she had run out of ideas. This was it. She opened the largest portal she ever had, and then she braced herself as the Jotunn charged into it.

The heat from the Jotunn crossing through her portal was intense, but its fire didn't burn her. It lumbered toward the glittering air in front of her, and in a snap, it started to be sucked through the panel.

"I hope Aunt Helen doesn't mind surprise visitors," Laurie muttered as the portal blinked closed.

After the last spark vanished, Laurie dropped to her knees, shaking. She hadn't been sure whether she'd get burned, *and* she'd never created such a massive portal. The combination of fear and excitement made her unsteady.

She looked up at Baldwin and Owen standing at her side again.

"Are you okay?" Owen asked. His hand came down on her shoulder.

"Not sure yet," she whispered.

The queasiness from opening several portals one right after the other was back—and this time, it had brought its friends: headache and chills. Her whole body felt *wrong*. It was like the awful case of the flu she'd had a couple of years ago. Then, she curled up in bed and switched between reading a stack of books, sleeping, and playing video games with Fen, who'd visited as much as her mother allowed him to. Now? None of that was possible. She was kneeling in the street in Mitchell, and the only light around her was from all of the things the Jotunn had set on fire.

"So far, Ragnarök sucks," she told Owen and Baldwin.

Baldwin nodded. "Died."

"Lost an eye," Owen added.

"Lost Fen," she whispered. She felt guilty. Dying or losing an eye was worse. She knew that, but losing Fen was a lot like she figured it would feel if she lost her arm or her lungs. She needed her cousin more than ever. The world was ending. The sky was black, and the buildings were on fire. She couldn't fix any of that, but she was going to try to fix the problem of Fen's loss. Thanks to her encounter with the Jotunn, she even had a plan.

She could open portals.

She could go anywhere.

Laurie wasn't used to thinking about her gifts for anything other than fighting monsters, rescuing friends, or chasing artifacts, but that wasn't all they could be used to do.

Resolved, she put her hands on the pavement in front of her and pushed herself to her feet.

"I need a Raider," she announced. "Catch one."

"You want us to...catch a wolf?" Owen asked.

"Human. Wolves don't talk."

Baldwin started, "Well, they sort of do. It's not English, but—"

"Human Raider," Laurie interrupted. She scanned the street. There had been a few Raiders lurking in the dark during the fight with the Jotunn. Surely there was one still around here now.

The street was mostly empty of people. Laurie wasn't sure if they'd fled this part of town or they were all hiding inside. A towering giant made of fire seemed to clear the area of everyone but the people who weren't surprised that monsters were real.

"Why do you want to talk to a wolf?" Owen asked from her side.

"Raider," she corrected. "I want to talk to a Raider."

Owen put a hand on her forearm. "There is an order to things, Laurie. You and Fenrir are both representatives of Loki. He was a god with two faces, a trickster, too complicated to be contained by only one descendant."

Laurie spun and faced Owen. She met his calm expression with fury. "You *knew* this?"

"Yes."

She wished she were the sort to punch people, because right now her temper was boiling up. She folded her arms and snapped, "So you're saying I'm Loki's heroic side, and Fen is the villainous one? Bull!"

"He's not like y—"

"Shut it, Owen." Laurie shuddered at the temper that filled her. She *liked* Owen. He was her friend. He was the first boy who had kissed her. He'd taught her how to use the bow now clutched in her hand. None of that changed the fact that he didn't understand that Fen was necessary to her—or that keeping huge secrets wasn't cool. Everyone was so focused on the fight, the shield, the hammer, the monsters, the serpent. She was, too, but right now, the lack of Fen in her life was more important than all of that.

"Next time you keep a secret like that, we'll find out how much of Loki's bad side I have, too," she warned Owen. "Fen and I both should've been told this as soon as you met us!"

Owen said nothing. He opened his mouth like he was going to speak, but then closed it without uttering a word.

While Laurie and Owen stared at each other, Baldwin had been concentrating on Laurie's order. With a mighty yell, he went hurtling across the street to the flickering shadows of a building with the front glass windows all smashed out.

Laurie followed him, grabbing Owen's hand and tugging him with her as she ran. She might be angry with him, but he was still her friend. She squeezed his hand and hoped he knew that was her way of saying "we'll be okay." Even though she was a girl, she was still a Brekke—and not as comfortable with words as with actions.

Inside the wreckage of the shop, they found charred and crushed shoes surrounded by shards of glass from the broken windows. Nothing was currently burning, but the smell of burned leather and plastic made her cough.

Standing in the middle of the destroyed shoe store was Baldwin, who had captured a Raider. The captive boy's arms were pinned behind his body by Baldwin's grip, but he still struggled to escape.

"I don't want to knock you down into all that glass," Baldwin said as Laurie walked closer. "But I will if I have to, so can you please stop trying to get free?"

Laurie shook her head. No one else could be so nice while they were holding someone prisoner. She lifted her bow and aimed it at the boy's leg. She wasn't really going to shoot him, but he didn't know that. "I need your help."

"No." He met her eyes and glared at her. "I'm not a traitor."

"Good," she said. "Because I'm not asking you to be a traitor."

He scowled in confusion, but he stopped trying to squirm out of Baldwin's grip.

"I need to see my cousin."

Owen started to ask, "Are you sure that's a good—"

Laurie cut him off. "I need to see Fen. I need to talk to him." She stepped a little closer to the Raider. "And you need to take me to him."

For a moment, no one spoke, but then the Raider nodded once. He told her, "The camp is out toward the Badlands."

Laurie opened a portal and nodded toward Baldwin. The grinning boy and the captive Raider stepped into the portal, and Laurie looked at Owen briefly. "You stay here, and tell Matt I'll be back."

She felt a surge of guilt at the hurt look on his face, but someone needed to tell Matt—and Owen wasn't a fan of Fen, or her plan, anyhow. Quickly, she added, "Trust me."

Owen sighed, but he nodded.

And Laurie stepped through the portal to find her missing cousin.

TWELVE

MATT

"POSTAPOCALYPTIC"

By the time Matt and Reyna made their way back to the others, the second Jotunn had been defeated. And according to Owen, Laurie and Baldwin were gone, having opened a portal to Fen.

Would Fen be ready to listen to his cousin and come back? Or would he try to persuade her to stay there? Matt had no doubt Laurie wouldn't stay, but what if the Raiders took her and Baldwin hostage? Matt had to trust that Laurie knew what she was doing.

"Off to find your uncle," Reyna said. "Finally. You know where he lives, right?"

"I have an address."

"But you've been there? He's your uncle, isn't he? Wait, Jake said something about not having seen him since you were a baby. How come?"

"There's . . . a family situation. With my grandfather."

"Shocking."

"The address?" Owen cut in.

Matt rattled it off. "I know the general area, too. Jake told me. But I've never been there."

"We'll find it," Owen said. "Just point us the right way."

They passed one smoldering building after another, but things seemed quiet. Everyone must have evacuated the city center. It looked like something out of a postapocalyptic movie. A kid's lunchbox dropped in the middle of one empty road. A nylon jacket caught on a signpost, flapping in the wind. Dumped trash and recycling bins, spilled contents on fire, tongues of flame licking out. The sizzle and pop of wooden building trim, embers glowing in the near-dark. And smoke. A fog of smoke, settled low but refusing to dissipate, the stink everywhere. Smoke and fire and destruction.

If this looks postapocalyptic, what would it look like post-Ragnarök?

The streets were eerily silent except for the crackle of smoldering wood and the snap of that abandoned jacket. A sudden yowl from up ahead had them all starting. A small tree smoked on one side, the faint glow of fire darting from a burning patch of dead foliage. The yowl came again. Matt hurried over and peered up the tree to see a calico cat, its green eyes staring down, as if in accusation.

"No," Reyna said, stopping beside him. "We are not rescuing the cat."

"But the tree—"

"—is on fire. I see that. Have you ever owned a cat? If they can go up, they can come down. Guaranteed."

Matt eyed the feline. It eyed him back, then yowled, as if to say *Well, hurry it up.*

"It might be too scared to come down," he said.

"It's a *cat*," Reyna said. "They don't get scared—just annoyed, which I'm going to get if you insist on playing hero and rescuing that faker." She scowled at the cat. "Yes, I mean you. Faker."

The cat sniffed, then turned to Matt, clearly sensing the softer touch.

Owen stepped forward. "If you'll feel better rescuing the cat, Matt, then go ahead. We aren't on a tight schedule."

Reyna waved her arms around the smoking street. "Um, Ragnarök?"

"And the longer you two bicker…"

"Fine," Reyna said. "I've got this." Before Matt could protest, she walked to the base of the tree, grabbed the lowest branch, and swung up. "Rodeo girl, remember? Also,

five years of gymnastics, which my mother thought would make me more graceful and feminine. Her mistake."

She shimmied along a branch. "Come on, faker. I'm your designated hero for today." She looked down at Matt. "And if you ever tell anyone I rescued a cat from a tree..."

Before Matt could answer, the cat sprang to the ground.

"Arggh!" Reyna said.

"You scared him out," Matt said. "He just needed the extra motivation. No, wait. It's a she. Calicos are almost always female."

"Are they? Huh." Reyna swung out. The cat sat on the ground below, watching.

"See?" Matt said. "She's grateful."

"She's gloating. Let's go."

They went. So did the cat, heading in the same direction, trotting along behind Reyna. Whenever she glowered at it, the cat would look around innocently, as if to say *What? I happen to be heading the same way.*

As they walked, Matt tried to talk to Owen. Not about anything to do with Ragnarök. Just talk. Conversation. But Owen deflected questions and instead turned them to Matt, asking how Matt felt about the coming battle. Which really wasn't his idea of distracting conversation.

"Give it up," Reyna whispered to Matt as he pulled back

to let Owen go on ahead. "If you're bored, you have to make do with me."

"I was just trying to get to know him better. But I guess all-knowing doesn't mean all-*known*, huh?"

When she looked confused, he said, "Odin is the all-knowing god."

"I don't think Owen's all-knowing."

"Yeah, but he knows more than us."

"True." She fell in step beside him. "How about you bring me up to speed on the myth stuff. Yes, I know, you've told me everything I *need* to know. But..." She shrugged. "I'd like to know more. You're the guy for that. And it also seems as if we have a bit of a hike here."

"Well..." He glanced back at the calico. "The Valkyries told you that Freya's chariot is drawn by two house cats, right?"

She smiled. "Right. I forgot that." She looked at the cat. "Hey, make yourself useful. Find a friend and a chariot, okay? My feet are getting sore."

The cat eyed her balefully.

"Do you want to hear how Freya got her cats?" Matt asked.

Reyna nodded, and he told the story about how Thor had found two motherless kittens and been asked by their father, a magical cat, to take them home. Thor had given them to Freya, and they became her boon companions, often depicted at her feet, when they weren't drawing her golden chariot.

"You know what that means, right?" Reyna said. "You owe me another cat."

Matt laughed. "I guess so. There's another part of the myth, one that says after seven years, she rewards her cats by turning them into witches. Maybe that's what this one is hoping for."

"Seven years?" Reyna looked back at the calico. "You try sticking around for seven years, and I'll turn you into something, all right. A pretty calico rug."

The cat only looked off to one side, as if to say *Whatever,* and they continued on.

The fire didn't seem to have reached Uncle Pete's street, but the smoke certainly had. And the blackouts. In the distance, Matt heard what sounded like a guy with a bullhorn.

"Stay in your homes," the guy was saying. "The fire department has managed to contain the blaze to the downtown."

"Um, no, that would be us," Reyna said. "You're welcome!"

The bullhorn man continued, telling people to keep their windows and doors shut, not to venture outside because of the high concentration of smoke still in the air.

They found Uncle Pete's bungalow and walked up the drive behind a Jeep that had camping gear and two bikes loaded up.

"Judging by that mud, it looks like he was four-by-four'-

ing with the Jeep. Cool." Reyna looked at the bikes. "I thought you said he wasn't married."

"He must have a girlfriend."

They walked to the door and knocked. When no one answered, Reyna jumped off the stoop and peered in the front window.

"Ooh," she said. "He likes old action movies. He's got posters for *Indiana Jones* and *The Terminator*. Whoa, is that an original *Blade Runner*?"

"Do you see any actual people inside?"

"No, but there's a sweet home theater setup."

The cat leaped up beside her and peered in, and Matt almost laughed, the two of them with their noses against the window. Reyna rapped on the glass and called, "Hello?"

"Is it dark?" Matt asked.

"Um, yeah, considering the lack of electricity."

"Exactly. Considering the lack of electricity, people would be lighting candles so they aren't sitting around in the dark."

"Ah, good point." She shielded her eyes against the glass. "I see light, but it's way back. A basement maybe?"

Matt knocked at the front. Then he went around the back and did the same. When both failed to bring anyone, he tried the doorknob. It opened.

The cat slid through his legs, nearly tripping him. It walked in. Looked around. Walked out onto the back porch. Meowed.

No one's home.

When the cat jumped onto the railing, Owen murmured, "Yes, stand watch. That might be wise," and Matt laughed softly, but Owen only frowned, as if wondering what was funny.

They went in, and Matt looked around the darkened house. "Uncle Pete?"

No answer.

A little illumination came from a solar-recharged night-light, glowing in the kitchen. Matt found the basement door and opened it to see pitch dark. In the kitchen, he paused at the fridge. There were photos of Matt and his brothers, neatly lined up in a row. As toddlers, then as kids, then teens.

The front room was empty. He left Reyna admiring the home theater setup while he checked the three closed doors. One led to a bedroom, one to a bath, and the third to an office. Most of the books seemed to be Norse history and myth. At least a third of them were stacked on the work-table. Papers and journals blanketed every inch of remaining space.

Matt picked up one paper. Handwritten words like *serpent* and *Mjölnir* and *rules of engagement* covered the page, with arrows between them and notations that looked like page references.

When Matt saw the cell phone, his heart picked up speed.

"No one goes out and leaves their phone," he said to Reyna as she joined him.

"They do if there's no cell service," Reyna said.

Reyna hit a couple of buttons, and then looked up. "Is your dad's name Paul?"

Matt nodded.

"There's a voice mail from him, dated yesterday." Her finger moved over the screen, then she stopped. "You should— Or if you'd rather…"

I'd rather ignore it. Which I can't, of course. Face the truth, whatever it might be.

"I'll take it," Matt said.

"You do that," Owen said, looking in from the hall. "Reyna and I will check the basement to be sure it's empty."

"Matt's uncle is a descendant of Thor," Reyna said. "He won't be cowering down there in the dark." She paused, as if catching a look from Owen. "Oh, you want to give Matt privacy. Just say that."

They left. Matt looked down at the message. He checked call logs instead, telling himself he was gathering data, not stalling. There were three incoming calls from his dad since Matt had left home. No outgoing calls since the message came in, though it had been listened to.

Matt hit the PLAY button.

"It's Paul. I'm not sure if you'll get this. I've just heard people in Lead and Wall lost power and cell service.

I hope you still have it. It's—" His dad sucked in breath. "Obviously, if you look outside your window, you know I haven't been entirely honest. Matt didn't just run off. It's Ragnarök. If I'd known it was coming so fast, you'd have been the first person I called. I'm sorry. But the seers selected Matt as Thor's champion and he took off with a couple of the Brekke kids. Dad said he got scared and ran. I…"

His father inhaled again, the sound hissing down the line. "That doesn't sound like Matt, but he *is* just a kid and I handled the whole thing badly. He found out he was going to fight the Midgard Serpent, and I patted him on the back and sent him to the fair with a hundred bucks. But if he did just get spooked, he'd have come back by now. He's a responsible kid. I'm just worried about him. I think there's more going on here with Dad."

A long pause. Then, "I'm going to ask you not to phone me back. I'm just…I'm being careful. I'll call you later, okay?"

The message ended. Matt stood there, staring down at the phone. Then he played it again.

Matt was heading to the basement to call up Reyna and Owen, when he heard the cat meow at the back door. He didn't even think, moving on autopilot, his mind still wrapped up in that call, and so he opened the back door to let the cat in.

Dad didn't believe I'd taken off.

He said that I was responsible. That he was worried about me, more worried about me than about Ragnarök.

"What the—?" Reyna said behind him.

He turned to see her stopped at the top of the basement stairs. The cat had zoomed past him—directly to the front door, where it was meowing.

"Seriously?" Reyna looked at him. "Let them in one door and they want out another."

Matt struggled for a smile. Reyna eyed him and said, "Did your dad say anything we need to know?"

"Only that he's starting to suspect things aren't right with Granddad."

She snorted. Owen cleared his throat, as if to back her off, but she only walked over to Matt, her voice lowering as she said, "Anything else?"

He shook his head.

"You okay?"

He nodded.

She paused, then said, "Do you want...I don't know..." She shifted awkwardly, voice dropping again as she said, "Do you want to talk about it?"

When he shook his head, she stiffened, as if she'd said the wrong thing, and she started to back away, but he said, "Maybe later?" and she nodded, color rising in her cheeks as he murmured, "Thanks."

The cat scratched at the front door.

"Hey, no," Matt said, jogging into the front room. "Don't—"

The door opened. It wasn't Matt's uncle, but a dark-haired, bearded guy in his thirties, wearing goggles against the smoke. He saw the kids and stopped as Matt lifted Mjölnir.

"Yeah," Reyna said. "See that hammer? Wrong house to loot. Move along."

The man pulled off his goggles. He smiled, a broad grin that creased his eyes at the corners. "Matt."

Matt froze. "You know who I am," he said, shifting Mjölnir to the other hand, making sure the guy saw it.

"Your picture's on the fridge."

"You aren't my uncle."

"No, I'm Alan." He put out his hand. "I'm a friend of his."

"Alan Dupree?" Reyna said.

A pause, then the man said, "That's right."

"There's an office downstairs," she said to Matt. "A diploma in pharmacology has his name on it."

"Right..." Alan said. "I'm your uncle's roommate. Well, housemate and—"

"There's only one bedroom," Reyna said.

"I...just moved to Mitchell a few months ago, so I'm taking the pullout couch until—"

Matt cut in. "Where's my uncle? I need to talk to him."

Alan hesitated, then he pulled himself straight and waggled the goggles from one finger. "We heard there were people trapped in apartments on the edge of downtown, and he had to go see what he could do to help."

"Which proves he's definitely your relative," Reyna said to Matt.

"Where's he now?" Matt asked.

"Still there," Alan said. "A couple of apartments are affected, and the fire department is AWOL. I drove back to grab cases of water and get him something to eat. Otherwise, he'll keep at it until he collapses. I can take you—"

"No," Matt said. "We'll go by ourselves."

"Matt's earned his paranoia," Reyna said. "Just point us in the right direction, and give us your keys. I'll drive."

Alan looked at Reyna. "How old are you?"

"Fourteen. Got my license last month."

"You won't mind if I ask to see it, then?"

She waved at the front window. "Um, apocalypse? Kind of forgot my wallet."

"Can we take your car?" Matt said. "We'll be careful, and there's not much out there to hit."

"All right, but I'm going with you." When Matt paused, Alan said, "I know you don't trust me, but unlike your friend there, I can show ID. If I'm sending you into a trap, at least you can take me hostage."

Matt sat in the back with Alan. Owen took shotgun. Reyna drove. Though she was really only thirteen, she obviously had experience, and she was careful, staying under the speed limit and obeying the stop signs even if there wasn't another car in sight. The cat sat in the back window, having hopped in and made itself comfortable as soon as a door opened.

"So that's the famous Mjölnir?" Alan said. "Is it true that only Thorsens can hold it?"

"No, anyone can," Matt said. "You just need to be a Thorsen to *lift* it."

"Right. I know all the lore." Alan quirked a smile. "Spend enough time with your uncle, and it's unavoidable." He sobered and cleared his throat. "If there's anything you want to talk about...about...me."

"Unless you turn out to be a Raider or a monster in disguise?" Matt shrugged. "It's a nonissue."

Alan nodded slowly, then he took out his wallet and flipped to his license. He paused, and instead passed over a photo of himself, grinning and covered with dirt, wearing a caving helmet. Beside him was a man who looked like a younger version of Matt's father.

"Is that proof enough that I know him?" Alan said.

"Not in a world with Photoshop."

Reyna chuckled from the front seat.

Alan shook his head. "You kids are tough."

"We've learned to be."

"I imagine you have. I—" He stopped short. Matt followed his gaze to see an apartment, smoke billowing from the windows, flames licking out.

"Let me guess," Reyna said. "That's where you left Matt's uncle."

"On the top floor. There were people trapped up there."

Before he could finish, someone ran from the sidewalk, waving frantically. It was a young woman, her face covered in soot.

Alan jumped out before the car came to a complete stop. "Is Pete still—?"

"He's in there," she said. "They were right behind me and then something happened."

"Of course it did," Reyna muttered.

"I need to go—" Matt began.

"Of course you do," she said. "And we're right behind you."

THIRTEEN

❖

FEN

"PROVOKING A DRAGON"

The Raiders' campsite was, as their camps always were, tidy and organized. This one was a little different, though, because they were settled in the Badlands. Craggy rock formations jutted up and looked a lot like the landscape of Hel. Usually a hike or run through the gorges and exploring the imposing cliffs was a treat for Fen. It was a perfect terrain to enjoy being a wolf. Now, however, it made Fen a little uncomfortable because of the similarity to Hel. He half expected monsters to step out of the gorges, but so far the only horrible creature he'd found at their site was the girl beside him.

Astrid was to be protected, according to the mayor, and Fen wasn't sure how seriously the pack was tied to the crazy old man. He needed answers, and although talking to Skull had clarified some things, the only one who had proposed trying to figure out a plan was...Astrid.

It could be a trick.

It could be true.

Either way, Fen saw no harm in talking to her. He hadn't hidden his thoughts on Ragnarök so far, and he couldn't actually make any decisions that would endanger his pack, so there were no secrets he could spill. If she knew anything about *wulfenkind*—and he guessed that she must, since she was traveling with them—she knew that already...which meant she might be honestly looking for a way to protect Matt.

Fen was silent as he and Astrid walked farther away from Skull's tent. He had the feeling that he needed more privacy than he'd get in camp. He motioned toward two of the Raiders who were watching him.

When the boy and girl came over, Fen said, "Astrid and I are going for a walk. No one is to leave camp."

They both nodded. The girl said, "Do you need an escort?"

"No. Just pass the word to stay in camp."

Then Fen turned to his former enemy and motioned toward the hills. "Killers first."

She rolled her eyes, but she said nothing as she walked deeper into the cliffs and ravines of the Badlands.

Temporary truce. He could do that. He wouldn't forget, though, not ever, and if they all got through Ragnarök, he'd find a way to make her understand that she should never ever hurt his friends again.

Astrid stopped in a clearing that was sheltered from view by the rock formations. "Before I say anything, I need to *show* you something."

Fen made an impatient gesture.

Astrid looked around the clearing and then gave Fen a glance that—on most people—would seem to mean they were scared. On her, he figured it was a trick. He couldn't do anything to her. She was under his pack's protection.

"I won't hurt you," Astrid said quietly. "Don't run or freak out, okay?"

Her eyes changed as she spoke. Instead of normal girl eyes, her eyes looked like a snake's or alligator's. They weren't human eyes. They weren't even *mammal* eyes. He was right that Astrid was something other than human. She was a shape-shifter of some sort, but she wasn't a wolf like Fen.

"What...what *are* you?"

"I won't hurt you," she repeated.

Then her skin started to change. What was smooth became scaled. Her pink-tipped hair vanished. Her fingers

stretched, and her fingernails became claws. Her jaw lengthened, and her teeth extended to fit her now extended mouth. Thin-skinned wings stretched from her back and flapped once, then twice, and then once more before folding flat against her back.

"You're a dragon," he breathed.

The pink hue on the tips of her hair when she was a human was a slightly paler shade than the color of her scaled body. She looked like she belonged in a kids' book or cartoon, if not for the scary-looking claws and giant teeth. Those were weapons.

His plans to make her understand not to threaten his friends suddenly looked more difficult...which made him realize that he'd been provoking a *dragon*. He'd been rude to her since he'd first met her. And right now, she looked like she could eat him alive. It made him a little queasy.

Astrid the dragon stretched her body out on the ground, watching him from reptilian eyes the whole time.

Fen hadn't moved. He hadn't run, but he wasn't moving nearer to her, either.

She exhaled a puff of sulfurous air from behind those gleaming fangs, but there was no fire or even smoke. Then in a quick moment, the dragon seemed to fold in on itself, becoming a girl again.

"You're a *dragon*," he repeated.

"I am." She didn't come any closer, but she watched

him carefully as she added, "My role as guest of the pack means you have to do what's in my best interest, just like the *wulfenkind*."

"I know," he said. A giant pit opened up in Fen's stomach. Whatever she was about to say was going to be something he really wouldn't like. Worse yet, he was powerless to argue. There were rules he couldn't break, no *wulfenkind* could.

"I had to... poison Baldwin. I *had* to make sure the myths stay on track," Astrid said, her voice sounding a little like she was trying to convince herself, too. "My family plays a role in this, too. I had no choice, Fen."

He thought about it. His mind rolled through every Norse myth he could think of. *Dragons? Where were dragons in the stories? There were other reptiles, but...* His mind clicked on what she was saying suddenly. "Reptile," he whispered.

"Reptile," Astrid agreed.

"*You're* the Midgard Serpent?" he asked, backing away so quickly that he almost tripped over his own feet.

"It's a little more complic—"

"All Matt needs to do is beat you?" Fen interrupted. There were some serious possibilities here. They could end this whole mess pretty easily. Matt could take her in a fight, right? The whole part where she was a dragon would be a little harder... or maybe not. Thorsen was a good guy. He might find it easier to fight a dragon than a girl. He laughed.

"So the big bad monster we were so afraid of is a girl our age? This is so awesome."

"Not exactly," Astrid said slowly. "My grandmother is the serpent right now, but...it's a family trait. You and Laurie are Loki's representatives; Matt is Thor's...." Astrid shrugged. "Everyone's a descendant of someone. My ancestor just happens to be a dragon. That's my role in the big end-of-the-world fight. I get to be the monster that kills Thor."

"Wait a minute! In the myth, Thor fights the serpent once before the great battle." Fen glared at her, folded his arms over his chest, and shook his head. "You...you came to us so you could fight him."

Astrid gave him a pitiful look, seeming far more vulnerable than any dragon should be. Her eyes widened imploringly, and she clasped her hands together. "I like Matt. I don't want him to get hurt. I grew up hearing about him. My whole life I was told about Thor, about him....They wanted me to hate him, but really, Matt is a hero."

Fen narrowed his eyes and stared at her. "You *like* him."

Astrid blushed, but then she looked straight at Fen and said, "He's brave, and he shouldn't have to die. I've been trying to follow the parts of the myth I have to. Maybe we can change the ending a little, though."

Something didn't add up. He wasn't sure what it was, but he knew that he was missing something. This was when he'd typically talk to Laurie or even Matt, but he couldn't. He knew things they needed to know, but he was magically bound by his role in the pack. He couldn't tell them, no matter how much he wanted to do so.

"How about you just let Matt fight you, lose, and then we can call off the whole ending-of-the-world part?" Fen suggested.

Astrid giggled.

Somehow that seemed almost as disturbing as the fact that she was a dragon. When the monster laughs, it's never a good thing. He'd read enough comic books to know that.

"What's so funny? I think..." He didn't get to finish telling her that he thought that his idea could work, because the air in front of him started to shimmer.

"Portal," Astrid murmured.

Fen glanced at her and then back at the opening that was forming in front of him. Seeing a portal open up was commonplace lately. What left him with his mouth hanging open like a gaping fish, though, was seeing Laurie and Baldwin step out of that portal at the edge of the Raiders' camp. They were the good guys, the heroes, part of the team that would defeat the monsters that *he* was supposed to lead into the final battle.

But there she was, his cousin. A Raider whose name Fen didn't remember stumbled forward, and Baldwin stood shoulder to shoulder with Laurie as the portal snapped closed. All three of them were ash covered, and there were smudges of soot on Laurie's face.

"What hap—"

"What happened?" Laurie cut him off. "What *happened*? Well, you'd know if you hadn't vanished on me!" She folded her arms over her chest, and the look on her face was one that made him want to tuck his tail between his legs and slink away.

Before Fen could answer, she stepped forward and hugged him, and then smacked him on the shoulder and said, "You have some explaining to do, Fenrir Brekke!"

FOURTEEN

MATT

"BATTLE CRY"

Owen stayed outside the burning apartment building. Matt, Reyna, and Alan went in. So did the
cat. Reyna muttered that if the feline had to hang
around, at least it could make itself useful and lead the way
and risk being first in line into a burning building. The cat
fell in at the rear.

"Here," Alan said, passing the goggles to Matt at the
front.

When Matt shook his head, Reyna dangled the keys.
"Trade?" Alan passed over the goggles.

Reyna slapped the goggles into Matt's hand. "Wear
them, Thorsen. Otherwise, you're going to get blinded by

smoke and lead us into a burning room." She turned to Alan. "That's how you need to do it. Don't tell him he's in danger if he refuses—tell him someone *else* is."

Alan grinned. "It must be a Thorsen thing. I was tempted to faint and pretend I'd collapsed from low blood sugar to get Pete back to the house to eat."

He led them to the stairwell, explaining that when they'd heard about folks stuck in this building, it had seemed an easy job. The stairwells were clear, no sign of smoke, the problem apparently just a jammed stairwell door, which Pete could handle with his Thorsen strength.

The woman outside had said Pete had gotten the door open and a bunch of them had escaped, only to reach the bottom and realize the rest weren't behind them. That was when the stairwell filled with billowing smoke.

Matt opened the stairwell door. Smoke swirled down, the stairs completely hidden under it. "Fifth floor, right?"

Alan nodded.

Matt hefted Mjölnir. "I can handle this."

"Um," Reyna said. "Did you hear the 'right behind you' part? That's not an option, Matt. Unless you tie me to the railing, I'm watching your back."

"Seconded," Alan said. "Except the part about the railing."

"And as Owen said, the longer we bicker about it..."

Matt nodded. "Come on, then."

Alan gave them bottled water to soak cloths he'd brought to hold over their noses and mouths, but climbing stairs while breathing through that cloth left Matt feeling like he was running uphill. They made it as far as the fourth floor. That's when the heat hit.

Matt glanced up to see the ceiling on fire. It looked like a roiling sea of flame. The cat raced past to the stairwell door and pawed at it.

"He says that way," Alan said, his voice muffled by the cloth.

"*She's* just trying to escape the flames," Reyna said.

"So she's not magical?"

"Huh?"

"Matt said you're Freya's descendant, and I know she has a cat...."

"Freya has two."

He smiled. "Maybe you get the second after Ragnarök. Like a graduation gift."

Reyna laughed. "Maybe, but I don't think that cat's magical."

"It's just randomly following you into burning buildings?"

Matt was already at the door, feeling it for heat. When he opened it, the cat ran through.

"Magic or not, let's presume she has good survival instincts and see where she leads us."

They followed the cat down the hall, into an open apartment and out to the balcony door. Matt reached for the cat to move it aside while he opened the balcony. When he opened it, the cat raced out and jumped onto the railing.

"Whoa!" Matt said. "Hold on!"

The cat balanced there, peering up. A portable fire escape ladder dangled from the balcony above. Before Matt could say anything, Reyna was on the railing, one hand braced on the wall.

"Careful," he said.

She nodded and gave the ladder an experimental tug. Then a harder one. When it held, she grabbed on and began to climb. Matt held his breath until she was up. Then he went. Alan followed. The cat did not.

At the top, Matt walked through the balcony door. Despite the smoke, he could see Reyna in the middle of the living room, staring at the hall door. Flames curled around the edges, like fiery fingers trying to pry it open.

"Wrong way," she said. "We—"

A tremendous crack cut her off. It came from the room to their left. They followed the sound into a bedroom . . . with a hole in the wall. An ax hacked at the hole. Matt took a step back, one arm going out to stop Reyna and the other hefting Mjölnir. The ax continued to chop a hole through the wall.

"Who's there?" Matt said.

The ax withdrew. A head ducked in—a man wearing

goggles, his red hair tied back, a Thor's Hammer dangling from his neck. He saw Matt and rubbed his goggles to clear the soot.

"Matt?" he said.

"Hey," Matt said.

Alan stepped forward. "He brought friends. Other—"

Uncle Pete cut him off with "Hang on" and pulled back, then kept chopping the wall. When the hole was big enough, he squeezed through. Matt could see people on the other side, looking on anxiously. His uncle motioned for them to wait.

"You okay?" Alan said.

"Sure. I need you to take the kids back down with these people. I got the ladder ready, as you saw. Then the fire engulfed the door. So…" He motioned at the hole. "Plan B." He said this all calmly, as if rescuing people from burning buildings was a daily occurrence.

"And you?" Alan said.

"There's a family trapped in an apartment."

"Of course there is," Alan said with a soft sigh, shooting a look at Reyna, who smiled and shook her head.

"I can help with that," Matt said.

"No, you'll—"

"I *will* help with that." He met his uncle's gaze and lifted Mjölnir. "This might come in handy. You can wield it, but I'm used to it."

Uncle Pete blinked, then he stared at the hammer. "That's . . . It's really . . ."

"My shield also fights fire with ice. Now can we go?"

His uncle still hesitated. Matt walked to the hole and climbed through. He heard Uncle Pete say, "Wait. No. You help Alan." He was turning to refuse when he saw Reyna coming through after him.

"Package deal," she called back to his uncle.

Matt was already moving down the hall, past the knot of people watching in confusion. Reyna followed. His uncle did, too, after telling the others that Alan would help them down. As they filed through the hole, Uncle Pete caught up and said, "Freya, I take it?"

When Matt glanced over, Reyna looked startled as she pushed back a rogue strand of black-dyed hair.

"Um, yeah," she said, and while she didn't add it, he could hear *How'd you know?* in her voice as she glanced down at herself—her faded jeans and Union Jack T-shirt and chipped black nail polish.

"Then I'm guessing that's yours," his uncle said, pointing.

They followed his finger to the calico.

"Where'd she—?" she began. Then sighed. "Yes, apparently, that's—Matt!"

Reyna wrenched him back as a tongue of flame shot through an open doorway. Farther down, they could hear a child crying. His uncle tried to move into the lead, but

200

Matt put out his arm. Then he inched forward, shield out, as the flames withdrew into the open apartment. As soon as he drew up alongside the door, another tongue shot out and his shield flew up and iced over just in time to meet it.

The flame pulled back again, almost like a living thing, but it wasn't alive, wasn't supernatural. Just fire doing what fire does, seeking new material to burn. He could see it inside the apartment, engulfing the ceiling in a sea of rolling flame. He carefully grabbed the knob to shut the door to keep the fire contained. Then he heard the crying...coming from within the apartment.

"They're in here, aren't they?" he said to his uncle, who nodded.

"Of course they are," Reyna muttered. When Matt went to step in, though, she stopped him and called, "Identify yourselves!"

"What?" Matt said.

"Random crying child in fiery room? Hello, trap?"

She called again, and the people within responded, but Matt couldn't make out what they were saying over the hiss and spit and crackle and whoosh of the flames. He thought he caught a boy's voice, yelling about fire and a bird.

"Did he say—?" Matt began.

Grim-faced, Reyna pointed across the room, and he could make out the shape of a bird cage on a pedestal. There was no bird perched inside. Given the smoke, it'd be on the bottom of the cage, which he thankfully couldn't see.

"Okay," he said. "But that identifies them as actual people, right?"

Reyna nodded, agreeing that a monster or Raider wasn't going to ask them to rescue the pet bird.

Matt stepped into the apartment, and it was like walking into a sauna as the heat from the flaming ceiling poured down. Through the smoke, he saw more fires ahead—a chair, a couch, a discarded sweater, burning piles dotting his path.

"Turn left," his uncle said. "They're in the bedroom."

They crept along, one eye on the ceiling, waiting for that fire to shoot down. It stayed where it was, crackling and spitting. Matt made it to the bedroom door. He handed Reyna his shield. Then he took the wet cloth from his nose and mouth and wrapped it around the scorching hot metal. The cloth hissed and spit. He turned the knob quickly, pushed the door open, and—

Flame leaped out. Reyna grabbed him by one arm, his uncle lunging to catch the other. As Matt yanked the door closed, his grip on the cloth slipped, his fingertips touching down on white-hot metal. He yelped. His uncle fumbled for the fallen cloth and got the door closed.

"There's no other way in, is there?" Matt said.

Uncle Pete hefted his ax. Matt nodded. "Okay, so we need to find the right place to—"

The cat let out a yowl. They looked down to see it staring at the wall, its fur on end, wire brush tail extended.

"I think she's saying that isn't a good spot," Reyna said.

His uncle chuckled. "Okay, Trjegul. Or Bygul, whichever you might be. Where should we break through?"

The calico just kept hissing and yowling at the wall.

"Apparently, cats are cats," Reyna said. "Magical or not, they don't take orders from humans."

The cat paced from the door to the corner twice, then stopped at a spot, sniffed it, then looked at his uncle as if to say *Well, get to it.*

"All right," Uncle Pete said. Then he yelled, "Stand back! We're coming through!"

He chopped a hole in the wall. When he went to look inside, Matt motioned him back and pushed the shield through, his head following. He saw a mother and two kids, maybe six and two, huddled on the other side of a flaming bed. The younger kid—a boy—pointed emphatically across the room. Matt could make out something burning on top of a dresser.

"Got it," he said. "We'll be careful. We're coming through as soon as we can."

His uncle kept chopping at the hole, while Matt helped

with Mjölnir. When it was big enough, Matt went through first. He started walking around the bed, then realized there was a very good reason the family was huddled there. A tipped basket of laundry had caught fire and blocked their escape.

"Bird!" the little boy said. "Bird!" He pointed, jabbing his finger.

"Don't worry about that," his mother said quickly. "He's concerned about his pet, but just...just get us out of here. Quickly. Please."

Reyna had stuffed water bottles in her pocket and was using them to put out the laundry fire as Matt beat it down with his shield. As soon as it was clear enough, the mother hustled her kids past. His uncle went back through the hole to watch the fire on that side as the family came through. Matt and Reyna guarded from the bedroom.

When the family was almost through, the little boy darted back into the room, his mother letting out a cry. The child scrambled and pointed one chubby finger at the dresser.

"Bird!" he said. "Bird!"

Matt looked. All he saw was the dresser, with something burning on top of it, something big, maybe three feet tall, reaching almost to the fiery ceiling. He was about to turn away, when he noticed something in the flames.

An eye? No—*two* eyes and then a beak and then, as he stared, the bird took form. A giant flaming bird.

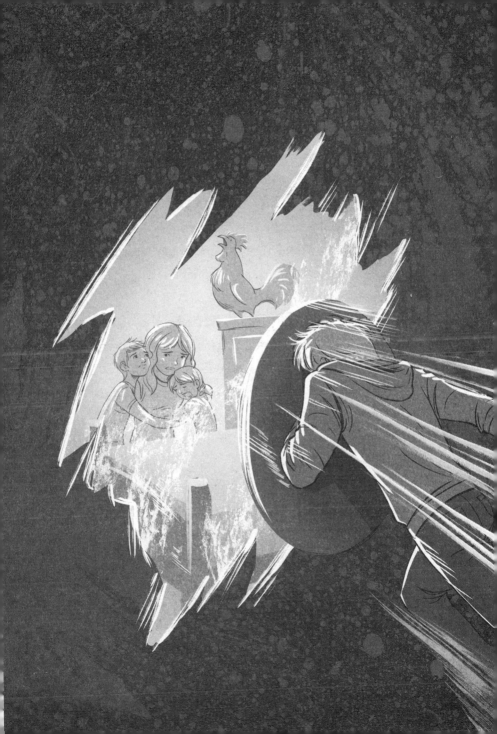

"Is that... a phoenix?" Reyna asked. "Do they have those in Norse myth?"

No. The only kind of flaming birds...

Matt swallowed. He remembered being in Hel when a bird had swooped at them. A chicken, Baldwin had said, and Fen had laughed, but that's exactly what it was. A giant soot-red rooster. One of three that would herald the coming of Ragnarök. That was the one that would alert the dead. The second, Fjalar, would alert the giants in their realm, and Matt presumed that had already happened. Then the third would alert—

The burning rooster threw back its head and let out a crow, so loud they both stumbled back, hands to their ears.

"Gullinkambi," Matt whispered.

The cat leaped through the hole and ran to the dresser, hissing with its fur on end.

"Kitty!" the little boy cried, running after it.

"No!" his mother shouted.

Matt dove for the child, but the toddler darted past. Gullinkambi rose: wings flying out, flame shooting from every burning feather, the walls igniting with a *whoosh*.

Matt dropped his hammer and shield and ran for the boy. He scooped him up as the child's mother screamed behind them. Matt wheeled toward the hole in the wall, but it was covered in flame. The fire was everywhere, engulfing the walls and the ceiling, lines shooting across the floor.

"Matt!" his uncle yelled.

"Working on it!" Matt shouted back. He handed the boy to Reyna. Then he snatched up the shield and hammer. The flames beat in, the heat unbearable, and the boy was howling, drowning out Matt's uncle and Reyna.

A wall of flame blocked the path back to the hole. The only other way out...

Matt saw the door just as the cat ran to it, dodging fire.

"Wrong way!" Reyna shouted. There was a reason they'd been unable to come in through that door. It was a solid rectangle of flame.

The cat yowled. Matt looked from the wall of fire to the flaming door. Then he threw Mjölnir. Threw it as hard as he could. The hammer crashed through the door, ripping it off its hinges.

That works, Reyna mouthed. Clutching the child to her chest, she started running for the door. Matt yanked her back as flames swallowed the opening, the doorjamb still on fire, the flames powered by magic now, burning hot and fast, devouring everything in their path.

He looked at Gullinkambi.

Are you supposed to alert me that Ragnarök is coming? Or stop me from making it that far?

The rooster only settled in, its dark eyes fixed on Matt, those eyes telling him the beast was neutral on the matter. It was merely the messenger, and if it set the room on fire and

Matt couldn't survive that, well, then he was hardly ready to fight the Midgard Serpent, was he?

Matt looked at Reyna. Her eyes were closed, lips moving, trying to cast a spell, but whatever she was doing, it wasn't working.

He thought of the fire Jotunn. Snow. Rain would work, too, but both required a sky for it to fall from. He looked at the burning ceiling. Nope. As he was about to look down, a chunk fell, heading right for Reyna. He pulled her out of the way, her eyes flying open as the chunk hit her shoulder. The boy shrieked as her shirt caught fire. Reyna put the child down fast. Matt smacked out the fire, hitting her hard enough for her to stumble, but when he tried to steady her, she grabbed him instead. Another chunk of flaming ceiling landed beside them.

"Matt!" his uncle called again.

"Still working on it!"

Matt wheeled on the door, his frustration surging, and when it did, he threw Mjölnir, as if reflexively lashing out. The hammer sailed through the flaming door and back into his hand, red hot, making him hiss through his teeth.

That won't help. It can't knock out fire. I need to—

The answer came in a flash, and he swung the hammer again, this time into his other hand, sliding the shield strap up on his arm. With his right hand free, he made a fist. Then he threw the other Hammer. The invisible one. It hit the flame and the fire withdrew. It lasted only a few seconds before flame swallowed the doorway again.

"Okay," Matt said. "You've got a five-second window. Can you do it?"

"I will."

Holding the boy again, Reyna got as close as she could to the door. Matt threw his Hammer, and she ran as soon as his hand shot out, and he tried to shout for her to hold on, to be sure it worked, but she was already racing through the flames. The Hammer blast hit the door. The fire recoiled. Reyna and the boy ran through.

Matt readied the Hammer again. He bent, prepared to sprint, then threw it and—

Nothing happened.

Out of juice.

"Matt!" It was Reyna now.

He tried again. Nothing. He was about to give it a third shot when a huge chunk of ceiling fell. He spun out of the way, only to step into a fire, slip, and barely avoid another falling piece of ceiling.

He swung Mjölnir back into his right hand. Then he lifted the shield, hunkered down, and ran, his shield raised to block his face. But that was all it blocked, the flames swallowing the rest of him as he sprinted through the door. He felt the incredible heat. Smelled the flames, inhaled them and smelled them and thought, *I'm dead.* But he kept going, running through to the next room and hitting the floor. He rolled fast. Something enveloped him, and all four limbs shot out to ward it off, but he realized it was a blanket, dropped over him, his uncle patting out the fire, saying "Hold still, Matt. Just hold still."

Matt did hold still. For about three seconds. Just long enough to be sure he was no longer a human torch. Then he pushed off the blanket and got to his feet.

"You heard Gullinkambi?" he said.

Uncle Pete nodded.

"Then we need to get these people out of here, fast, because I have someplace I need to be."

After they made sure the rescued families were safe, they returned to his uncle's house, where they washed up and Alan got them something to eat. No one said much. Matt had told Owen about Gullinkambi, but he'd only nodded, as if he'd heard the rooster—or already knew what was coming. With Owen, either was equally possible.

After they ate, Uncle Pete announced, "I'd like to speak to my nephew," which even Reyna knew meant *alone.*

They went inside the study. Uncle Pete closed the door. "I'm sorry," he said.

"For what?"

His uncle gave a short laugh. "Everything. I'm sorry I

wasn't part of your life, and I'm sorry that when we finally do meet, it's under the worst possible circumstances. But more than that, right now, I'm sorry you need to go through this."

Matt nodded. There wasn't anything to say, really. No undoing what had been done. No stopping Ragnarök.

"Ever since I got your dad's message, I've been looking for a loophole." His uncle gestured at the paper-strewn table. "I've been trying to figure out if someone else can take your place. Namely me. But every reference I've found to the prophecy says no. I thought maybe I could try, but there's one"—he lifted an old book and opened it to a marked page—"that says no one except the champions can step on the battlefield. If they try, it'll be trouble for their side."

"A penalty," Matt said.

"Right. So..."

"It needs to be me, and we can't take the chance of putting someone else in my place. It's okay. I'm..." He glanced down at his hammer and shield. "I won't say I'm ready, but I have what I need. I can't get any more ready. Not in time. The next step is finding the battlefield. The Norns said you'll show me where that is."

"That's up to you."

"But—but I have no idea where to go."

"I mean it's up to you where the battle will be held. The descendants choose." Uncle Pete pulled an atlas from the shelf. "And we'd better do it fast."

FIFTEEN

FEN

"TRAPPED BY MAGIC"

Aside from the obvious bad timing of Laurie's arrival while he was talking to Astrid, her appearance complicated things. On one hand, Fen really wanted to whoop in joy. She was here and apparently still speaking to him. On the other hand, she couldn't stay. He wasn't going to try to persuade her to fight *against* Thorsen. Matt needed help if he was going to win, stop the Midgard Serpent to save the world and all that.

Obviously something had alerted his pack to Laurie's arrival, because *wulfenkind* in both wolf and person shape were headed toward him. Fen straightened his spine and squared his shoulders with more self-assurance than he felt.

More than a few of his pack members were watching with a mix of curiosity and hostility on their faces.

It wasn't safe for her to be here—or for Baldwin.

"You don't belong here," Fen told Laurie. "Go away!"

"Neither do you, you…you…nitwit!" She stepped forward and poked him in the shoulder, hard.

Baldwin stayed at her side, but he shot an unreadable look at Fen and said, "Hi."

A sudden growl just beside Fen's left side made him look over his shoulder, where he found Hattie snarling as if she was ready to bite someone, probably his cousin.

"She has a weapon," Hattie muttered. "She brought it here."

Her gaze was low, and without even looking Fen knew what she'd seen. Still, he looked in the direction of her glare and saw the bone bow in his cousin's hand. It wasn't upraised, but it was in her hand and could be lifted in a blink.

This day just gets better and better.

If she raised the bow, there would be a flurry of violence that he wasn't entirely sure he could stop. She was an intruder in their camp; worse yet, she was an *armed* intruder.

"No one touches her," Fen yelled. "Anyone who does will be exiled."

Growls and grumbles greeted his words.

"What about him?" someone called.

"I'm impervious," Baldwin answered cheerfully. "*And* just back from the dead."

"As expected," a very unwelcome voice said. Astrid had to draw the attention to herself. She couldn't just stay silent and hidden.

Fen winced as a hurt look crossed Baldwin's face. Astrid's involvement was like adding gasoline to a fire. "Not now," he barked.

"*You!*" Laurie half screamed, half snarled. Her bow hand tightened on the magical weapon, and she started to straighten her arm.

Fen caught her wrist. "No."

He couldn't help but flinch at the look of pure betrayal in Laurie's eyes.

"Why?" she whispered, and he knew it wasn't just about this moment. There were a number of questions in those three letters. *Why was he here? Why was he defending the enemy? Why hadn't he talked to her? Why was he a loser now?*

All he could say was, "This is where I belong now."

"*Why?* Why are you here with them? You owe me some answers, Fenrir."

"It's not that simple," he started.

"Guys?" Baldwin's voice interrupted them.

Fen and Laurie both turned to look at Baldwin.

"The wolves are growling...and more of them are actually wolves now. The evil one there"—he gestured toward Astrid—"makes me nervous, and Laurie looks like she's going to start firing those arrows any minute now. Do you think we can talk somewhere else?"

Fen dropped his gaze to where his hand was still wrapped around Laurie's wrist and then back to meet her eyes. "Please?"

Silently, she nodded, and he felt her relax under his grip, no longer fighting to raise her arm and the weapon in it.

"Step back, everyone." Fen glanced behind him.

They snarled and growled a bit, but they listened.

As they retreated, Fen told her, "I won the pack from Skull. I need to stay here and lead them."

"Are you..." Laurie shook her head. "I'm not even going to ask if you're crazy. Clearly, you are. They are trying to end the world, Fen. Did you forget everything?"

He took a calming breath. "As their alpha, I *have* to do what's in their best interest." He wished he'd taken the time to explain their heritage a little more, so she understood. The best he could say for now was, "I have no choice. It's magic."

"No. You will not stay here. You listen to me"—Laurie poked his shoulder again—"you are coming back with me right now."

Astrid stepped forward to stand shoulder to shoulder with Fen. "He has a role to play in the great battle. We all do."

Laurie snapped her attention to Astrid. "*You* do not talk to me." If she could've hissed or snarled, he was pretty sure she would've. That look of sheer fury that was on Laurie's face never boded well.

Astrid is a dragon. My cousin is yelling at a dragon.

"You need to leave, Laurie," Fen said, trying to defuse the situation. "Go back to Thorsen and—"

"Fine." Laurie opened a portal quicker than he'd ever seen her do it. Apparently, fury made her faster. Then with a kick to the pink-haired girl's legs, she shoved Astrid through it.

As Astrid fell through, Laurie looked at Baldwin and said, "Grab him."

"Sorry, man," Baldwin said cheerily, and threw himself into Fen, propelling them through the portal.

Before Fen opened his eyes, he already knew where his cousin had taken them: to Thorsen. He didn't know what town this was at first, or what ruins of a town it was, but he knew who would be there. He looked around at what he quickly realized was Mitchell, SD. Shakily, Fen came to his feet and looked not at the one-eyed boy staring at Laurie in obvious disapproval, but at Matt.

The mix of relief and fear was a familiar one at this point. It's how he'd felt when Matt learned that Fen was supposed to turn him over to the enemy, how he'd felt when he was standing before his Aunt Helen and the then-dead Baldwin, and how Fen had felt when he'd won his fight with Skull. Familiar wasn't the same as *good*, though.

"We need to talk," Fen told Matt.

"I figured," Matt said, seeming surprisingly calm. Then he looked at the other person who'd come through the portal with them. His calm expression faded, and he blanched. All he said, though, was, "Astrid."

Owen stepped up and grabbed one of Astrid's arms. "I'll keep an eye on her," he said in a cold voice. "The one I still have…"

Astrid went with him quietly. Baldwin walked away from them, still unusually quiet. Fen wanted to say something. He'd gone to Hel for Baldwin, but he had also been harboring his friend's murderer. Fen didn't know what to say…to any of them, really. Astrid was one of the rare people that all of the descendants of the North disliked. She'd pretended to be Owen's girlfriend when he wasn't around to deny it, lied to them, tried to steal from them, and killed Baldwin. Then, while they were all in Hel rescuing Baldwin from the death *she* caused, the enemy had taken Owen captive, and he'd lost an eye.

And I'm supposed to protect her.

As much as he loathed saying it, he still had to speak. "She's under the Raiders' protection. I can't let you h—"

"Shut it!" Laurie yelled. Then she turned to Matt and announced, "I can*not* deal with him, Matt. My cousin apparently hit his head or something, because the only other answer is that he's a complete fool."

Oddly or not, this made Fen grin for the first time since

he'd been forced to take over the pack. He'd followed the rules as much as the magic could force him to. Now he was standing in front of Laurie and Matt. She was frustrated with him, but he was still relieved. They could help him figure out a plan. That's what he needed.

"Come on," Matt said.

The three of them walked toward a building that wasn't on fire, and they stood in the shadows of the constant night. It reminded him of being in Hel. The world around them certainly didn't look like Mitchell normally did. This wasn't the nice, clean city he'd visited for a school trip. It was a nightmare land with cars on fire and broken chunks of buildings littering the street. Fen's eyes widened as he took in the destruction.

"What happened?"

"Jötnar," Matt said.

"Two of them," Laurie added.

"Good idea getting rid of yours," Matt said to Laurie, and Fen felt a flicker of resentment at being left out. Maybe Matt knew that, or maybe he was just that good of a guy, because he looked at Fen and said, "She portaled it to Hel."

Fen laughed. "You sent it to Aunt Helen? That's awesome."

Laurie looked sheepish for a moment. "It's not like there weren't already jötnar there!"

At her anxious expression, Fen butted his head into her shoulder, not caring that Matt stood with them, simply needing to let her know that he still felt the same toward her. Quietly, he told her, "I was worried that you would be hurt or need me—"

"I do!" she interrupted quickly. She tilted her head toward Matt. "We *both* need you here."

Matt nodded and brought up the hard question: "Why were you with the Raiders? I saw you."

Fen took a deep breath. "I know." Quickly, he explained about the fight with Skull, the rules of being alpha of a Raider pack, and then the difficulty of figuring out what to do since he couldn't endanger the pack *and* he didn't want to fight for Mayor Thorsen.

Matt winced a little at the reminder that his grandfather was the enemy, which Fen sort of understood. A lot of the Brekkes were Raiders, which meant they'd been Fen's enemy until he'd become alpha against his wishes. Family could be confusing.

"I'm trapped by magic," Fen said after he'd explained everything. "Unless fighting *with* you becomes better than standing against you, I can't do anything."

The surge of relief at getting to tell them the truth was overwhelming. Big end-of-the-world battles could mean they all died. In the myths, it was awful: Loki dies, the serpent kills Thor, Fenrir swallows Odin, Frey dies, even Garm dies. The descendants had changed small pieces of the myth so far, but Ragnarök was "the twilight of the gods." It was a story of endings, and going into a fight where most of them were supposed to die without them knowing that he cared was scarier than talking about *feelings*.

Matt was quiet for a moment.

"Astrid wants to help you," Fen told Matt. "Change the end of the battle or something. At least that's what she's saying. I don't know if I really trust her, but…there are things she needs to tell you. It could be good."

"What things?" Laurie prompted.

"I can't tell you," he said after a moment. "Magic. Seriously, Laurie, it's not like I want to keep secrets, but I can only do what's best for the pack. *Astrid* could tell you, though, because she's…not a wolf."

He looked at his cousin, hoping that she caught the pause, hoping she'd think, *Well, if she's not a wolf, is she something else?* That didn't work, though, because she just stood frowning with her lips pressed tightly together. She seemed like she was ready to erupt in yells.

Fen bumped her shoulder again. "No matter what happens, the Raiders know not to touch you."

Instead of being happy, his cousin looked furious. "Why is that?"

"You're my cousin, so you're not to be touched."

"So they can attack Matt, Baldwin, Owen, the twins, the Berserkers, and anyone else…just not me?" Her arms were folded over her chest again, and Fen knew that meant she was angry about something. He wasn't sure why she was, but she clearly wasn't seeing his protection as a good thing.

"I can't protect everyone," he said. "You're my family. You're *their* family."

"It's okay," Matt told her. He sort of hugged her, but with only one arm. Seeing Matt comfort Laurie made Fen angrier. He should be the one who got to stay at her side. He should be the one who made her feel better and protected her. That's the way it had been their whole lives.

"I hate Ragnarök," he said.

"Agreed." Matt nodded.

"Double agreed," Laurie said. She seemed to calm down then, like the anger all faded away as quickly as it had come. She met Fen's eyes and asked, "We'll figure it out, though, right?"

"Definitely," Fen lied. He wasn't at all sure that they could, but he wasn't going to say that aloud, not to her. "I can't stay here. You have to send me back."

"The battle is coming," Matt said.

"I figured it was soon," Fen said.

"Pretty much *now*."

Fen nodded. "If the tide turns so it's better for my pack… I just need to do what's best for them. That's the rule. I have to do what is best and safest for my wolves. Right now, they're fighting on the side most likely to win, but if who's winning *changes*…"

"Got it," Matt said, immediately understanding that

Fen couldn't help even though he wanted to, but that there, hopefully, would be a time when that would change.

"You'll be careful, right?" Fen started. "They all know the myths and—"

"Yes," Matt interrupted. "And we'll be careful."

"I don't want any of you to die," Fen admitted.

"We know. We should've known that you weren't a traitor," Matt said. "Laurie never doubted you."

Fen looked at her, but his cousin said nothing. She was staring at him, arms folded over her chest, and her eyes were wet. She wasn't crying outright yet, but it was coming.

"Try to be safe," Matt said.

Fen nodded. He felt better for having talked to Matt, but he still needed to talk to Laurie. Matt obviously knew how they were, so in the next minute he said, "I'll see you at the fight, then. I need to go deal with Astrid."

Matt turned to Laurie then and asked, "Can you get Ray? Reyna's worrying, and we need him with us for the fight."

And then he was gone, and the cousins were left alone again.

"I didn't mean for this to happen," Fen told her.

She turned away, her back to him and her mouth closed. He didn't want to fight with her, but he couldn't undo the magic that came with being alpha of the pack. He couldn't stay here.

And he had no idea how to persuade her to open a portal so he could lead wolves and monsters into battle against her.

SIXTEEN

MATT

"MONSTERS"

Matt was pacing. The others had moved away, leaving him alone as they waited for Gullinkambi to return. According to his uncle's books, Gullinkambi would crow once to alert them to prepare, then it would return to say, "Stop messing around and get your butts in there."

He peered around for Reyna. She'd been off to the side, talking to his uncle and getting details on her role. Thoughts of Reyna cheered him up, but the mood didn't last. He kept thinking about Astrid. He was about to start the biggest fight of his life, and the last thing he needed was to be distracted.

A footfall crunched behind him. He turned to see Reyna heading his way with the cat at her side. He grinned at them, and Reyna stopped short, glancing over her shoulder as if looking for the cause of his grin.

"Someone spike your prefight Gatorade?" she asked.

"No, I'm just happy to see—" He rocked back on his heels. "Happy to see the cat is still with you. Have you picked a name yet?"

"What are my options again?"

"Trjegul, Bygul, and Heyyu."

"Tree-gool and Bee-gool?" she said. "And Hey-yu?" She stopped. "Hey, you. Oh. Ha-ha. Leave comedy to the professionals, Thorsen."

He shrugged. "You could always ask the cat what her name is."

"Nope. I pick Trjegul." She looked down at the calico. "You're Trjegul now. Even if you're really Bygul."

The cat only blinked.

"So if I call you by your name, you'll come, right?"

Trjegul got up and wandered off in the other direction.

"Watch out or I'll trade you for a swan!" Reyna called after her. "A giant, killer stealth swan that eats ungrateful kitties for breakfast."

Matt chuckled and when she turned back to him, he wanted to continue the conversation. It didn't matter how. Tell her another story about Freya's cats. Tease her about Trjegul.

Keep her engaged and joking, and stretch this moment as far as he could. Like a locker room goofing off before the big bout. Yet even as he thought that, a shadow passed overhead. He looked up sharply to see a bird winging past. His breath caught. Then he realized it was only one of Owen's ravens.

Raven. Owen. Astrid.

"Matt?" Reyna said.

"Astrid's here." He blurted the words.

Reyna stiffened. "Did you say—?"

"Astrid. She came back with Fen."

"Oh, and let me guess. She's here to tell you what a big mistake she made and how she's so sorry and she's totally on our side now. *Your* side, that is. Fortunately, you'd know better than to buy that."

"I'm not stupid, Reyna."

"I never said you were."

He shifted his weight. "Maybe, but sometimes you make me feel…" He shrugged it off. "Never mind. The point is that I know her well enough to be careful. But Fen brought her back. She's under Owen's guard. As far as I'm concerned, she's a prisoner of war. A possible source of valuable intel on the enemy."

Reyna barely seemed to have heard him. "Do I make you *feel* stupid, Matt?"

He adjusted the shield on his back. "Nah, not really. Ignore me. I'm just…" He shrugged. "Lots of things on my mind, and I'm feeling…" Another shrug. "Whatever. I should go talk to Astrid."

He got about three steps before Reyna said, "I've never met a guy who was less stupid, Matt. Or less brave. Or less…everything."

He turned slowly.

"Oh gods," she said, rubbing her face. "That came out wrong. I don't mean—I just wanted—" She stomped her foot. "Can I say something nasty to even it out? Please? I'm so much better at that."

He gave a small smile. "Sure, go for it."

He was only teasing, but she looked away fast and mumbled, "I don't mean to be nasty. I just…I just wanted…" She looked at him. "I wanted you to hit back, Matt. I wanted you to stand up to me, because the one thing you need is the one thing I've got in spades. Self-confidence. Only you never hit back. You just take it. But I hoped you understood that I don't really think you're stupid or anything like that, because if you were, I wouldn't stand at your side. I trust you like I don't trust anyone except my brother." She paused. "Does that sound lame?"

"No."

"If I make you feel bad, tell me off. I can take it."

"Okay."

She exhaled. "Good, enough of that, then. We need to go talk to Astrid."

"I...I'm not sure you should..."

"I've got your back, remember?" She looked at him. "Always, Matt."

Not always. You can't. Once that rooster crows, I'm on my own.

"She's going to try to trick you," Reyna said. "It'll help if I'm there to make sure you see through it."

As soon as Matt saw Astrid, he realized Reyna was right—if Astrid pretended to have seen the error of her ways, he'd be tempted to believe it. He needed someone to keep him on track, and no one did that better than Reyna. Plus, of everyone there, Astrid had the least issue with Reyna. They hadn't connected or clashed.

When he walked over, Owen having slipped off to give them privacy, Astrid saw him coming and she smiled. It was a nervous smile, her eyes alternately glowing and shadowing, as if she was happy to see him but knew he wasn't happy to see her. Playing a role. He got that now. He'd gotten that for a while, but it was interesting to see it in action.

That's when Astrid noticed Reyna at his side. She looked from Matt to Reyna and back. Then she pulled herself straight and turned, just enough to cut Reyna from her field of vision.

"Hey, Matt," she said. "Bet you were hoping not to see

me again, huh?" That shy smile. "Thank you for coming. I know I'm the last person you want to talk to—"

"No," Reyna said. "You're the *first* person he wants to talk to, because you're going to help him win this battle."

Astrid turned, slowly and deliberately, toward Reyna. She looked her up and down, and then frowned, as if she couldn't quite place her.

"Reyna? I didn't recognize you without the emo girl costume. Still not quite the goddess of light and beauty, are you? Big heels to fill. It'll take a while to grow into them." She looked Reyna over again. "Maybe a long while."

"Oh, I fit my shoes just fine. Today, they're a sweet pair of combat boots, because today, I'm playing a different aspect of Freya. Goddess of kick-your-butt-if-you-mess-with-me. Or mess with anyone else."

"Anyone in particular?" Astrid slid a sly look at Reyna.

"Yep," Reyna said. "Matt. Oh, wait. Did you think I wouldn't admit it? Sorry to disappoint. I like Matt. I like him a lot—because he's an awesome guy, *not* because he's a cute boy. He's a friend. The concept may be unfamiliar to you. Just go with it."

Astrid's eyes narrowed, and she opened her mouth. Reyna cut her off with "Stop."

"I'm not—"

"Whatever you're about to claim you aren't doing? You're totally doing it. And we're going to stop right here. Two girls hissing at each other over a boy? Cliché. Doing it when we should be strategizing for a save-the-world battle? That's an insult to girls everywhere. Catfight, done." She turned to Matt. "You have the floor, sir."

"Uh..." He blinked. "Right. Astrid? I need to know—"

"A lot of things. But first, there's one very important thing I need to tell you. Alone." Astrid looked at Reyna.

"Seriously? Did you even hear my girl-power speech?"

"It's a private conversation. Unless you're suggesting he can't handle me himself? I think he's a big boy, Reyna. Strong enough to fight me and smart enough to outwit me. Are you suggesting otherwise?"

Reyna just looked Astrid in the eye as if to say *Nope, not playing your games.*

Astrid glanced at Matt. Her eyes pleaded with him to intercede. He didn't.

"Just tell me, Astrid," he said. "We don't have much time—"

"I'm the serpent."

He paused. "You're..."

"The Midgard Serpent. It's me."

"What?" Reyna said. "Oh no. Don't you dare pull that. The Midgard Serpent is a fourteen-year-old girl?"

Astrid turned on her. "What happened to 'girls can do anything'? A pretty sentiment...until it doesn't serve your purpose."

"Being a girl has nothing to do with it. I'd say the same if you were a boy. Thor is dead; Matt is his replacement. The Midgard Serpent? Not dead. It's a logic problem, not a gender one. Unless you aren't really a fourteen-year-old girl."

Astrid bristled, as if this were the worst possible insult Reyna could have dreamed up. "I'm a girl, just like you, who went to school, right up until a few weeks ago, when I was told I was destined to fight Thor at Ragnarök." She turned to Matt. "Sound familiar?"

"But Reyna's right," he said. "The Midgard Serpent isn't dead. I felt it rising—saw it rising—near Blackwell. Deep in the earth. If you're telling me that was you—"

"No. It was my grandmother. She's the..." Astrid struggled for words. "I'd say the 'real' serpent, but then you'll think I'm lying about myself. The Midgard Serpent isn't one creature. It's a hereditary responsibility, passed from generation to generation. Like being the descendant of Thor, except we have an actual role to play, all the time. Then there's the starring role. At Ragnarök. That one, apparently, is mine, whether I want it or not. Which I don't. No more than you want to be Thor."

"Prove it," Reyna said.

"That I don't want to be part of this?" Astrid turned to Reyna, her eyes snapping. "The fact I'm here should prove—"

"It proves nothing except that you have a story to sell us. But I didn't mean that. I mean prove that you're the serpent.

Matt says he saw your grandmother. If you want us to believe you are the Midgard Serpent—at least for the purposes of the battle—there's an easy way to prove it. Shape-shift."

Astrid bit her lip. She looked at Matt. Then she closed her eyes and when she opened them, they were green, with slits, like a snake's.

I've seen that. I caught a glimpse of it—

The fight. When Astrid tried to steal his shield. They'd fought, and she'd hissed, as if in pain, and he'd caught a split-second glimpse of her eyes and—

Matt swallowed.

That was the myth, wasn't it? That Thor faced the Midgard Serpent twice. The first time, he overcame it and left it alive. He'd lived to regret that. *Died* regretting it. Thor had seen the world end because he'd been a decent guy. Because he'd shown mercy.

I should have—

His gut clenched so hard he staggered, and he heard both girls say "Matt?" but only dimly.

I should have killed her? Is that what I'm thinking?

He looked at Astrid.

She's a kid. A regular girl with friends and family and a future and . . . and I'm supposed to kill her?

"I . . . I need a minute," he said.

He stumbled away. Astrid ran after him and grabbed his arm.

"Matt, please. I just want to talk to you."

"Later."

"There won't be a later, Matt. Please. We can work this out."

Isn't that what he'd expected her to say? What Reyna warned him she'd say? And what he'd told himself he wouldn't fall for? And yet as soon as she did say it, he thought, *Yes. That's the answer. We'll work it out.*

I'd let you trick me. Kill me. Kill my friends. Because I can't deal with the alternative. I can't kill—

"Five minutes," he said, pushing her off. "I need five minutes."

Matt went as far as he dared and then sat on a rock. Something brushed his leg and he jumped. Trjegul wound around his feet, purring. He reached down, expecting her to take off, but she leaped onto his lap and rubbed against his hands, purring louder.

He glanced over and wasn't surprised to see Reyna about twenty feet away.

"Don't worry," she called. "I'm not interrupting you. I'm just..."

"Making sure Raiders don't appear over the hill and drag me off before the battle?"

"Right. I'll stay here." She fidgeted. "Unless you want company. And don't say yes because you think you should."

He waved her over. The cat hopped off his lap and went to Reyna as she sat on the ground.

"The Midgard Serpent is a kid," Matt said.

"Seems like it."

"Do you think she isn't? That Astrid's pretending to be a kid? It's a disguise?"

Reyna shook her head. "No. Trust me. I know enough girls like her to be sure that's not an act."

"Oh."

She looked up at him. "Which isn't what you wanted to hear, is it?"

"I . . . She's . . . It's supposed to be a monster. A real monster. Like a Jotunn or a troll, and sure, I wouldn't go around killing them for fun, but if I had to, well, they're monsters. This . . ." He met her gaze. "She's a kid, Reyna. Just like the Raiders. A girl who can shape-shift and this is what's expected of her, and it doesn't make her a good person, but even if she's lying about not wanting to do it? That doesn't make her a monster, either."

"I know." She absently patted Trjegul. The cat rubbed against her hand. "Is there a loophole? Can you just take her out temporarily?"

"A TKO?"

"Exactly. You—" She caught his expression. "Oh. You were kidding."

"Not kidding. Just . . . no. According to my uncle, there

are no loopholes. We must fight. I kill her or she kills me. Or, like in the myth, we both die. We can't just shake hands and walk away. Or score a TKO." He ran his hand through his hair. "I know I said I wouldn't listen to her. That I wouldn't believe her if she said she wanted to help us. And I'm not saying I would now, but..."

"You need to hear her out."

"I do. I'm sorry if you thought I'd be stronger than that."

She looked at him. "I'd never want you to be strong enough to kill a kid, Matt. *Never.* When I said you need to hear her out, it wasn't a question. It was a statement. You need to hear her out. It's the only chance we have to avoid you doing something that would make you..."

"A monster?"

She nodded, her face grim.

Astrid told Matt exactly what he expected. That she was as much a victim of circumstance as he was. As much a victim of birthright. Like him, though, she'd risen to the challenge. She'd done as she'd been told by his grandfather. That's whose orders she'd been following. Not her grandmother's, because her grandmother was no longer really her grandmother—she was the Midgard Serpent.

Astrid explained that the last time she'd seen her grandmother as a human, she'd been too young to remember her.

Her grandmother had volunteered for the role because she'd been dying of cancer. To become the serpent was, as Astrid explained, a kind of death. Instead of being able to shift from human to serpent, she sacrificed herself to be reborn a serpent.

"If I was to see her, I'd run the other way before she killed me," Astrid said. "She wouldn't recognize me. My real grandmother is dead. She volunteered so no one would have to."

"But for the purposes of Ragnarök, you're the serpent," Matt said. "Right?"

"My people are fair, whatever you might think of us. I'm supposed to take her place to level the playing field. I'm..." A wry smile. "A little smaller than her, as you'll see."

"But once you take her role, *are* you her? The serpent? If you survive, can you shift back?"

"No one expects me to survive, Matt. Certainly not your grandfather. If you think, for one second, that he's on my side, you're wrong. He's told me I can't defeat you. That it'll end as it does in the myth—we both die. The world will be born anew. The Thorsens and the Brekkes and the Raiders and the serpent-shifters will survive and thrive together. That's his dream." She looked at him. "If someone honestly believed the myth couldn't be avoided, like he does, it's not a bad dream. Unless you're the ones who have to die to make this happen."

"So how do we avoid that?" Reyna asked.

"Well, originally, I hoped to convince Matt to switch sides. He jumps to ours and helps us, and that would mess everything up."

"Except for the 'monsters win' part?" Matt said.

"There is that." She sighed. "Not all of us are monsters, but I came to realize that didn't matter. You'd never help the Midgard Serpent and jötnar and the trolls and the rest of us defeat your friends. So there's only one other option. I'm the one who flips."

"Seems the obvious choice," Reyna said.

"Does it?" Astrid looked at her. "That means I turn on my family. You might not think much of the Raiders, but I have friends there. I will betray my entire family and all my friends. That's not simple. Not one bit."

Reyna nodded. "You're right. I'm sorry. Tell us what you have in mind."

Matt was still talking when a voice said, "Hey, sis, still bugging poor Matt?" They both turned. Then Reyna leaped up and ran to Ray, throwing her arms around him. Matt started to lead Astrid away, to give the twins time to reunite, but Ray called, "Hold up. I need to talk to you, Matt."

Matt turned.

Ray walked over. He hesitated a second, on seeing Astrid, but someone must have explained it to him, because he didn't ask about her, just said, "I found a few things in my research in Blackwell that might help Reyna and me in our battle. But I'm not the mythology expert. Can I run them by you? Get your input?"

Matt glanced at Astrid. Reyna caught his look and said, "Astrid? Why don't you come with me," and as they left, Matt turned to Ray. "Let's find someplace private and talk."

Ray had indeed dug up a few things to help his Ragnarök battle. Matt was impressed. He might not be much of a fighter, but he definitely had a good head on his shoulders. He helped Matt adjust his plan with Astrid, too, though the scheme was incredibly simple.

When Gullinkambi crowed, Laurie would open a portal to their chosen battlefield. They'd go through...and Astrid would join them. She would walk onto that field as their ally, not their enemy. She'd forfeit her battle with Matt. While that wouldn't let him walk off the field, he had no intention of doing so even if the chance was offered. He'd fight alongside whichever descendant needed him most, as would Astrid.

At Ray's suggestion, they didn't tell Astrid where the battlefield would be, just in case she was still trying to trick them. That meant she couldn't zip off and warn the others. Nor did they share martial strategy. The only possible way to trick Matt would be to pretend to fight alongside him and then turn on him. As Ray pointed out, that was a problem easily solved. Matt wouldn't take his eyes off her. He'd stay behind her, at all times. She understood that and agreed to his terms.

Convincing the others was easier than he expected. Reyna drilled Astrid and found her answers satisfactory. Same for Laurie. Matt gave everyone the chance to ask whatever they wanted and make whatever stipulations they wanted. Even after all that, he still didn't trust Astrid, but he agreed, as Reyna said, that this was their only chance to avoid the unthinkable. They had to take it. Eyes wide open, but take the deal.

They'd barely finished when Gullinkambi arrived. It perched on a dead tree and crowed to the night sky and that was it. The battle horn had been sounded. There was nothing left to do. Nothing left to say.

It was time for war.

SEVENTEEN

LAURIE

"FROST GIANTS"

hile Matt and Reyna were off talking to Astrid, Laurie had to return her cousin to the enemy. She hated that Fen had to leave, but she knew he had to go back to lead the Raiders. Part of her wanted to insist he ignore the magic that made him need to return to his pack, but the rest of her knew that trying to stop Fen *and* overcome magic wasn't realistic. Plus, of course, the Raiders were kids like them. Maybe Fen could save them somehow. He *was* a hero in her opinion.

I just wish we weren't on opposite sides.

"I don't like this," she mumbled.

Fen, in a surprising moment, grabbed her tightly and

hugged as hard as he could. "I don't, either. I wish I could tell you to go home to Blackwell, but you're Loki's champion. You can do this. You can defeat..." His words faded because the forces she needed to defeat included him now.

"I won't fight you," she whispered. "No matter what. I won't."

"I'm going to delay arriving as long as I can," Fen promised. "It's the best I can do.... Then I guess I'll fight the goats or something. I don't think I can fight you or Baldwin *or* Matt." He grinned. "I wouldn't mind taking a swing at Owen, though."

"You wouldn't hurt him, either."

"Looking for a silver lining," he said with a forced lightness.

Laurie sniffled against his shoulder. "Jerk," she said, knowing Fen heard what she really meant: I love you.

"Be safe," he ordered her. He pulled away and looked at her. "All you need is to be safe. If Thorsen wins, it's all good, and... if he doesn't, you'll come with my pack. Either way, you'll be okay after the fight. I swear it. You just need to get through the battle, okay?"

She didn't bother arguing that there was no way she would live with the monsters if Matt lost.

"The myths aren't always right," Fen reminded her. "You *will* be okay."

"You too," she half ordered, half asked. She knew that

Loki and the wolf Fenrir both died in the great battle of Ragnarök. They'd focused so much on Matt and the Midgard Serpent, but Fenrir was ripped apart by Odin's son and Loki was killed by Heimdall, another of the gods. Laurie figured that they all knew that. Ragnarök wasn't only about that one battle. The word itself literally meant "twilight of the gods." It was the story of how the gods died. Obviously, it wasn't completely accurate, because the gods themselves were already long dead.

"Stupid gods, leaving us to fight these battles," she muttered.

Fen laughed. "Call Aunt Helen when the battle starts. Stay by her side."

"Loki led the monsters, and you fight for the monsters, so..."

Fen gestured to Laurie's bow. "She gave this to the one she will help: Loki's daughter, not me."

There was nothing left to say then, so Laurie opened a portal to the Raiders' camp and Fen stepped through it. She stood there alone for a moment, and then she straightened her shoulders and headed to the others. The descendants picked the battleground, and when they arrived, the fight would begin.

She wasn't ready. Honestly, she didn't think she'd ever be ready, but it was time. The Berserkers were going to arrive there, although they couldn't enter the actual field;

Ray was back with that group. Owen was here. Everyone was ready, even the Midgard Serpent—who was currently watching Matt like she was a lost puppy, not a world-ending monster.

Laurie met Matt's eyes and nodded.

Then silently, she opened a portal into the Badlands. It was the right place and time to do this. Helen's monsters could fight better on familiar terrain, and nowhere on earth looked as much like Helen's domain as the strangely beautiful and frightening Badlands.

"Owen first," Matt said.

One by one, the descendants and the dragon-girl went through the portal until it was only Laurie and Matt standing in Mitchell.

"This is it," she whispered as she looked at him.

"We can do it," he assured her. "We have a plan."

Then he went through the gateway to the battle that would either save or doom them all. She tried to believe that they'd win as she fell through the portal, letting it close behind her. It felt far more *final* than any other portal, but she clung to Matt's words: *We have a plan.* She chanted the words in her head like they'd make the hope into a fact: *We have a plan. We have a plan. We have a plan.*

Of course, it took all of five minutes for that plan to fall apart.

Laurie looked around at the group that stood at the edge of the Badlands: Matt, Baldwin, Owen, Reyna, Ray... and no one else. Astrid wasn't there.

"Where is she?" Reyna asked, looking around for the dragon girl who was nowhere to be seen. "I knew—"

"Astrid came through," Laurie interrupted, meeting Matt's eyes. "She did. I saw her step in, and I *felt* her go through the gateway."

"There is an order to be upheld," Owen said.

They all turned to look at him, but he seemed unperturbed by their collective stares. He simply shrugged. "I told you that there were things that could and could not change. It's why I stayed away so long." He met Laurie's eyes briefly. "It's why I didn't tell you that Fenrir would defect. Astrid is bound by the same things we all are: there are only so many things we can change."

"Says who?" Laurie challenged. "We aren't mindless players in Ragnarök. We *will* change it. We *will* win. We *will* live through this."

"I hope you're right," Owen said.

Astrid was supposed to be the one Matt would fight. She was the version of the Midgard Serpent who was to take the field, but now Astrid was missing.

The thunder of hooves rattled the ground so intensely that Laurie thought the buffalo were stampeding again.

They did roam the Badlands, but not the part where the descendants of the North now stood. Here, on the edges of valleys and eerie-looking rocks, there were no buffalo.

Instead, there were mythic warrior women on enormous horses bearing down on them. Fortunately, the Valkyries were on the same side as the descendants. The horses came to a sudden stop, dust and dirt kicking up around them. Hildar, the one who seemed to speak for them, looked down at the kids and nodded.

"It is time," she pronounced. "Son of Thor, come."

Laurie expected to hear a low whisper at the oddity of her ordering Matt to heel like a house pet, but Fen wasn't there to crack a joke. *What if I never see him again? What if he dies? Or I die?*

"Where is Astrid?" Matt asked.

"Not here," Hildar replied, as if that part weren't already obvious. "I believe Odin's child explained." She nodded toward Owen. "He is the one closest to the Norns and their insistence on rules."

Hildar didn't *quite* say she was irritated by the Norns, but Laurie was getting good at reading between the lines when it came to mythical creatures. The Valkyrie wasn't entirely pleased by the Norns' apparent interference.

"Freya's daughter, you and your sibling will come as well." Hildar's stern expression seemed to soften ever so slightly as she met Laurie's gaze. "I wish you good battle, daughter of Loki. I am pleased that you fight with the right side in Ragnarök."

Laurie lifted her chin a little higher. "There was never any doubt."

Hildar smiled. "You remind me of Loki's . . . better traits." The moment passed, and she looked at Matt again. "Come," she repeated.

Matt and the twins were swept away with the Valkyries, leaving Laurie, Owen, and Baldwin alone. She'd known that they wouldn't all be hip to hip in the great fight, but that didn't make the moment of separation any less scary.

"Laurie?" Owen said quietly from her side.

She turned and glanced at him. He looked ready to bolt: hands clenched, lips pursed. Silently he inclined his head, and she looked to where he was now staring.

Baldwin whistled.

"Seriously?" she asked no one in particular. Laurie wasn't as up on mythology as a lot of people, but she knew enough to know that the towering creature headed their way was a *hrímthursar*, a frost giant. Like the towering monsters made of fire that they'd faced in Hel and in Mitchell, this was a Jotunn . . . but of frost and ice. It was one of the creatures that she remembered far too well from the stories her father told her when she was a little girl.

"Is that actually a *hrímthursar*?" Owen murmured from her side.

She couldn't tear her eyes away from it. "Uh-huh."

"Any idea how we're to fight it?"

Laurie shook her head. "When will the Berserkers arrive?"

"Soon," Owen promised. "I've sent the ravens to summon them."

Soon might not be fast enough. She didn't know what to do. The last giant had only been handled by sending it to see her Aunt Helen, and Laurie wasn't sure how well that had gone over. She didn't want to risk angering the ruler of Hel by sending a flood of monsters to her domain. In the myth, Helen fought on the side of the monsters. Laurie really wanted to avoid that part. That meant coming up with a plan to get rid of a frost giant.

Right, piece of cake, she thought.

Portaling it would work, but she needed a location she could visualize or a descendant she could zero in on. If not, she'd be portaling it blindly, and she wasn't going to send it somewhere where it could kill people. She couldn't think of any volcanos, and Hel was out. That left stopping a *hrímthursar* on her own.

Admittedly, Matt was going to face a dragon, but Laurie was facing a *frost giant* and who knew what else—and she felt exceptionally under-armed. Matt had the Valkyries, the goats, the shield, and Mjölnir. She had a one-eyed boy with his currently absent acrobatic fighters, another who was impervious to harm, and a bow made of bone. Somehow, every fight she'd been in up to this moment seemed easy in comparison.

The battle hadn't even properly begun, but there was a mammoth creature of ice and frost stalking toward her. Who knew what else would be coming? The world was teetering on the edge of its own destruction. That certainly didn't bode well for anyone's ability to have an easy time of it.

"Does anyone else think it's strange that we can *see* in the total darkness?" Baldwin asked, pulling her attention from her building terrors and self doubts. "I mean, the sky is black, but I can see just fine."

"Me too...well, with the eye that still works," Owen added.

"Hey, guys?" Baldwin pointed. "The frost giant is bringing friends."

Following at a great distance behind the *hrímthursar* were trolls, mara, and wolves. They couldn't move as quickly as the towering creature, but they were coming. That alone was enough to make Laurie want to run screaming in the other direction. She could fire endless arrows from her bone bow, open portals, and apparently turn into a fish. Owen would have Berserkers who could catapult into fights and ravens who would spy. Baldwin simply couldn't be hurt. None of that seemed to be anywhere near enough when she thought they were facing *one* monster. How could it be possible to fight a battalion of them?

"Plan?" Owen asked her.

"What's the myth again?" Even though she'd heard it earlier that day and several times before this in their various conversations, she wanted to hear it *now*. There had to be something she wasn't thinking of, and that meant hearing it from someone else, hopefully so as to trigger her memory or theirs.

Owen started, "Thor and Odin are separated. Loki fights Heimdall; Odin fights Fenrir; Thor fights the serpent. We all die." His voice was calm, even as they all watched the horde of monsters approaching. "Does that help?"

"Maybe we could avoid the death part," Baldwin interjected.

"Anything *useful* in that myth?" Laurie asked, looking at the enemy troops. They were maybe fifteen minutes away.

Owen grabbed Laurie's arm and tugged. "Do you think we could keep recounting the myth somewhere a little less in their line of sight?"

The three of them started toward a fissure in the nearest rock formation.

"What about thermite?" Baldwin asked as they crouched behind a rock.

"Thermite?" she echoed.

"You need to watch *MythBusters*. The source of all useful

knowledge...well, at least the sort my parents won't let me have." Baldwin grinned. "If you mix rust, aluminum oxide, and a sparkler, it makes a sort of modern Greek fire. Completely and utterly inappropriate for us—or even most adults—to make *or* use."

"Where would we get *any* of that?" Owen asked as Laurie eased out of the fissure to see how far away the monsters were.

The frost giant was still ahead of the other monsters, and none of them seemed to be in a hurry. "Ten minutes, tops," she told the boys as she moved back to their sides. "It'll see us in *maybe* ten minutes. We need to hurry."

Baldwin opened his bag from Hel and dug around inside it. "I have sparklers." He tossed them to Laurie and kept digging in his bag. "Now I need one of those Etch A Sketch things."

"Why can't we just get modern weapons from the bags?" Owen asked.

Baldwin paused and shot a disbelieving look at him. "Because Helen didn't provide them when I opened the bag. Maybe she wants the monsters to have a sporting chance? Maybe she wants us to prove ourselves? Or maybe whatever magic the bags have doesn't work with grenade launchers"— he glanced into his bag hopefully and then sighed—"even though it would be kind of neat."

"Neat?" Owen echoed weakly.

"Do you have a better plan?" Laurie gave him a look that made her feel like she was turning into Fen. She'd only used that I-dare-you stare a few times in her life, but it always made people back down. Today was no different.

"No."

"Look in my bag for rust." She tossed it to him. "I need to crack these open." She started grabbing the Etch A Sketches and sparklers that Baldwin was tossing out of his bag like it was an endless vending machine.

Baldwin paused, glanced at Owen, and asked, "Do you think we can light the thermite and then send it toward the frost giant with your ravens?"

"No."

"Clay pots," Baldwin yelled.

Laurie noticed Owen raise both brows, but he didn't ask, and Baldwin didn't answer. After a few more minutes, Baldwin was giving them instructions to assemble what he was calling "modified thermite bombs meets Greek fire."

"Greek fire?"

"Early warfare tactic," Baldwin said, digging through his bag. "Byzantine War maybe?" He shrugged. "A lot of theories about it: generally delivered via earthen pots or siphons, possibly ignited *by* water, but mostly thought to burn on water. Aha!" Baldwin pulled a small vat of some sort of old-fashioned jar from his bag and exclaimed, "Thanks, Helen."

"How do you know all this?" Owen asked.

"We might have about six minutes before it sees us," Laurie reminded them. "Less history. More explosives."

"*MythBusters*, the History Channel, and chatting with Helen when I was dead," Baldwin answered as he opened the jar, grinned, and pointed at it. "You need to dip your arrows into this and—"

"They're ghost arrows," she interrupted. "I don't ever *see* them until they hit a target."

"Hmm." He sat back from his makeshift science lab. "That's a problem."

They stood staring at the miscellaneous pots, jars, broken toys, and sparkler boxes. The giant was getting closer by the moment.

"Four minutes," she reminded them.

"Try," Owen murmured. "There's no other plan. Better to try than not. According to the myth, I'm going to be swallowed by your cousin...and you will die fighting. Baldwin is already meant to be dead. I know you would rather Fenrir be at your side, but we're here. We believe in you as much as he does."

Baldwin nodded, and then crouched down to open another jar and waited.

"You can do this," Owen added.

In that moment, all of her irritation at him seemed to vanish.

She didn't know if she could, but the arrows flew true, and the best weapon against a creature of frost was an incendiary one. Laurie lifted her bow, pulled back the string, and whispered, "To light the arrow, I need to see it." She wasn't sure *why* she thought to say it, but as soon as she spoke the words, an arrow appeared.

"Yes!" Baldwin punched his fist into the air. "Test one, we'll use the Greek fire. The precise ingredients are unclear, but I *know* that's what it is. Helen is helping us."

It wasn't the sort of help Laurie had hoped for, but it was the only way they were even getting a chance to defeat the *hrímthursar*, so it was enough.

She dipped the arrow into the jar. "Three minutes, guys. This *needs* to work."

"It will!" Baldwin flicked a lighter and set the tip of the arrow on fire. "Fire in one... two... three."

When he said "three," she let loose, and the flaming arrow went sailing through the sky. She saw a flash of light when it hit the *hrímthursar*. She wasn't sure where or if it even mattered enough to notice. Maybe a small flaming arrow was like a gnat to such a creature. She didn't know. All she did know was that she had no other plans.

"I need arrows," she said, and flipped the top of her bag open with her foot. Arrows spilled out of it, and soon the three of them had an assembly line. Owen dunked the

arrows into the Greek fire or thermite, and Baldwin lit them for Laurie.

After being hit by the twelfth arrow, the frost giant roared and started to run toward them.

"Now," she whispered, and began firing as fast as she could. "It sees us *now*."

"Hurry!" Owen urged.

The *hrímthursar* ran faster and faster, ice spreading from the ground where its feet touched, extending out like frozen lakes that seemed to stretch closer and closer.

Laurie sent a volley of arrows, shooting two or three at once without even realizing that the boys had given her several in each turn.

As the *hrímthursar* got closer, Laurie could feel the cold start to hit them in arctic waves. Her hands were shaking, and her teeth were chattering. Every bit of exposed skin started to burn with the cold. Still she fired.

"It's working," Owen told her. "Just keep going. *Please*." His words were wavering as he forced them through lips that had to be as cold as hers now were. "Again."

Baldwin's fingers were slipping off the button as he tried to hold and squeeze the lighter with shaking hands.

It *was* working, though. Sections of the frost giant were blackened from fire, and some fires were still burning. When the flames went out, the exposed parts of the *hrímthursar* were turned to stone.

She targeted the feet and ankles. If it couldn't walk, it couldn't run.

Then she targeted the *hrímthursar*'s mouth, eyes, and hands. Little by little, parts of the frost giant turned to stone as the thermite-Greek fire solidified the frost. As the frost warmed, they could see the creature under the ice, as if the ice thawing revealed an entirely new shape.

Fiery arrow after fiery arrow turned the frost giant to stone—first in patches, and then an eye, a finger, an ankle— until it was completely solidified. There, in the Badlands of South Dakota, a new rock formation was made, this one as a result of the descendants of the North trying to stop the world from ending. She wasn't sure if it would freeze again and go back to its home, but right now, she'd stopped it.

She shivered all over, and for a brief moment, they stood staring at it—but that was all the time they had. The rest of the monsters were still coming, and what they lacked in size, they made up for in sheer number. At the back of the horde, a second *hrímthursar* walked. The moment of victory that she'd felt vanished as she looked at the monsters still approaching.

"One down...way too many left to go."

EIGHTEEN

MATT

"THOR'S CHARIOT"

They'd lost Astrid. Lost their best chance at an easy win.

Did you really think it would be easy, Matt? After all this?

No, not easy, but perhaps easier. Was that too much to hope for?

He looked out at the Badlands, the dust so thick he could barely see what they were about to face. Barely dared consider what they were about to face.

Nope, easier was definitely too much to hope for.

"So, without Astrid…" he called to Hildar. He rode

behind her as her steed raced across the field. "Now that she's gone, what happens?"

"Her family will appoint another to take her place."

"Another kid?"

"No."

He exhaled. "Good."

"They will send an adult. One better trained in the art of war."

"W-what? But...but the battle...it's supposed to be fair. That's why Astrid's fourteen and—"

"And you turned her against them."

"I—"

"While I understand it was her idea, the fact remains that she joined the opposing side, and one can argue she was influenced by that side."

"Could you have warned me about that?" Matt glowered at Hildar's back. "In advance?"

Hildar glanced over her shoulder. "Would it have made a difference? Would you have fought and killed her?"

He didn't reply.

"I thought not."

They continued on. After a moment, Hildar looked at him again. "I will be honest, son of Thor. I thought your ploy might work. I would have warned you otherwise. But I believed it was..."

"Worth a shot?"

The faintest tweak of her lips, something that might even be called a smile. "Yes, I thought it was worth a shot. It was a worthy strategy. I am proud. Of you and of Astrid."

"Will she…She'll be punished, won't she? When she goes home?"

"We will ensure she is not, son of Thor. Provided she still has a home to return to and you do not lose to your new opponent and see the world encased in ice."

"Umm…"

"You would rather I did not mention that possibility?"

"Kind of."

Another twitch of a smile. "I will not, then, because I am confident that your chances are very good. At least sixty percent."

"Sixty?"

"At least. Perhaps even sixty-five."

She offered a bigger smile now, as if she'd just paid him the highest and most reassuring compliment.

"Any last-minute advice on how to raise those odds and—"

The horse reared suddenly. Matt flew off its back. He dimly heard Hildar let out a cry and saw her grab for him, but it was too late. He hit the ground. A horse screamed. Another whinnied. A hoof skimmed Matt's shoulder.

"Whoa!" Reyna shouted from behind her Valkyrie. "What the—?"

Trjegul yowled. Matt was pushing to his feet, but the thunder of hooves shook the ground so hard the vibrations knocked him down. He peered into the dust. Around him, he heard shouts of surprise and the whinny of frightened horses. He started rising again, but a horse leaped right over him and he barely ducked in time.

The horse came down in front of him...and kept going. Kept *dropping*. The Valkyrie on its back was holding tight, her eyes wide with horror as her steed plummeted into what looked like solid earth.

Matt managed to get onto his knees, scrambling toward the fallen horse, certain he'd see it lying on its side, hoping it hadn't stumbled because of him.

His hands touched down on air. He jerked back. Then, blinking hard against the dust, he slowly reached forward again, his hand moving along the ground until it reached the edge.

The edge of the ground. Beyond that? Nothing.

He heard Reyna calling for her brother, who replied, and then they both yelled, "Matt!"

Something landed on Matt's back. He raised Mjölnir just as Trjegul ran a sandpaper tongue over his cheek. The cat bounded off into the dust cloud. When Matt looked again, the dirt had settled enough for him to see he was lying on the edge of a chasm. Below, he caught a flash of the white horse and heard a shout and a whinny. The Valkyrie and her mount had fallen into the fissure, and were standing on a ledge below.

The earth shook again. Yet it wasn't the pounding of hooves. He could make out the dim figures of the horses all around him, some milling about in confusion, another fallen with a Valkyrie bent beside it. When the earth shook, the horses neighed and whinnied and stamped. And the earth was shaking because...

Something moved deep in the chasm. The horse below screamed, and its Valkyrie let out a bloodcurdling battle cry. Her sword flashed, but whatever moved below was too far down for her to reach.

Matt leaped into the chasm. As he hurtled down, the thought *What am I doing?* did pass through his mind, but it was too late to change course. He shot past the Valkyrie, who shouted something he didn't hear. He landed on the thing whipping through the earth and the force of it knocked him off his feet onto his hands and knees. He looked down to see green scales under him. Emerald green.

Um, you're on the serpent. The Midgard Serpent.

Which was a problem.

He crouched on the serpent as it tore through the earth into a hole too small for him to follow, leaving him stuck atop a conveyor belt moving sixty miles an hour, battering him against the walls of the chasm.

"Matt!" Reyna shouted down. "Get out of there!"

He looked up. *Way* up.

How *was* he going to get out?

A problem to be solved later. Right now, he had something else in mind.

He looked up at the Valkyrie and shouted, "Your sword?"

"My...?" she replied.

"Drop your sword. Quickly. Before the serpent—"

He didn't need to finish. She let go of her sword. It embedded itself in the dirt wall just above his head. Matt positioned himself, then jumped, grabbed it, and dropped. The fact that he managed to do so without slicing himself in half proved some higher power was still on his side. When he landed, he had both feet dug into the sides of the chasm, with the serpent passing beneath.

He readied the sword, knowing his chance was escaping, fast.

With both hands wrapped around the hilt, he slammed the sword down. *Into* the serpent. A tremendous *boom* rent the earth, like a scream trapped below ground. The serpent writhed. The ground shook. Above him, horses whinnied in panic, and the Valkyries shouted to calm them.

Matt closed his eyes and shoved the sword into the beast, pushing it right up to the pommel. The serpent writhed and screamed and the ground quaked, but it couldn't escape, nor could it back up and come after him.

Matt wrenched the sword out for another blow, but the

beast shot into the earth, Matt sailing backward, landing against the side, dirt flying up around him. Something landed behind him. He glanced back to see Hildar, with another Valkyrie dropping beside her. Both lifted their swords to plunge them into the serpent, and then—

And then there was no serpent. A flash of a tapered end, like a tail, and it was gone.

Matt struggled to his feet, the ground still trembling as the serpent slithered away. Panting, he pointed at Hildar's sword.

"You aren't supposed to do that," he said between breaths. "It's against the rules."

Her chin shot up. "I am not permitted to aid you against the serpent on the battleground. This is *under* the battleground. A matter of interpretation, and I am very precise in my interpretations." She returned her sword to its sheath. "It was a good idea, son of Thor. You have wounded it."

"Seriously?"

"Yes, I am always serious."

"No, I mean did I *seriously* wound it."

She paused. "I do not know. You may have mostly angered it."

"Great…"

"It was already going to be angry. But with anger comes rage, and with rage comes weakness. The best warrior is dedicated and passionate yet clearheaded. It is not about revenge or victory. It is about honor."

"Uh, guys?" Reyna called down. "You still need to get out of there."

"Yes, we do." Hildar looked at Matt. "I trust you have a plan, son of Thor?"

"Um...sure. Just...give me a minute."

Matt figured out a way up, with help from Ray and Reyna. Ray suggested "dirt climbing"—in the absence of rocks—with some kind of rope to help. Reyna used the horse's reins. Which sounded obvious enough, except that the reins were made from threaded finger bones, which was kind of gross.

The Valkyrie who'd fallen in went first. Hildar had to order her to leave her horse behind. A Valkyrie never abandons her steed...unless there's a battle brewing and her leader needs her and her horse is safe enough where it is and she can recover it later. While their horses could "fly" across the ground, it was a power of speed, not actual flight. So the horse stayed. The rider went. Matt followed.

He crested the top of the fissure to see a terrible sight through the clouds of dirt. An army of the dead marched toward them.

At least fifty warriors tramped across the earth, the entire ground shaking under their boots. Draugr warriors. Zombies, if you wanted to get pop culture about it, but draugrs were ten times scarier than any Hollywood zombie because they retained the power of human thought—plus they could grow to double their size.

The draugrs wore the rotted remains of their armor. And the rotted remains of their bodies. Leathery strips of skin hung from their skeletal frames, nearly indistinguishable from the leathery strips of, well, leather. Some wore helmets on heads with matted hanks of hair. Some wore helmets on heads of skull. Missing limbs, missing eyes, missing jaws... none of those infirmities slowed them down. They marched in step, relentless and slow. A wall of death. Coming straight for them.

Matt scrambled up from the crevice. And the draugrs... He'd have said they stopped dead, but that might be disrespectful. They were, after all, great warriors who'd given their lives in Viking battles.

Now they stopped. Absolute silence fell across the plain. Even the dust settled, and Matt caught sight of a distant bird, too high for him to make out. A huge bird, it seemed, but maybe it was a trick of perception; and besides, he shouldn't be gaping up with fifty undead warriors standing less than a hundred feet away.

The draugrs had gone completely still. Not so much as a shield or sword clanked.

Matt hefted Mjölnir. He didn't wield it or swing it. Just raised it high.

"Vingthor!"

The cry went up from fifty throats. Or as many of the fifty still whole enough for their throats to form words. Then, as a single body, the draugrs dropped to one knee, the impact nearly knocking Matt off his feet again.

Matt looked out over fifty draugrs on bended knee, heads bent to him, and he didn't see fifty rotting zombies—he saw fifty Viking warriors. Soldiers who'd died for their country. Who'd fought battles as big as the one he was about to face. True warriors.

That's what I need to be. A true warrior. Willing to die for my people. As much as I'd really rather not.

As Matt walked toward the draugrs, one in the middle rose.

"Vingthor," he said. "We have come to escort you to the battlefield."

"Thank—" he began.

"That is our task," Hildar said, walking forward, her chin up. "The Valkyries escort the son of Thor."

The draugr lowered his gaze. "And we wish you no disrespect, queen of the shield-maidens. But the way to the field will not be clear. Already, they gather to stop you."

He extended a bony hand. At first, Matt saw only clouds of dust. Then, above those clouds, the heads of trolls, an army of them, marching their way.

"Trolls, jötnar, mara, and more," the draugr said. "They

267

are not permitted to fight alongside their champions, but until you are at the battle proper..."

"Yes, yes," Hildar said with some impatience. "They may impede our progress. We expect that. We are prepared for it. I will dispatch my troops to deal with them, and *Vingthor*'s goats will assist."

She waved, and as if from behind a curtain, a swarm of Valkyrie and battle-goats appeared, the ground thundering with hooves, the air ringing with bleats and whinnies and war cries. They bore down on the troll army, stopping it in its path as the shouts and grunts and clangs of conflict took over.

"And our warriors join yours," the draugr said, pointing as another cloud appeared from the opposite direction. Draugrs ran at the trolls with their shields and swords and maces and bows raised.

"That's great," Ray said. "Can we go now? Before that fight gets to us?"

Hildar grunted and eyed the draugrs. Matt had seen that same expression when she'd had to deal with Helen. Hildar's domain was Valhalla, land of the honored dead. Helen's was Hel, the lower realms for everything else, which included the draugrs.

"The more the merrier?" Matt said to Hildar.

Her brow wrinkled. "It is war. It is not meant to be merry."

The lead draugr smiled, showing rows of rotted teeth. "Then, my lady, may I suggest you have not been doing it correctly?"

All the draugrs laughed. It was not necessarily a pleasant sound, given the condition of their windpipes, but Matt smiled and said, "The more the *better*, Hildar. That's what I meant. And Ray's right. I don't mind a warm-up bout before my championship title, but I'd rather not face that." He waved at the roiling mass of combatants. "Onward?"

"Yes," she said. "Onward. You"—she gestured at the lead draugr—"cover us from the rear and do not expect to keep up."

They mounted the horses. Matt sat behind Hildar again, Ray and Reyna with the two Valkyries immediately behind, the others fanned out in a protective circle. At a word from Hildar, they were off.

The draugrs could not keep up. While they were faster than Hollywood shambling zombies, the Valkyries rode at a pace that turned the ground to a blur. For all her grumbling, though, Hildar wasn't eager to leave allies quite so far behind, and periodically slowed to "survey the battlefield," which gave the draugrs a chance to close the gap.

During one of those slowdowns, the lead draugr shouted, "My lady!" and pointed overhead. Matt looked up to see that distant huge bird, still too far away to make out anything more than the shape of wings and a body.

Hildar grunted.

"What is it?" Matt asked.

"None of our concern," she said. "It won't attack. Not yet."

"Okay, but I should know what—"

"We are nearly there. Onward."

Hildar began to spur on her horse, then pulled it up short. There, rising over the cloud of dust, were three huge trolls. Or so it seemed, until the monsters' shoulders appeared, and Matt realized it was one troll. Three heads. Not so bad, then…if it weren't at the lead of six more trolls, all with single heads, but not one less than ten feet tall. Mountains of rock. Moving straight for them.

He hoisted Mjölnir.

"No, son of Thor," Hildar said. "We will handle this."

"I wasn't kidding when I said I could use a warm-up bout."

"And we will leave you a fight. But the time draws near and you will not have a chance to rest before…" She glanced up at the distant creature still circling above them. "Before the time comes. Dismount."

She motioned wordlessly to the draugrs. The lead warrior nodded and separated his troops. Most were to go with the Valkyries. A few, himself included, were to remain behind with the three champions, now on the ground beside their escorts.

"This will be quick," Hildar said. "Keep your eyes open. All of you. Shout and I will return."

Matt nodded. Hildar rode off. She looked back only once. That's all she had time for. Then the trolls charged and the Valkyries charged, their battle cries splitting the air and drowning out the roar of the draugrs at their heels.

Matt looked at the leader of the draugrs, who was clearly waiting for instructions.

"Form a circle around the three of us," Matt said. "Watch for attack from every direction. Reyna? Ray? Can you give us some fog cover? The dust isn't quite going to do it."

"Aye-aye, captain," Reyna said.

They took up positions. All except Trjegul, who slunk off through the fog and dust to do whatever magical cats did. Or just to stretch her legs.

Matt tried not to focus all his attention on the draugrs and the Valkyries battling the trolls. There were other fights raging around them, distant clouds of dust and cries and shouts. He thought of Laurie and Fen, Baldwin and Owen, and wondered if any of those battles were theirs. After all this time fighting together, the thought that the others might be in danger made him strain to hear their voices, as if he could race to their sides if he heard trouble. He couldn't. That part of his journey was over.

Once Matt reached his battle ring, he'd lose even Reyna and Ray, who would be led off to their own fight. Ragnarök was for champions. Champions fought alone. Had some-one warned him of this a few weeks ago, he'd have looked at them askance and said "Okay…" not understanding the problem. Alone was the only way he fought. He was a boxer and a wrestler, not a football player. Not a team player. Now thinking of fighting alone was hard enough. Thinking of his *friends* having to fight alone? Almost unbearable.

A hand brushed his, and he jumped. He looked over to see Reyna beside him. She gave his hand an awkward squeeze.

"It'll be okay," she said.

He nodded.

"I know I should say more," she said. "Something better."

"No, *I* should have. Earlier. A better speech. Rousing words of motivation and support for those about to…"

"Die?" She quirked a smile.

"Yeah, sorry. Forgot that's how it goes. For those about to win?"

"No, for those about to vanquish the enemy and return triumphant, ready to face an even greater trial: eighth grade."

Matt laughed.

"No kidding," Ray said. "Seems weird, doesn't it? We could be back in school next week." He squinted out at the darkness. "Well, if they get the lights on."

"And if we manage to—" Matt began.

Reyna clapped a hand over his mouth. "Uh-uh. We will. Next week, we'll be back in class, facing down nasty teachers, bully boys, and mean girls."

"I don't think you need to worry about that," Matt said.

Her brows shot up. "Why? Because you think I *am* one of the mean girls?"

"No, because I can't imagine anyone messing with you."

She laughed and looked down as Trjegul trotted back and yowled. "She agrees."

"No, sis," Ray said. "I think she's warning us about that."

He pointed. At first Matt saw nothing. Then he looked just above the dust clouds to see a swarm of something coming at them. White and feathery like...

"Mara, incoming!" Matt shouted.

"Hold hands!" Reyna said. "Matt? Close your eyes. Ray and I will work on—"

They disappeared, and he started to turn her way to see what was wrong, but when he did, he kept spinning, whirling right off his feet and falling into—

Snow. Matt landed in a snowbank. He lay there, on his back, fingers digging in, snow melting against his warm fingers.

Did I do this?

"Reyna?" he called. "Ray?"

His voice echoed back to him. That's when he realized everything had gone silent. So silent that he rubbed his ears, as if they were plugged.

He pushed to his feet, sliding on the snow. It was so dark he could barely make out the white snow.

But I can see it, meaning there's light coming from somewhere.

He craned his neck back to see one cluster of stars. Just one. The Big Dipper. Also known as Thor's Chariot.

He blinked hard, and the world got brighter. Or as bright as it was going to get, because there was nothing to see. Snow and ice stretched in every direction.

"Reyna? Ray?" Then, "Hildar? Owen?" Louder. "Fen? Laurie?"

Silence answered. Absolute silence. When he took a step, the crunch of snow beneath his shoes sounded like a gunshot, and he wheeled, hammer raised.

Nothing there. Nothing at all.

Then a sound. A voice. A very weak cry. He started toward it, running, shoes digging in and giving him traction as he raced across the snow-covered ice.

Gaze fixed on his path, he saw white, white, more white, and then...black. A crevice in the ice, nearly as wide as he was tall. That's where the voice came from. Someone trapped in the fissure, like the Valkyrie had been.

He dropped to all fours before he reached it and crawled forward, carefully. When he reached the edge, he peered down and saw...

Faces. Dozens—no, *hundreds* of people partially embedded in the ice, moaning and waving their free arms. Faces going down, down, down into darkness.

One looked up and its eyes were black pits of despair.

Matt couldn't even tell if it was a man or a woman. Ice spiked its hair and covered its face, leaving only those dark eyes and a gaping mouth.

"Help us," the person moaned. "Please, help us."

Help them? Hundreds of people trapped in ice and all he had—

He raised Mjölnir.

Maybe I can't free them all, but I can try.

He lowered himself carefully into the icy fissure. It was easier than with the dirt one—this almost had steps leading down. He kept going until he reached that first person. Then he drew back his hammer and slammed it into the ice wall and—

The entire wall shattered. Bodies tumbled out, people screaming, falling, pitching, and dropping into the blackness below.

"No!" Matt screamed.

"You can't help," a voice said.

Matt looked to see the person who'd called to him—a woman—suspended in midair, as if by magic.

"You can't save us. You're the one who doomed us."

She reached out and grabbed the hammer and yanked Matt into the crevice. As he fell, turning end over end, tumbling into the blackness below, he saw Thor's Chariot dimming against the night sky above him.

Then it went out.

NINETEEN

FEN

"TURNING TIDE"

Fen had thought a lot about the final fight, the big showdown, the epic moment when he and his friends would face impossible odds and *win* because that's what heroes do. Now that it was here, he didn't feel like a hero. He felt afraid. He didn't want to die or let anyone down—but he wasn't sure that was possible. If he won, that meant his cousin and his friends would lose and probably die. *They* were the heroes now, and he was a villain...except he didn't *feel* like a villain. He felt the same way he'd felt when he was with Matt and Laurie and Baldwin, but now they were on the other team. It wasn't as simple as "teams," though. This wasn't gym class. These were legions of people and monsters who were fighting to decide if the world would end. Today.

Initially, ahead of the front of the horde of monsters was one of the frost giants, but it had charged forward when flaming arrows started hitting it. He knew Laurie was there, facing a monster without him. He could tell by how the arrows all hit the frost giant; every arrow flew sure and true.

"Wait!" he called, when the rest of the troops started to speed after the *hrímthursar*. It was the best he could do—buy her a few minutes of time.

The monsters all stopped. Even the second frost giant halted. They looked to him and listened. They didn't even ask why. He was Loki's champion for these monsters, and if they defeated the descendants of the North, it *would* be a better world for the monsters.

I am not a monster, Fen reminded himself. He had to do right by his pack, but that was all. He tried to think of how to make his duty to his pack mesh with the way the horde of monsters waited for his command. He couldn't tell the monsters not to attack. He couldn't think of anything to do other than say, "Raiders near me, not in the front."

No one questioned him, although both Skull and Hattie looked a little pleased.

Quietly, he told Skull, "I protect my pack. The monsters are bigger than us."

Skull grinned, looking a little horrific with his discolored bruises.

But then a chattering noise came from the ground by his feet, and Fen looked down to see an enormous squirrel staring up at him. No, not at him, but at the sky. If this had been any other day and any other place, Fen would've gotten far, *far* away, but this was Ragnarök.

Fen followed the squirrel's gaze to the sky—where he found the largest eagle he'd ever seen.

"Wretched inchworm," the eagle called.

At first he thought it was talking to him. Aside from the oddity of such oversized animals existing, the fact that it was *talking* was enough to make Fen unable to move or speak. Then the squirrel chittered and dove into a hole in the ground. The eagle circled overhead almost lazily.

As weird as it was, Fen couldn't stay any longer. He motioned his pack forward. A bird shrieking insults wasn't reason to stop advancing, even if that bird was as big as a dairy cow. He started to march forward again, not in wolf shape because he didn't really want to rush, but not exactly dawdling, either.

He'd gone a few more yards when the squirrel popped back out of the ground, chattering and staring at the sky again.

The massive eagle dove toward the ground, talons outstretched and screamed, "Lazy decay feeder."

Again the squirrel vanished under the ground.

The eagle swooped low enough that a gust of air from its wings made several Raiders stumble. No one seemed overly concerned, although the Raiders were moving closer to Fen. He wasn't sure if they were intending to protect him or hoping he'd protect *them*.

When the earth started to break open a third time, Fen's irritation boiled over. "That's it! Someone make that…"

His words dried up as the ground rumbled. Dirt and rubble scattered like shots as an enormous white reptilian head came to the surface.

"You were saying?" Skull muttered from his left-hand side.

"…squirrel shut up," Fen murmured.

"That's not a squirrel."

Fen shot a glance at his second in command. "You think?"

The snake's vibrant blue tongue flicked out, tasting the air like any snake would. It might be acting like an average reptile, but it sure didn't look like one. Slithering out of a vast hole was the strangest creature Fen could imagine, like some sort of zombie snake with wings but twice as long as a reticulated python. The enormous, more than forty-foot-long snake was white like bone, and it moved toward him with the rustling sound of dried grass like on the South Dakota prairie.

"I thought Astrid was the Midgard Serpent that Matt has to fight," Fen said quietly.

Skull raised his eyebrows in surprise—either at the revelation or that Fen said it aloud. He didn't say anything, so Fen continued a little louder, "If she's the serpent, what's *that*?"

The trolls and the Raiders who were in human form all laughed.

"Nidhogg," Skull said. "Eater of corpses. It gnaws on Yggdrasil, the world tree." He gestured at the dog-sized squirrel. "That's Ratatoskr. He carries the eagle's insults to Nidhogg."

"Uh-huh."

"And at Ragnarök, Nidhogg kills Thor's son."

Fen tore his gaze from Nidhogg, who was now hissing at the eagle. "I thought the Midgard Serpent killed him?"

"No," Hattie clarified. "The Midgard Serpent kills *Thor*."

"Well, that's clear as mud." Fen snorted. "What do we do with it?"

The oversized snake turned its slitted eyes on Fen and flicked its weird blue tongue out close enough that Fen gagged. He thought he'd smelled the worst stench when he'd faced the cave bear on the way out of Hel, but this was a whole new level of nasty.

"Corpse eater," Skull reminded Fen, who turned away from the smell, choking.

Nidhogg turned its mammoth body away from Fen and started slithering toward the rocks where Laurie was. The rest of the troops followed. All Fen could do was go with the monsters. To do otherwise would be horrible for the pack. With these odds, there was no way that switching sides could be in the *wulfenkind*'s best interest.

"I'm so sorry," he whispered to his friends, although there was no way that Laurie or Baldwin or Owen could hear him.

The trolls and wolves all around him sped up, and he knew he couldn't let this happen. There had to be a compromise, a way not to hurt Laurie or the kids at her side. Even though he disliked Owen, even he didn't deserve the slaughter headed toward him faster and faster.

"Take them prisoner," he blurted out.

"What?" Hattie screeched.

"There are, like, *three* kids," Fen continued. "It's not even a battle. It's a massacre."

Yips and growls came from some of the wolves.

He looked around at them and all but snarled his next words. "If anyone hurts my cousin, there *will* be consequences."

"Not wolf," a troll grumbled. "Not listen. Will crush enemy."

Before Fen could try again to argue that taking prisoners made more sense, Owen's seemingly endless crowd of fighting clowns arrived. There was no way he could convince his side to take Laurie and the others prisoners now. The

Berserkers were already hurtling into fights as they started the skirmish with the monsters.

Fen growled and gave in to the inevitable. He launched himself into battle with the rest of the wolves, swinging fists at Berserkers and trying to reach Laurie. He knew he could fight his wolves, but he hoped that they would obey his orders. There was no way that he'd let a troll or anyone else hurt her, though.

I'll throw Berserkers in their path if they try.

As far as plans went, it wasn't any worse than most of his fight strategies.

"Be on the lookout for the goats," he called out.

"Snacks!" ground out a troll.

"Where?" asked another, scanning the crevices in search of the pants-biting beasts. "Where?"

If the enemy won this battle, it wouldn't be because of superior intellect.

"The goats aren't here yet," he clarified for the trolls. "They fight for Thorsen, though."

"Yum," a troll said.

"Hi," Baldwin called as he clambered up a troll cheerily. He waved at Fen. "Sorry you turned to the dark side, but I don't really want to fight you."

Fen smothered a groan and punched a Berserker. That, he could do. In fact, if he was going to have to fight on the wrong side, he thought he might take a little fun in it.

He didn't mind hitting the boy who seemed to be pursuing Laurie. If Fen had to fight someone, it was going to be Owen.

After a quick glance to see that Laurie wasn't in immediate danger, Fen scanned the crowd, looking for blue hair as he kicked, growled, and punched.

Several Berserkers later, Fen was feeling full of energy and standing eye-to-eye with Owen.

"Fate can't always be avoided," the one-eyed boy said calmly.

Fen snorted. "Especially when you hide what you know."

"True. Here we are, though. It was fated." He spread his feet and took a boxer's stance. "I'm not surprised."

"Who does Odin fight at Ragnarök?" Fen had a suspicion that he knew the answer.

"Fenrir."

Fen laughed in a mix of amusement and bitterness. "No wonder you tried to turn Laurie against me. Do I need to guess who wins?"

Owen swung. Fen ducked and returned a punch of his own.

"They both lose eventually," Owen said.

"I'm not going to lose," Fen promised. "This"—he swung and hit Owen in the mouth—"is for trying to make Laurie doubt me."

No more words were exchanged as they fought on.

Fen had to give Owen credit: he was more than an average fighter. Fen had been getting into scrapes since he could stand. It was just how his childhood was. Owen, however, didn't go down easy, and when Fen did knock him to the ground, he popped back on his feet in some sort of gymnastic move that Fen envied—not that he ever intended to tell Owen that.

"Son of Loki," said a voice behind him.

He turned, taking a one-two punch to the head as a result of the distraction, and there stood Helen.

He grunted and shot a dirty look at Owen. The boy simply smiled at him.

"That's not a very polite greeting," Helen pointed out as he spat blood from his mouth.

Before he could reply, she looked away and fixed on Laurie approaching from across the field of battle. "I am here to honor my promise. In the myths of old, they say Hel opened wide, and I brought my forces to fight for Father Loki."

"I know," Fen said quietly.

It seemed likely that Helen's arrival was either very good or very bad. Her dress, which had been covered in insects when he last saw her, had been replaced with a long white coat that seemed to writhe. She lifted an arm like she was going to hug him—and he realized that she was draped in some sort of tattered shroud that was crawling with maggots.

All around them, fights stopped as both sides realized that Helen was standing in their midst.

"She is Loki's champion," Helen said in a raised voice, motioning to Laurie with one maggot-covered arm. "And I will do as my father would have: I fight on the side of his champion."

Still, no one moved.

"Nephew," Helen murmured meaningfully as Laurie reached them. "You appear to be on the losing side."

"The losing—"

If she had picked me, Fen realized, *we'd have won, and the world would end.* She hadn't, though. The ruler of Hel, Loki's daughter, had chosen *Laurie* to back—and Helen's idea of support was to bring forth the monsters that lived in her domain.

"Hi, Helen! Best. Fight. EVER," Baldwin yelled as he ran by to launch himself at Nidhogg.

Helen smiled and shook her head. "He has a fondness for snakes. Something about a snake garden?"

Fen laughed. "Maybe we could take a field trip back to Reptile Gardens after the world doesn't end."

"It still might end," Helen said. "We'll tend to these creatures, but Thor's child has to deal with the Midgard Serpent on his own." She gave Fen a smile that looked unnervingly like Laurie's and confided, "Father Loki never suggested that *his* children must play by the rules, though. Rules are more suggestions to work around than absolutes to obey, according to Father Loki."

She lifted her hands and the earth split open in wide gorges.

"Pick your side, nephew."

Garm was at the front of the line of monsters emerging from the fissures. The immense dog met Fen's eyes and said, in a reference to their first conversation back in Hel, "This is not play, either, but it will be fun."

Since he was in human form, Fen was surprised that he understood Garm, but now that he was alpha of the wolves, this seemed to have changed, too. "I'm glad you're on our side."

Garm offered a toothy smile.

Fen watched as the fire Jotunn stepped out of the cracks and various dead warriors pulled their rotting bodies out of the earth. The myth had made clear that Helen had brought her forces to fight on Loki's side, but with two champions, it had never been clear *which* champion she'd back. They'd hoped that it would be Laurie, but until this moment, they couldn't be sure—and Helen had never committed for certain.

With a giant grin, Fen looked at the *wulfenkind*. "Helen fights to stop the world from ending. The tide has turned.

As your alpha, I tell you that we will fight *with* my Aunt Helen—as in the myth." He met Skull's gaze and added, "It's what's best for our pack." Then he looked at his cousin, who was smiling at him with the happiest expression he'd seen in a long time, and added, "Our pack will be on the *right* side."

Skull yelled, "You heard our alpha!"

The wolves immediately stopped fighting the Berserkers.

Fen strolled over to stand beside Laurie. "Which should we take first? A troll, another Jotunn, or the big creepy snake?"

She bumped her shoulder into his. "Jerk. I saw you fighting Owen."

"No boys allowed near you. Your dad made me promise," Fen said. When she gave him an "oh really" look, Fen added, "Plus, I don't like him."

Laurie rolled her eyes. "Come on. Monsters to fight. I'll yell at you later."

He wasn't sure if they'd stop the world from ending or not, but it was a lot less scary now that he was beside his best friend. "Snake first."

TWENTY

MATT

"WARM-UP BOUT"

Matt lay facedown on rock. Cold dark surrounded him. The moans and screams of the dead filled his ears.

I'm in Hel. No Valhalla for me. Straight to Hel with all the people I doomed to death when I let the serpent win. When—

Something tugged at the back of his jeans. Pulling at the waistband. He flew up, Mjölnir in hand. Then he heard a bleat. A hard butt in the rear knocked him forward into something solid and warm and covered with soft hair. Another bleat. Another butt in the butt.

Matt blinked hard. The darkness lifted and the cold dissipated, and he found himself standing in a wide crevasse amidst jagged rocks. Except...the rocks rested on ground level and only reached to his head.

What had happened?

Mara.

A third bleat, impatient now, and he turned to see a snow-white goat with golden horns and black spots under its eyes.

"Hey, Tanngrisnir." He hugged the goat. When he realized what he was doing, he pulled back fast, but Tanngnjóstr pushed forward, clearly expecting the same greeting his brother got. Matt gave it to him—after checking to be sure no one was watching.

"Thanks for the wake-up call, guys," he said. He grabbed the edge of the rock and hoisted himself up for a careful look around. "Mara cleared out?"

Tanngrisnir snorted, as if to say *Of course*.

"Lead the way, then," he said.

Tanngrisnir showed him the best path out of the rocks, while Tanngnjóstr brought up the rear. After a few yards of picking through rocks, Matt could see the battlefield. Hear it, too, in the distance.

"How far did I wander?" he said.

Tanngrisnir bleated.

"Yeah, far enough, obviously. Okay, well, since I doubt you guys brought Thor's chariot..."

He trailed off, thinking of Thor's Chariot in the nightmare.

The end of the world. The end of him and everything and everyone else. He shivered. Tanngnjóstr rubbed against him.

Matt nodded. "No time for that, I know. My job is to make sure that's one nightmare that never comes true. Let's get moving—"

Tanngrisnir reared up, his golden hooves pawing the air. Then he fell. Right at Matt's feet. Fell with an arrow through his throat.

"No!" Matt dropped beside the goat. Tanngnjóstr leaped over him with a wild snort and Matt looked up to see the goat charging—

It was charging a draugr. One armed with a bow and nocking an arrow to fire at the goat. Matt shouted "No! They're with me!" and as the words left his mouth he realized the futility of them. Of course the goats were with him. The draugr had to know that Tanngrisnir and Tanngnjóstr were sacred beasts.

Matt launched Mjölnir. It slammed into the draugr and knocked it back, bones shattering, but it was too late. The arrow struck Tanngnjóstr in the throat. The goat went down. Matt raced forward, catching Mjölnir without even thinking. He ran and skidded to his knees beside his goat, its golden eyes wide as blood poured from its throat.

Matt buried his hands in the goat's long fur.

"You're immortal," he whispered. "You're supposed to come back."

The goat lay there, still and silent.

At a noise, Matt leaped up. A draugr strode forward, flanked by two others. It was taller than the rest, with tangled reddish yellow hair and a long matted beard, one side of its face had rotted to bare skull. This was no anonymous dead warrior. This one Matt knew. This one Matt had fought. Fought and defeated and watched Helen exile to Hel.

"Glaemir," Matt said.

The former king of the draugrs smiled. "Did you think you'd won that easily, Matthew Thorsen?"

"How did you—?"

"Escape?" A rotting-flesh grin. "It is Ragnarök. Everything that wishes to escape can. I had help." Glaemir waved and a half dozen draugrs appeared from the dust. The half dozen who'd stayed behind with Matt when the Valkyries rode off.

"Some of my men are still loyal to me," Glaemir said. "And still loyal to my cause. Which, sadly, is not yours. Now, I believe my men heard you say you wished a warm-up fight?"

Eight draugrs clanked their weapons against their shields and stood at attention.

"Enough of a warm-up for you, boy?" Glaemir said. "I think so. In fact, I think it will be such a warm-up that you'll never see the battle ring."

At Glaemir's signal, his men charged. Matt ran. That

was the only thing to do when faced with a troop of undead warriors on open ground. Behind him, Glaemir whooped with laughter.

"There is your champion. A little boy who runs away. Fitting, I think."

Matt jumped over Tanngnjóstr's still body and then Tanngrisnir's, trying not to think about the dead goats. He raced into the rocks, wound around two smaller ones, and found the place where he'd woken, ringed by stone. He stopped there and backed against one rock.

When the first draugr ripped around the corner, Matt started counting to five. He'd barely reached two before a second draugr appeared. Matt launched Mjölnir. It slammed into the first, knocking it backward against the second and ramming both into the rocks behind them.

The impact of hammer against bone? It wasn't pretty. There was cracking and crunching and shattering, and then two draugrs on the ground, in pieces, as Mjölnir whacked into Matt's outstretched hand. Another draugr appeared. Matt counted, but at four he realized he couldn't wait any longer and threw it.

The hammer hit its target just as another draugr came around the corner, too far to catch the impact and too close for Matt to wait for Mjölnir's return. He hurled his magical Hammer. That only knocked the draugr off balance. By then, Mjölnir was on its way back, and it slammed the

draugr in the side of the head. Matt flinched at the cracking of the warrior's skull as it fell.

"Four down!" Matt shouted. "Do you want to talk, Glaemir? Or let me keep warming up?"

The draugr king didn't answer, but Matt swore he heard the gnashing of teeth. Another draugr appeared, this one on the rocks over Matt's head, and he hurled Mjölnir with a little too much confidence—and at the entirely wrong angle. The hammer sailed over the draugr's head and kept going.

Matt launched his amulet power, but the Mjölnir mistake distracted him and the Hammer fizzled. The draugr leaped in front of him and raised its sword, chuckling a horrible wheezing chuckle. It peered at Matt with one good eye, the other a dried blob hanging on its cheek. Then it charged. Matt dove. He hit the draugr in the legs and knocked it back. Out of the corner of his eye, he saw the sword swing down and he slammed its arm with a blow hard enough to knock the bone from its socket. The draugr snarled... and switched the sword to its left hand.

Matt jumped to his feet and backpedaled just in time to avoid the draugr's swing. He was dodging the next when Mjölnir slapped back into his hand, which would have been awesome, if he'd seen it coming. As it was, it knocked him off balance, his hand barely closing in time. He started to swing the hammer, when two more draugr appeared. Matt slammed Mjölnir into the first and ducked the sword of the second and—

A shadow passed overhead. A fourth draugr? He couldn't take on four. He danced backward, considering his options, when a leaping figure hit the one-eyed draugr with an angry bleat. It was Tanngnjóstr.

Matt's sigh of relief was cut short as *he* was nearly cut by a sword aimed at his midriff. He spun out of the way just in time.

One whack of Mjölnir knocked the sword out of the draugr's hand. A second blow caught it in the side with a horrible crunch. A third broke its femur, and it went down. Matt pulled the hammer back to aim at the fourth draugr, but Tanngrisnir leaped from the rocks and toppled it. A wild stamp of hooves made sure the draugr stayed down, groaning and alive, but making no move to rise.

"Two left," Matt said to the goats as they surveyed the zombified bits littering the ground. "If you guys can focus on the last two regulars, I'll take Glaemir."

The goats bleated. This time, Matt knew exactly what was out there—namely the draugr with the bow and arrows. He warned the goats, and they dodged arrows as they galloped toward the distant draugr.

Matt surveyed the open ground. Glaemir stood to the

side, brandishing his sword. It looked more like a dagger, barely the length of Matt's forearm…because Glaemir himself had grown to twice his already impressive size.

"No one left to hide behind," Matt called. "If you want to run away, I'll let you."

Glaemir laughed. "You are indeed Thor's champion, boy. As delusional a braggart as your ancestor."

"It's not delusional if it's true. But I can see why you'd hide behind your warriors. I beat you once. Rather not face me again, I bet. Especially now that I have…" He hefted Mjölnir.

Glaemir charged. Matt walloped him in the knee, which was at the perfect height. Glaemir barely staggered before recovering and swinging his sword. The problem with being twice Matt's size? Matt could easily strike his kneecap, but Glaemir had to bend to swing his now-undersized sword. It was an awkward move, handily avoided.

Matt slammed Mjölnir into Glaemir's other kneecap. Now the draugr king stumbled. A third blow and he fell to his knees.

"The bigger they are…" Matt said, raising Mjölnir for a final blow, but as he swung, Glaemir suddenly shrank to his normal size and Matt flew off his feet from the force of his missed blow. The tip of Glaemir's sword tore through his shirt. This time Matt met it with his shield. The clang was enough to set his arm quivering, but he managed to get to his feet and face off against the draugr king.

"You know what's missing from this warm-up?" Matt said. "The warming part. I'd really like to at least break into a sweat before my real battle."

Glaemir swung. Matt blocked.

"So if you could step it up—"

Another block.

"I'd really appreciate it, and I think the serpent would, too. Otherwise—"

Whoosh. Clang.

"—I think she'll be disappointed. It *is* Ragnarök, after all."

"Hey, Matt!" a voice yelled. "You talking or fighting?"

He caught a glimpse of Reyna, running through the dust with Ray at her heels.

"I can do both," he called back.

"Yeah, well, maybe less of one and more of the other?" She pointed toward a mangled draugr crawling toward them.

"Right," Matt said. "Okay, then. Gimme a real fight, Glaemir. Get my blood pumping and—"

Glaemir snarled and swung. The sword cut so close Matt felt the wind of it.

"Um, Matt?" Reyna said. "You want some help?"

"Nope. Unlike some people—some *undead* people—I fight my own battles. Thanks for the offer, though."

"Anytime. But if you could hurry it up…"

Another swing. Another block. Matt heaved Mjölnir

back. Glaemir rushed him, grabbing a shield off a downed draugr. The zombie ducked Matt's blow and when he spun off balance, it slammed him with the shield. Matt went down, flat on his back.

"Matt!" Reyna rushed forward.

"Got it," Matt said . . . as Glaemir put his sword to Matt's throat.

The twins and the goats lunged toward the fighters. Matt raised his shield hand.

"Really, I've got it," he said. "I think Glaemir and I can discuss this reasonably. I'm willing to accept his surrender with no hard feelings."

Glaemir laughed. "You truly are Thor's child. Arrogant to the core. I have you pinned, boy. One thrust of my sword—"

"A truce, then?"

"You are amusing. Perhaps even brave. But it is time to admit defeat, boy, and prepare to meet Hel on the other side, an ignoble fighter cut down by a true warrior—"

Matt smacked Glaemir's sword away with his shield and leaped to his feet. "Can't resist the urge to gloat, can you? Thanks, I was counting on that." As he spoke, he swung Mjölnir. It caught Glaemir in the side of the head—and both kept going, hammer and skull, knocked clean off Glaemir's neck. The draugr's head shot across the plain, disappearing into the dust.

"Hey, hear that?" Matt said. "The sound of silence. Finally."

He hefted the shield over his shoulder as the twins stared at him. "Oh, don't worry. He can put it back on." Matt waved at the draugr's body, crawling pathetically in the wrong direction. "As soon as he finds it. By then? We'll be—"

The thunder of hooves cut him short. Hildar rode up, her normally impassive face drawn with worry. Then she saw Matt and reined to a stop.

"Son of Thor." She exhaled. "Finally."

"Sorry," he said. "Old business to attend to. But I got my warm-up."

He motioned to the disabled draugr king crawling their way.

Hildar sniffed. "I knew they were not to be trusted."

"No, you just don't like them. But with these few, you had good reason. Now, I think I have a real battle to get to."

"You do," Hildar said, and reached down to swing him onto her horse.

"So this is the spot?" Matt said, peering around in the near dark. It looked a lot like the place where he'd found the draugrs, with both open land and rocks for cover.

"We were granted the right of choice in this as well," Hildar said. "You approve?"

Matt slid off the horse. The others were gone. Even his goats weren't permitted to join him here. Just Hildar, and only for transportation services. Matt climbed to the top of a rock and looked out.

"Seems good. Is there a foul line?"

"When the serpent arrives, your battle-ring will become warded."

Matt looked at the expanse of open earth to his left. "Is there a depth barrier, too? I mean, I'm hoping the serpent can't just burrow in the ground if I injure it."

"It cannot. The boundary applies to the ground and to the air."

He squinted up. "Um, okay. That's not going to block my powers, is it? Sure, I can't fly like the comic book Thor, but if there's an upper barrier, can I still invoke weather?"

"You can."

"Let me rephrase that. Will that weather still reach the battlefield?"

"It will."

"Good. So the sky barrier...? Why...?" He trailed off as he saw the giant bird, high in the night sky. "Is that so *it* can't attack? Whatever it is?"

Hildar did not reply. When Matt looked at her, she tugged a strand of hair anxiously. Then she caught him looking and tossed the strand back, her chin lifting. Yet she said nothing.

"Hildar…this is a one-on-one battle isn't it?"

"Yes."

A distant crack, like thunder. The bird was descending. No, not a bird, he realized. It was an odd shape, almost like an airplane, long and thin with wings. He blinked hard, trying to focus, but the night was too dark and the creature too high.

"I don't have to fight that thing, right?" he said.

Silence.

"Hildar?"

"Yes." A pause. "Yes, son of Thor. You must fight it."

"But…?" The creature dropped lower and let out a horrible cry, one that nearly knocked Matt off his feet. When he recovered, it had swooped down, and he could see it clearly.

It was a dragon. A huge, serpentine dragon with bat-like wings and a massive head. Matt stared up at it.

"That…That…" He swallowed. "That's the Midgard Serpent?"

Hildar didn't answer. He looked over to see her staring as the creature swooped again, its shape blocking every star above.

"No," she whispered.

"That's not the serpent?" he said. "Thank the gods, because—"

"No!" she shouted, punching the air with her shield. She swung and yelled into the open expanse around them. "It is to be the *champion*. The chosen champion."

A voice answered, slithering from all around them, an unearthly voice that didn't come from the dragon, but from the earth itself. "You stole our champion."

"No, Astrid betrayed you. Not us. Your side must choose a new champion."

"We have."

"That is not—" She wheeled, roaring now into the emptiness. "That is not a champion. It is the *serpent*. The true Midgard Serpent."

Laughter floated all around them. "So it is. So it is." And, in a blink, Hildar and her horse vanished, and Matt was left alone, staring up at the creature above.

Not Astrid in dragon form. Not her cousin or her mother or an aunt. Her grandmother.

No, not even her grandmother. The thing that had consumed her grandmother, that her grandmother had died to become.

The real Midgard Serpent.

That's what he had to fight.

TWENTY-ONE

LAURIE

"ENEMIES BECOME ALLIES"

When Helen had arrived, Laurie hadn't known whether to cheer or weep. The myths told that Helen worked with the monsters to bring about the end of the world, but she'd seemed to favor Laurie over Fen. She'd gifted her with the incredible bone bow and ghost arrows, and she'd given her the map to exit Hel. Still, one could never be completely sure about any of the children of Loki, and Helen was his actual daughter.

But she'd opened the earth and brought forth her monsters, not to fight *for* the end of the world, but to stop the world from ending.

"I'm glad you're with me," Laurie told Fen. "I wish we could be with Matt, too."

"He'll be fine," Fen told her. "Come on. We have a world to save...starting with Baldwin."

To their right, Baldwin was trying to wrap a rope around Nidhogg's neck. Laurie couldn't tell whether he was attempting to strangle the corpse eater or ride him like a war horse. Either way, he wasn't doing too well. The cheers of glee were to be expected, but he looked like a small toy in a swimming pool: he was tossed about with no control at all.

"Baldwin!"

He looked down at her and grinned—but then he looked at Fen beside her. "Are you evil, too, or is Fen good again?"

"We're on your side," Fen yelled back.

Their yelling caught Nidhogg's attention, and the oversized white serpent turned its gaze to them. The long blue tongue shot out, and both Brekke cousins ducked just in time.

"Pull back and help the Berserkers," Fen ordered his pack. "Hattie and Skull, give the orders."

Hattie nodded and instantly started deploying wolves to attack the trolls that they'd just been calling allies. Laurie knew Fen still didn't like the girl, but he hadn't liked the twins or Owen, either. Both Hattie and Owen were on their side, as was Skull and the rest of the pack. Liking teammates wasn't necessary if he could work with them.

That was Fen through and through, and Laurie was glad of it today.

Skull hadn't budged. He stayed at Fen's side, leveled a glare at him, and pointed out, "You're my alpha. My job is not to blindly obey, but to *help* you." He motioned at Nidhogg and at the Jotunn that was lumbering toward them. "You two need all the help you can get."

Fen nodded.

Then two wolves launched at them.

Skull snarled, "Not our pack."

The two boys were side by side and punched the wolves simultaneously. Fen grinned and looked around them. The Berserkers were led by Owen—who was keeping his distance from Fen—and Fen's pack was being directed by Hattie. Garm and Helen were rounding up trolls, and that left the four kids facing Nidhogg.

Baldwin was still managing to stay on top of the serpent, but Laurie was watching the *hrímthursar* that was headed toward them. That frost giant would need to be defeated, too, but right now, she had other plans.

"What are you thinking?" Fen asked.

She glanced at her cousin just as Skull clotheslined another wolf. Fen winced in sympathy at the gagging noise from the fallen wolf. Laurie met his eyes and said, "Chicken."

"Playing chicken with a *hrímthursar*? That's your plan?" Fen clarified.

"Yep."

He laughed and shrugged. "Okay."

It was moments like these that reminded her that they were both Loki's descendants. She quickly explained that she needed him to play chicken so they could "steer" the creature and anger it enough to use its frost as their weapon.

Fen glanced at Skull and said, "Shift and stick with me." Then he told Laurie, "Be right back."

Once they were gone, Laurie looked at Nidhogg. What she was about to do would be easier without Fen being his usual overprotective self. She pulled out her bow, nocked an arrow, and called to Baldwin, "Slide down. New tactic."

Baldwin didn't question her. He simply let go of the rope he'd been using as a makeshift bridle and reins. In the next moment, he was sliding over the side of the white serpent and tumbling to the ground. He rolled to his feet and ran to her side.

She had to restrain herself from puking at the smell. A thick pinkish slime coated his clothes from riding the corpse eater. "Breathe through your mouth," Baldwin offered. "It helps until you get used to it."

Laurie nodded. She wasn't a prissy girl, but she was pretty sure that she wouldn't *ever* get used to the stench of rot that currently coated her friend's clothes. She took small breaths through her mouth. It helped a little.

Nidhogg started to slither away, picking up speed as it moved toward the thick of the fight. It was far enough away that she was starting to worry that it would begin eating the still-living fighters. Unfortunately, it wasn't far enough that she could say that she was at a "safe distance" for what she needed to do.

"Just like in Mitchell," Laurie whispered. "Be ready to run."

Come on, come on, come on, she silently urged Fen and Skull. The two wolves were darting toward the Jotunn and then retreating. Slowly but steadily, it turned on its path and veered to the left—away from the area where she now stood and where most of the Berserkers and Fen's pack were battling with the enemy.

"In three...two...one..." At each count she launched an arrow at Nidhogg. It turned to see what was attacking it, and then at one, she let a volley of them fly toward its face. As arrows stuck in its face and eyes, it lurched toward them, pulling its massive coils into the air and darting toward them in a move between a hop and a slither.

"Go! Go! Go!"

Laurie and Baldwin ran full out, but there was no way to completely dodge the serpent. It was bigger, faster, and angrier. She didn't have a better plan to lead it away from the crowd, and the only weapon she had other than her bow was her mind. If she could get it near the *hrímthursar*, she could use one monster's weapon—the frost—against the other.

Then one of the Berserkers went flipping by her and

tossed a black feather to her and Baldwin. "Odin's ravens' feathers," he yelled.

As Laurie and Baldwin grasped the feathers, she realized that they were suddenly moving so quickly that their feet barely touched the ground. They weren't exactly *flying*, but they were moving fast enough that they were sailing over the ground.

Nidhogg was surging toward them, its hisses loud behind her. Apparently, like many snakes, it didn't need to rely on its sight to locate them.

The Jotunn was chasing Fen and Skull now, firing blasts of ice at them as they darted and dodged in front of it.

And it felt like everyone was going to converge in one big heap of chaos and pain.

"Fen!" she yelled. "Incoming!"

Her cousin ran toward Nidhogg.

The Jotunn finally saw the massive white snake headed its way. Wrongly interpreting it as an attacking enemy, the *hrímthursar* roared.

Nidhogg hissed and raised its gaze to the giant.

The blast of frost was so close to her that Laurie heard a crinkling sound as some of her hair froze.

The snake and Jotunn flew at each other in a battle that was far better matched than kid versus either one. Nidhogg twined around the Jotunn, crawling up its body rapidly at first but growing sluggish by the time it reached the *hrímthursar*'s neck. Until that moment, Laurie hadn't known if the corpse eater was cold-blooded like other reptiles, but as it grew slower in its movements, she realized happily that it was.

Icicles fell to the ground like spears as the slime of decayed things that clung to Nidhogg's body froze and sloughed off.

Still, Nidhogg didn't give up. It tightened its coils around the *hrímthursar*'s throat and simultaneously tried to sink fangs into the Jotunn's face.

The blast of cold and snow knocked all four kids to the ground.

"Way too close to them," Skull said from Laurie's left side. She flinched without meaning to. He'd been the enemy since before she knew he existed. Seeing him at her side any day before now would've been dangerous.

"What were you thinking?" Fen snarled at her. "It could've killed you. I thought you had given *me* the danger-ous one."

Laurie flashed her cousin a grin. "I did. I just gave me an equally dangerous one."

Skull laughed, and Laurie's discomfort with him decreased a little.

As snake and Jotunn wrestled, seeming almost evenly matched, Laurie looked at the rest of the fights. The Berserkers and *wulfenkind* that fought on her side were winning. Various trolls were sitting around looking dazed or fleeing. One was facedown with Garm sitting on its back. The gate guardian from Hel was surveying the fights, too. The doglike creature flashed teeth at her when their gazes crossed in what she thought was a smile.

Garm made a growling noise, and Helen turned to stare at Laurie.

The ruler of Hel started to stride toward Laurie just as the Jotunn got a good grip on Nidhogg and tossed it.

The massive serpent hit the ground hard enough to crack the earth—and create a crater.

"Hush, you," Helen told the snake as it hissed and started to move slowly toward the kids again.

The cold had obviously made the great reptile all but unconscious. Its tongue flicked slowly, and it moved at a near glacial speed. It might be struggling, but it wasn't done.

"I told you this was a bad idea," Helen continued as she approached Nidhogg. She patted it on the nose gently. "My niece is a clever little beast, I said. My side is with her, I said." She *tsk*ed at Nidhogg. "Now, do we kill you or will you retreat?"

Although Laurie was no expert on reptiles, when it eyed her and flicked its thin blue tongue, she was pretty sure there was hatred in Nidhogg's expression.

The serpent hissed something else, and Helen smiled.

With a flick of Helen's hand, the two-headed fire Jotunn

that Laurie had seen in Hel came lumbering forward. At its approach, the snake almost glowed. Laurie could see it warming back up.

All that for nothing! she thought.

But then, instead of turning to face the kids who had tricked a frost Jotunn to attack it, Nidhogg slithered off and vanished into the crack in the ground that Helen had opened.

"Silly thing," Helen murmured as it vanished back into the earth. Then she turned and flashed them a smile. "Well done."

Of course, this still left the *hrímthursar* to contain.

Laurie pulled out her bow and, as before, mentally requested arrows she could light.

"We could light it off that," Baldwin said, pointing at the flaming Jotunn that was now talking to itself. The two heads were discussing whether the Badlands looked like home or home looked like the Badlands.

"Hey, you're a big wolf," Baldwin said to Skull. "How about you shift, and I'll ride you? You run toward the fire and—"

"How about *no*." Skull shook his head. He was staring at the ground. "I just need a couple of good rocks..."

"Or we could simply do this," Helen suggested. With another wave of her hand, she sent the two-headed Jotunn toward the frost Jotunn. "Come, dears, we need to finish up with the trolls."

Then she strolled away, humming a little song like Laurie's mother did when they went walking to go to an afternoon picnic.

"Your aunt is scary," Skull said.

"You're related to her, too," Laurie told him.

The once-intimidating Raider shivered.

Anything he might have said was lost under a roar, as behind them the two-headed Jotunn from Hel clashed with the *hrímthursar*. Fire and frost smashed together, and soon the air was hazy. It rolled out like a fog around them and made it hard to see at all. It was like standing inside one of those steam rooms at the gym that her mom liked—hot and hard to breathe.

"Back up," Laurie ordered.

"Be careful of the crevice," Fen added.

A rumble shook the ground under their feet and the earth seemed to rip open again. The movement sent them all tumbling to the ground. Laurie rolled down a sudden hill, stopping with a jolt as she slammed into a rock.

"What was that?"

"Thor's child is facing the Midgard Serpent." Helen's voice carried across the distance. "It doesn't sound promising."

No one else answered or even spoke.

When Laurie got to her feet, she couldn't feel any of the boys near her. She said their names, swept her arms around, and...discovered that she was alone at the bottom of whatever hill she'd tumbled down.

The clash of fire and frost also made loud hissing noises over and over...which was scarier than usual when they'd just faced a giant snake. In a matter of moments, Laurie could barely see in the fog around her. Several times, she stumbled, fell to her knees, and got back up.

Even though the haze made it hard to see, she could still hear cries and grunts. Waves of cold and heat surged at her, and flashes of red from the fire Jotunn lit up the mist like explosions.

"Fen! Baldwin!" After a grudging pause, she added, "Skull?"

No one answered. All she heard was the sounds of fighting and the hiss of steam.

Carefully, Laurie started crawling back up the inclined ground to where she thought she'd been, hoping to at least get herself back to the rocks so no one could sneak up behind her. She'd gone about ten feet when she felt the brush of fur against her arm and yelped in surprise. The wolf nudged her hand with its muzzle and then nipped her sleeve and tugged.

"You'd better be Fen," she muttered as she allowed the wolf to lead her out of the small ravine where she'd fallen when the ground under her feet had convulsed.

TWENTY-TWO

MATT

"UNFAIR ADVANTAGE"

The serpent landed. No, not a serpent. A giant snake was certainly nothing to scoff at, but if you stayed away from the fang-bearing end, it could be managed. This? This was a dragon the size of Matt's school.

He'd seen the serpent, twice, wriggling through the ground, and very clearly, this was no earth-dwelling snake so it could not be the Midgard Serpent, right? Yet it took only one close look to realize that excuse didn't hold. It might have the head and the wings and even the front legs and claws of a dragon, but the rest was pure serpent—emerald green on the back with a pale green stomach—and that's what he'd seen in the ground.

A serpentine dragon. Able to burrow through the ground or soar through the air. A dragon with wings that could batter his puny body against the rocks. A dragon with claws that could rip him to shreds. A dragon with fangs the size of his forearm, one scratch of which would send deadly poison racing through his veins.

The serpent landed. Matt raised his shield. It was the size of one massive dragon nostril.

This. Was. Not. Fair.

The dragon opened its mouth. Matt saw tendrils of smoke and a faint red glow, deep in the creature's endless black throat.

No. No way. Please don't let it be the kind of dragon that breathes—

Fire blasted from the Midgard Serpent's mouth. Fortunately, Matt already had his shield up. Unfortunately, it was like blocking a geyser with his finger. The flames whooshed past the shield and wrapped around its icy surface, and Matt fell back with a yelp.

The serpent took a deep breath, preparing for blast two. Matt dove behind a rock, barely making it in time. Then he crouched there, his brain spinning.

Not fair. Not fair. Not fair.

The words kept looping through his brain. Meaningless. There was no crying foul here. Hildar had tried. The Norns

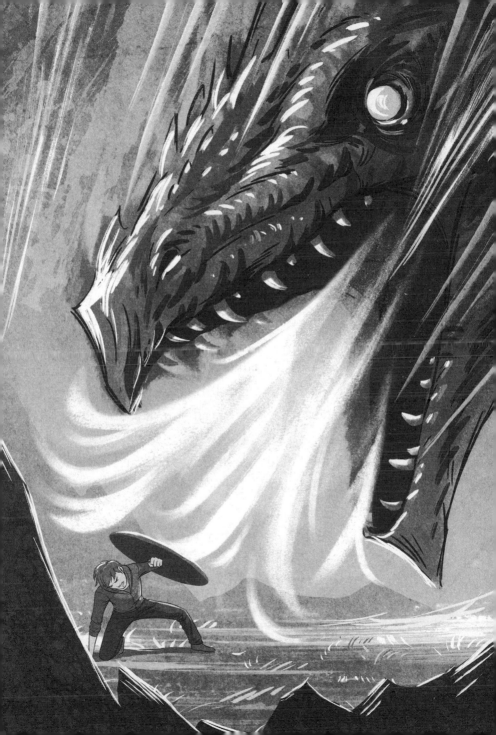

apparently couldn't do anything to fix this. All's fair in war and the apocalypse.

Matt took a deep breath. He hefted Mjölnir. Then he carefully peeked over the—

A wave of flame engulfed the rock. Matt hit the ground. He lay there, on his stomach, pondering his options.

Options? What options? I'm pinned behind a rock by a hundred-foot-long fire-breathing dragon.

Well, no, that might be a slight exaggeration. The dragon wasn't quite a hundred feet long. Maybe eighty. The pinned-behind-a-rock part, though? Matt lifted his head again, not even getting his eyes over the top before the serpent blasted him.

Yep, that part? Totally accurate.

Shield raised, Matt started lifting up again, seeing if he could just take a look, his head shielded, and throw Mjölnir—

The next blast of fire hit the shield with enough force to knock him flat on his back.

Okay, new plan.

As Matt rose, the ground shook. For a second, he thought it was him, quaking in fear. But despite the rather dire predicament, he wasn't the one trembling. Meaning the serpent—

Matt scrambled between two rocks just in time as the serpent lumbered around his original hiding spot. It stopped, eyes narrowing as it looked at the now-empty place. As he stared at it, he swore he heard Reyna's voice in his ear.

Um, Matt? You've faced fiery monsters before.

Right, but...

Then his coach, when Matt panicked once on heading into the ring against a guy who looked twice his size.

That only means you can't expect to knock him flying on the first blow, Matt. Focus on what you can *do.*

Ignore the size of the dragon. Focus on the current problem. The fire-breathing part.

Matt closed his eyes and imagined a blizzard—snow and sleet and gale-force winds buffeting the hapless dragon. He concentrated as hard as he could and after a minute, a snowflake landed on his nose. Grinning, he opened his eyes to see...

Big, fluffy snowflakes, gently falling from the sky.

Not quite what I ordered.

Still, buoyed by the quick—if not entirely overwhelming—response, he squeezed his eyes shut and pictured the worst storm he could remember. Three years ago. They'd been at school when it whipped up, dumping so much snow that the kids had to spend the night there.

Fluffy snow continued drifting lazily down.

No problem, just keep—

Thunder cracked. Wind whipped past, grabbing his shield and lifting him onto his tiptoes. He yanked the shield

down and ducked his head against the incredible gust blowing past.

Well, you asked for gale-force winds.

True, but he really needed snow with it, and even those
useless big flakes seemed to have stopped. Wait. No....He
could see them. Falling somewhere else. Just not on him.

Matt looked up to see the dragon. Right over his head.
Flying. Blocking the light snowfall. Its beating wings caus-
ing those gusts as its jaws opened to—

He dove just as the Midgard Serpent loosed another
volley of flame.

It's not supposed to fly in the ring.

No, it just can't fly very high. Actual flight? Not a regula-
tory violation.

The dragon shot another fiery wave, one that ignited the
dry grass around the rocks. Matt ran onto the open ground,
racing as fast as he could, struggling to think, just think,
think, think—

"Matt!"

Was that someone calling his name? He wasn't slowing
down to find out.

"Matthew!" Then, "Matty!"

Matt's gut went cold. He knew that voice. But it couldn't
be. No one was allowed here except him and the dragon.

No rules, Matt. No refs. Not now. Anything goes.

The dragon swooped, jaws opening, teeth glittering. Matt hit the ground and rolled.

"Matty! Over here!"

As he came out of his tumble, he glanced over. His grandfather stood on one of the rocks, waving madly. Matt took one look, leaped to his feet—and ran the other way.

Granddad? Here? In the fight?

Did he actually think Matt stood a chance against the real Midgard Serpent? That the outcome was not guaranteed and the dragon needed *help* beating the puny mortal kid?

"Matt! Over here! I'm trying to help you!"

Matt turned to stare at his grandfather.

"I'm sorry!" Granddad yelled. "I made a mistake, but I'm here for you now."

Of everything Matt had been through, nothing was worse than hearing those words. With his mind spinning, his confidence shattered, unable to even think of a strategy against the monster circling above him, he'd still had hope. Crazy and completely groundless hope, but hope nonetheless. *I can do this. Somehow, I can do this.* Then he heard those words and something inside him cracked, and it took everything he had not to drop to the ground, put his head down, and cry.

You did this to me. And it's not enough to want me dead. You have to help me die, by preying on the one flicker inside me that

*still hopes, the little kid that loved his granddad and can't believe
you've sent him off to die.*

Matt did not drop to the ground. He did not cry. He
did not stop running. But he did answer. An answer that
his grandfather would never have imagined coming from
his lips. An unrepeatable answer. But the only one, in that
moment, that Matt could give.

Matt raced into another outcropping of rock. He got into
it just as a tongue of fire slid around the rock and scorched
his leg. His jeans ignited. He started dropping to put out
the flames, but the serpent hit him with another blast and
he barely got his shield up in time. It turned to ice again,
protecting him, but Matt had already been dropping to
the ground, and now his knee gave out and he went down
and—

A hand grabbed him. He swung Mjölnir up, but his
trajectory was wrong and by the time he lashed out, his
grandfather had him by the shirt, Matt unable to reach him
as he was dragged across the ground.

Matt twisted and fought, and then he remembered his
other Hammer. His hand shot out to launch it, but his
grandfather had already dropped him into a gap between
rocks. Matt hit the ground and scrambled up, only to knock
his head on more rock.

A cave of sorts. That's where he was. A weird cave-like
rock formation. Matt started lunging to get out, then stopped.

He was safe. Shielded above and on three sides by rock. The fourth side was open, but a scattering of nearby large stones meant the dragon couldn't get to him. The beast was, perhaps ironically, too big.

I'm safe.

No, you're trapped.

True. He was wedged in, the only exit leading to the dragon, but while his grandfather had doubtless meant to trap him, he'd inadvertently given Matt a place to catch his breath and think.

The ground thumped as the dragon landed.

"You aren't supposed to be here!" Granddad boomed to the monster. "This isn't your fight."

The dragon hissed and beat its wings, drumming the air.

"There is another chosen," Granddad said. "She waits outside the ring. The proper champion. A serpent of your lineage. You are to retreat and allow her to take your place."

A snarl. Then a cry of pain from his grandfather and Matt lunged forward before catching himself.

It's a trick. Even if it isn't, he's only trying to play by the rules and let one of Astrid's family take her place.

"Begone, serpent!" his grandfather shouted. "Or if you take your champion's place, I will take mine. The Norns have allowed me on the field because you broke the rules. Unless you retreat, I am permitted to stay."

Matt shot from his hiding spot, yelling, "No!" He

clambered onto the rocks to see his grandfather at the dragon's feet.

"It's all right, Matt," Granddad yelled back. "I can do this. Give me Mjölnir, and I'll fight the serpent for you."

Matt almost laughed at that. "Give you Mjölnir?"

"I was allowed in on the condition I'm unarmed except for my amulet. But I can wield Thor's hammer. Give it to me, and I can do this for you."

"You honestly think I'd believe that? You aren't going to use Mjölnir to fight the dragon. You're going to take it from me so I'm guaranteed to lose. You think I have a chance of surviving, of winning."

"Yes, I do. You've proved I was wrong, that this doesn't need to end the way the myth says. You brought Balder back from the dead. You won Astrid to your side. The outcome of the fight can change. I see that now, and I'm here to help you."

"I don't believe you." Matt raised his shield. "I am Thor's champion, serpent. I'm the one you'll fight. The *only* one you'll fight."

"Matt, no!"

The dragon jetted into the sky, as high as it could without hitting the barrier. Then it swooped at Matt. He threw Mjölnir and dove back into the rock shelter. A roar of pain as Mjölnir hit. The hammer sailed back into his hand.

Matt's hiding place went dark as the dragon hovered

over it. Fire engulfed the rocks. Matt pressed back as much as he could with his shield blocking his face. Sweat poured off him.

Then the beast let out another cry of rage and pain.

"Yes!" his grandfather shouted. "Over here! If you break the rules, then we both break them. You have two of Thor's descendants to fight today, serpent. Come and—"

A howl from his grandfather. Matt ran out to see him on the ground. He had no shield. No hammer. Only his Thor's power, and it wasn't enough. Matt saw him lying there, knocked down by the dragon, and he didn't care if his grandfather was on his side or not. This was still his grandfather.

Matt hurled Mjölnir. It bounced off the serpent's flank, and if the creature felt it, it gave no sign, just hovered there, gaze fixed on its target. Fixed on Granddad.

The dragon opened its jaws. Matt shouted a warning. The beast let loose a wave of fire, but his grandfather managed to roll out of its path and scramble behind cover.

Matt climbed onto the tallest rock. He looked up into the sky and called on the power of Thor. The true power. Not ice and snow and wind, but rain and thunder and lightning. The power of the storm god. He threw everything he had into calling on that power, into believing he had that power. And the skies opened and rain poured down in torrents.

The dragon dropped to the earth as if shoved down by a giant invisible hand. It let out a roar. Then it stomped toward Matt. He pitched Mjölnir, hitting the dragon on the snout, and it let out another roar. Then it drew breath, its chest inflating, and Matt heard his grandfather shout for him, his words drowned out by the torrential rain.

The dragon's jaws stretched as wide as they could. Fire kindled in its throat, filled its mouth, shot out, and…disappeared.

The dragon stood there, as if confused, a bubble of fire roiling from its mouth, going no farther. Matt swung Mjölnir. The hammer launched and the beast sprang. It leaped with the grace of a cat, and the hammer flew harmlessly past it. Matt jumped off the rock into his hiding hole.

The hole went dark. Wind buffeted the rain as the dragon hovered above the rock. Then its giant claws reached down, as if to land. Those claws, each as long as Matt's forearm, wrapped around the top rock as he wriggled back farther, out of their reach. But they didn't swipe for him. They grasped the rock and they wrenched, and the stone disappeared above him.

Matt ran out from his ruined hiding place. He looked up to see the dragon hovering there, the massive rock clutched in its claws. It flew directly over him and those claws began to open.

"Matt!" Granddad shouted.

Matt didn't move. He readied Mjölnir. The beast dropped the stone. His grandfather screamed, a terrible raw scream.

But Matt was already launching Mjölnir and his amulet's power, one right after the other. Mjölnir hit the rock and exploded it into a hundred shards. The Hammer power struck those shards and hurled them into the dragon's belly. And Matt got out of the way before gravity took over and brought that rain of stones down on his head.

As the dragon screeched in pain, Matt ran for his granddad, knocking him out of the way, the rock shower falling harmlessly behind them. Then Matt spun back to the dragon, and saw tears in its abdomen where some of the sharper rocks had embedded themselves. Its wings flapped, lashing the rain into hail-like bullets. Matt didn't stop the storm, though. However much the rain hurt Matt, it hurt the beast just as much...and extinguished its flames.

Matt threw Mjölnir again. This time, he aimed for the dragon's eye, and the beast was too enraged to see it coming. The hammer hit. The dragon bellowed, the sound crashing like waves, Matt's hands flying to his ears, nearly missing Mjölnir as it sailed back. He caught it and threw it again at the same eye, but the dragon saw it and flew off awkwardly, struggling to keep itself up against the downpour, veering to one side as if half-blind.

Hands grabbed Matt. He wheeled to see his grandfather.

"We can—" Granddad began.

"No," Matt said. "There is no *we*."

His grandfather's face crumpled at that, but there was no shock in his eyes, just grief and understanding.

"If you're serious about fighting the serpent, then do it," Matt said. "I'll do the same. Just not together. I don't trust you. Don't expect me to."

"I was wrong. I—"

"No." Matt stepped back, shaking his head. "If you're going to fight, then fight. Anything else is a distraction. And probably a lie."

"I—" His grandfather's eyes widened. "Matt!"

Matt heard the dragon first. Heard the loud beating of its wings. He was ready, though. Nothing his grandfather said would distract him, and he'd been listening for that sound. He wheeled and threw Mjölnir. It smashed into the side of the dragon's skull with a crack like thunder. The dragon screamed and rose, wings flapping fast and hard. Then it dove.

Matt dove, too. He faked the dragon out, starting one way, then twisting and diving the other, rolling behind a rock.

He heard a scream. Not from the dragon. From his grandfather. Matt jumped to his feet and turned to see his grandfather caught in the beast's giant claws. Matt ran from behind the rock.

"No!" he shouted so loud his throat hurt. "He's not the champion. I am! I'm the one you—"

The Midgard Serpent threw his grandfather to the ground. Hurled him at the rocks below.

Matt let out a cry. He ran at the beast and loosed Mjölnir. It cracked against the giant snout. The dragon pulled back. The sudden move threw it off balance, and the beast thudded to the ground. Matt raced to his grandfather, who was lying on the rocks, groaning.

Matt grabbed his grandfather and carried him to an outcropping of rock. He laid him down between two rocks as he listened to the distant thumps of the dragon.

As soon as Matt laid him down, his grandfather collapsed. He tried to raise his head but couldn't.

"Just wait here," Matt said. "I'll end this."

"I know." His grandfather's lips curved in a pained smile, his blue eyes glowing with pride. "I know you will. You can win this, Matt. You *will* win this. I see that now, and I'm so sorry—"

"Shhh. Don't talk. I'll be right back."

He tried to leave, but his grandfather caught his hand. "I made a mistake. I thought I was doing what was best for our people. Saving them. And yes, that meant letting you go, but that wasn't my choice—you were the chosen champion, and I didn't see any way to save you. I told myself you'd go to Valhalla and take your place with Thor himself, and you'd be better off there, not here after Ragnarök, fighting for survival with the rest of us. I accepted our fate and yours because I thought it was inevitable. But I was wrong. Now I know why you were chosen, Matt. You have the power of Thor and the bravery of Thor, but it's more than that. You will win this because you have the heart of Thor. I am so, so proud of you, and so, so sorry for everything."

For a moment, Matt couldn't move. It was everything he'd wanted to hear, everything he'd dreamed of hearing, everything he'd told himself he was a fool for imagining. Whatever happened with the Midgard Serpent, *this* was Matt's real victory. His real reward, and he crouched there, mouth open, unable to get out the words he wanted to say.

"Go," Granddad said. "You can't turn your back on it."

Matt nodded. He reached down to hug his grandfather.

"I'm going to really make you proud," he said. Then he pulled back, ready to do exactly that, to kill the dragon. But when he moved away, Granddad's head lolled, his blue eyes open, his breath stopped.

"No," Matt whispered. "No!"

Behind him, the dragon roared.

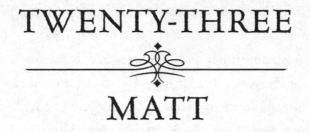

TWENTY-THREE

MATT

"FATE"

Granddad was dead.

Dead.

Matt leaped to his feet. He barely saw the dragon through the rain and through his rage. He ran at it, and he launched Mjölnir, and he blasted his Hammer power, but both missed, Mjölnir flying wild, the Hammer fizzling. Even the rain seemed to slow, coming in fits and starts as if riding the roller coaster of his emotions, the fury and the grief and the fear and the confusion.

A fresh rush of anger, and he threw Mjölnir again. The dragon ducked it easily and flew at him, sending Matt scrabbling to get behind rock as flames shot out. The fire sputtered away, but slower now, sparks still showering Matt's face and hands.

Mjölnir returned, and Matt readied to throw it again. Then he stopped. He heard Hildar's words—*with anger comes rage, and with rage comes weakness*—and he replayed his last few moves. They'd been fumbling and blind.

She's right. I might feel better, hurling this hammer at my grandfather's killer, but what am I doing besides tiring myself out? And giving the dragon time to recover?

What else had she said? *The best warrior is dedicated and passionate yet clearheaded. It is not about revenge or victory. It is about honor.*

Honor. A fine word. But was this really about honor? No. A fight for honor was a fight to defend some nebulous ideal. The stakes here were not nebulous at all. Matt flashed back to the nightmare the mara had sent him, and he shivered as if he'd been thrust into that icy wasteland again. He remembered the chasm, the voices, the cries, the people trapped in the ice, falling into Hel, all because he'd failed this fight.

Honor was a fine word, but this was a battle for life. If he lost...? He glanced up at the stars, at Thor's Chariot, yes, but mostly at the stars behind it, billions of stars, billions of lives.

Matt hefted Mjölnir. He looked into the sky again, and he focused, clearheaded as Hildar said. Simple and pure focus. He had to know what he wanted and then make it happen.

The wind picked up, and it might have been the dragon beating its wings, but Matt wouldn't believe that. Wouldn't accept that. For once in his life, he wouldn't doubt and deprecate his abilities and his powers. That wind was his. He controlled it. He *owned* it.

The sputtering rain began to fall straight and true. Then the wind caught it, blowing it like icy cold bullets, and Matt thought of earlier, when the dragon's beating wings seemed to turn the rain to hail, and that's what he asked for. No, that's what he *demanded*.

And it fell. Slow at first, slushy rain that soaked him to the bone. Then the rain hardened, and he lifted his shield over his head as he strode from his hiding place. The hail beat down like golf balls, pounding against his wooden shield, the sound deafening, but Matt kept going. He walked straight into the middle of the open stretch of land. The dragon flew above him. He couldn't hear it, but its shape cast a shadow, blocking what little light the storm let through.

Then he saw the beast, diving straight at him, its claws extended. He whirled out of the way and launched Mjölnir. It hit one of the gaping wounds on the dragon's chest, and the dragon let out a roar that resounded over the pounding hail.

Matt caught the hammer. The beast dove again. Matt spun—and slid on the sleet-covered ground. One foot shot left, the other right, and he started to go down. The dragon let out a piercing cry of triumph. Giant claws wrapped around Matt. His shield fell. He fought madly, swinging the hammer wildly, but the claws closed and the dragon lifted him into the air.

Matt twisted and looked up and saw only darkness. A sky of endless night. He knew that wasn't what he was seeing at all—it was the belly of the dragon blocking everything else—but in his mind, he saw that nightmare sky, every star extinguished, and he thought a clear, calm, deliberate *No.*

I will not let those stars go out.

He lowered Mjölnir, testing the weight as if it were a baseball bat. Then he swung it at the dragon's thin, birdlike leg. The beast screeched. He hit it again, in the same spot, and the claws opened.

Matt fell. He didn't look down to see how high he'd been. He didn't let himself look. He closed his eyes, and he focused on the wind and a gust of it lifted him, slowing his fall. He still hit hard enough to gasp in pain as his knees screamed with the impact. But he landed on his feet.

He saw the shield and left it where it lay. The hail pounded down like softballs now, and with each hit, he felt a future bruise and he thought, *So I'll have bruises. I'll live to see those bruises, and that's all that matters.*

The dragon landed. The hail was too much, covering its back in icy sleet. It landed right in front of him and met his gaze, one of its eyes half-closed, its snout bashed in on one side, pain and rage blazing in its good eye. It looked at Matt, standing there, and it let out a noise, a deep rumbling noise, and it wasn't a growl or a snarl. It was a laugh.

The dragon looked down at him, a mortal boy, no bigger than its head, holding a puny hammer, this boy, standing his ground, far from any shelter. And it laughed.

Then it snarled, opening its jaws as wide as they would stretch, giant fangs flashing... and Matt threw Mjölnir. He threw it straight into the gullet of the beast.

The dragon stopped short, its injured eye widening. Then it began to choke. Matt stepped away, looked up at the sky, and stopped the hail.

The dragon's head swung wildly, jaws still wide. Matt jumped back, and again he slid on the ice. When he twisted to catch himself, the serpent's fangs slashed at his jeans. As he felt the fabric rip, his mind flashed to the mural back in the Blackwell hall—Thor versus the Midgard Serpent at Ragnarök. The god defeating the beast, only to turn away and have it, with its dying breath, bite him with its poisoned fangs, killing him.

Matt danced out of the way, his brain screaming, "No!" But the serpent had only ripped his jeans. It slashed down at him again, still choking, still dying, but fighting with everything it had.

Matt looked up into the sky, at the stars, and he made his final demand to the god of storm and thunder. The skies opened in answer. One perfect bolt of lightning shot down, striking the dragon. It lit up, blazing red against the darkness. The giant body convulsed. Then it fell.

The serpent dropped onto the earth, splashing up mud and water. It kept convulsing, the very ground shaking beneath it. Matt tensed, his Hammer power at the ready. But then, with one final shudder, the beast lay still. Poison dripped from its fangs and a puff of smoke curled from its throat. Then Mjölnir came hurling out and smacked into his hand.

Matt looked down at the hammer, dripping wet.

"Serpent drool," he said. "Great."

Then he laughed. He threw back his head and laughed.

There was a moment, holding Mjölnir over the dead Midgard Serpent, when all he could think about was that he'd won. He'd defeated the serpent. He'd defied the myth.

And then he remembered the others and their fights. As fear crept in, he remembered something else. His granddad. Lying dead in the rocks.

Matt clenched his hand around Mjölnir, and any last

traces of that victory laugh died in his throat. He picked up his shield and started toward his granddad's body. As soon as his foot touched down, burning pain shot through it. He looked down to see the pant leg the serpent had ripped. Under it, blood dripped down his leg. Blood and poison, burning a trail down to his sneaker.

"No," he whispered. He fell to one knee, dropping the shield and the hammer. He ripped back the torn fabric. There it was. A single puncture wound, blistering now as the poison worked its way through his body.

Did you think you could cheat fate, Matty? Really?

Exhaustion washed over him. He blinked hard and felt himself toppling. He tried to stay upright, but the darkness fell, and as it did, he swore he heard the serpent laughing.

TWENTY-FOUR

FEN

"AFTER THE FIGHT"

The worst of the monsters were contained, and Aunt Helen was coordinating the stragglers with an almost cheerful efficiency. Fen, however, still felt the lingering threads of fear twisting throughout his body. He'd just seen Laurie roll down a hill and dangle perilously close to that gash in the earth. He'd rather face more monsters than anything like *that* moment ever again.

He decided to keep her by his side by any means necessary as he led Laurie away from the gorges that led down to Hel. Honestly, Fen was ready to bop her on the head and send her home whether she liked it or not—and he already knew that her answer would be a big *not*. Unfortunately, she was the one with the ability to open portals, so he was left linking his arm with hers to keep her from falling to her doom again.

Being around her now that she was acting…well, acting like *him*, was almost scarier than watching her being pursued by a massive snake that had arrows in its face. If they survived the end of the world, he was going to assign some of his pack to guard her twenty-four hours a day. This whole adventure had turned his previously trouble-avoiding cousin into a girl version of him. It was not good. Not at all.

"She could lead the pack," Skull said in awe. "Are you sure she's not a wolf?"

"I'm a fish, actually," Laurie interjected.

"*Fish?*" Skull echoed. His mouth gaped open.

Fen shrugged. "Dude, our family is weird in so many ways, and it's the fish thing that surprises you?"

"Salmon," Laurie added.

"Oh." Skull stared at her and then shook his head.

Fen glared at him. It was bad enough that Owen looked at her in awe; he wasn't going to tolerate any of the wolves looking at her, too. Family kept family out of danger. Skull and Owen were both dangerous—especially now that Laurie seemed to enjoy battles and adventures. There was no way those two weren't both likely to end up in peril. Owen had a horde of fighters; Skull had been pack alpha.

Fen pulled Laurie closer to his side. Bopping her on the head and putting her in a fortress sounded like a better plan by the minute.

The remaining small fights were fading. Most of the monsters were finding their way to Aunt Helen, who looked like an orchestra conductor directing the lot of them into that gash in the earth that would lead them to her domain. She was meandering around the crags and crevices, her face seeming almost lifelike for the first time. The ruler of Hel looked strangely *happy*.

"She's as much a hero as anyone else," Laurie murmured, catching the direction of Fen's gaze.

Helen looked up, finding them unerringly. "I expect visits, children. I'll even spare you the journey next time since you've proved that you can complete it successfully."

Fen gaped at her.

"It was a test," Laurie said, half questioningly.

"Of course," Helen agreed with a smile that Fen had seen on his own face often. They really *were* related. There was something strange and a little awesome about realizing that this immortal being really was part of his family. She nodded at him and went back to herding the monsters into Hel, where, as she put it, "They'll be more comfortable."

"Thank you," Laurie told their aunt.

Helen looked suddenly sad and added, "Father would have enjoyed it."

Fen didn't know what to say to that. Loki, their long-dead ancestor, was just a name and stories to them, but to Helen he had been a person, a parent, someone real. Before he could figure out what to say, Helen turned away and was gone.

"We need to get to Matt," Fen said. "The wolves are helping...Aunt Helen." He paused briefly, newly comfortable with calling her his aunt.

"Let's go," Laurie said.

Fen was ready to crawl into bed and sleep for days. First things first, though: they needed to go check on Thorsen. He'd obviously beaten the dragon, but in the myths, he died because of that fight.

As if she could read his mind, Laurie said, "He'll be fine. He has to be."

All Fen could do was nod. He wasn't as optimistic as her.

MATT

"Matt? Matt?"

Someone was shaking him. He opened his eyes and saw...

Sunshine.

A cat jumped on his chest and peered down at him. Then a face blocked the sun. Reyna, grinning.

"Hey, champion, you done napping yet? I'm sure your fight took a lot more out of you than mine did, but I think you've had enough rest."

Matt lifted his head. Ray stood behind Reyna. On his other side, Hildar was swinging off her horse.

"You've slain the serpent," Hildar said.

"Dragon," Matt croaked. "It was a dragon."

"Of course it was," Reyna said.

She grinned again, a huge one, as bright as the sun, and he stared at her a moment before pushing up, blinking. He lay on the battlefield with the Midgard Serpent in a heap twenty feet away. The beast's mouth was open, fangs jutting. Seeing those fangs, Matt pulled up his pant leg. The mark was still there, red and swollen, but nothing more.

"You fell into the river," Hildar explained.

"River?"

"In Hel."

"Um, sure, but…"

"You swallowed the poison there. Do you remember what I said when you told me?"

He struggled to recall. "You said that was as it should be. So it inoculated me?"

She frowned at the unfamiliar word.

"The poison I swallowed built up a tolerance for this one," he said.

"Yes. Everything was as it should be."

He blinked harder and as he did, he realized there were others there—Laurie and Fen, along with Baldwin and Owen. Behind them were Tanngrisnir and Tanngnjóstr.

"Everyone's ... okay?" he said.

Laurie smiled. "Seems that way."

"We did it."

Laurie hugged him. She was filthy and smelled like wet dog and smoke, but she was alive. "Yes, apparently we did."

"So what happened?" Matt asked. "How did you guys—?"

"Later," Hildar cut in. "Come now. Others wait."

LAURIE

There were a million and twelve things they would all have to talk about. Some were simply tales of the fights they'd had, but some were questions. They could talk later. Right now, well... right now, they could go home. They'd all survived. They'd stopped the end of the world, and they'd actually *survived* it.

"Are you okay?" she asked Matt.

He nodded. "You?"

"We're alive, and Fen's not a traitor." Laurie bumped his shoulder like she did with Fen.

Matt gave her a small smile. "We did it."

"Of course we did," Fen said. "Never a doubt."

Laurie rolled her eyes, and Matt shook his head. It felt good to be back to normal...or as close to normal as possible surrounded by Valkyries, magic goats, and descendants of dead gods.

"Are we ready to go home?" she asked.

Hildar spoke up. "I'll see Freya's daughter home."

"*And* my brother," Reyna interjected.

"Later," Baldwin said. He looked at Owen and asked, "Can I travel with you guys?"

Owen nodded and hesitantly said, "The threat is over, though, so you don't have to—"

"Friends, dude. We're friends now, right?"

At that, Owen looked a little stunned. "I suppose we are."

Laurie grinned at the boys. Somehow it had been easier with monsters than with everyday things. "We're *all* friends," she told them, her voice making it very clear that it was an order. "And we will keep in touch, *right*?"

Fen slung an arm around her. "Whatever you want, Laurie."

"It's like she's become even scarier," Baldwin said in what he might've thought was a whisper.

"I like it," Owen said quietly, earning warning looks from both Matt and Fen.

"I expect e-mail!" Laurie told them all, and then she opened the portal to Blackwell and told her *two* pseudo-brothers, "Let's go home."

MATT

Matt stepped through the portal. His uncle stood there, holding a bottle of water and a sandwich.

"Alan insisted I bring this," Uncle Pete said, handing them over.

Matt laughed. He uncapped the water and took a deep drink before saying, "Where is he?"

"Home. This next part's just for family."

"He is family."

Uncle Pete smiled. "Thank you. Next time, though. Eat your sandwich and come on. We don't want an audience for this."

Matt said his good-byes to Laurie and Fen. Temporary

good-byes. This wasn't like an out-of-town championship match where you say you'll keep in touch and never do. They would. Always. There was no question of that.

After the farewells, Matt walked with his uncle. A figure came running toward him. For a split second, Matt froze, his fingers wrapping around Mjölnir. Then he looked up at the sky. The sunlit sky. No more battles. No more enemies. And with that, he saw who was coming—a teenage boy with red hair and a wide grin.

"Hey, kiddo," Josh said, racing up to him. "You did it, huh?"

Matt didn't get a chance to answer before Josh's arms grabbed him, lifting him in a hug so suddenly that Matt dropped Mjölnir. Onto Josh's foot.

"Ow!" Josh said, releasing Matt and hopping away, holding his foot. "Big hammer. Heavy hammer."

Jake strolled over, chuckling. "Doofus." He reached down for Mjölnir. His fingers wrapped around the handle sticking up. He had to heave to get it off the ground, the tendons in his neck straining as he handed it back. Matt took it easily and Jake smiled. "And that proves who it belongs to, doesn't it?" He reached out and clapped Matt on the back, leaning in to keep his toes out of hammer range.

"Matt?"

Another voice. A soft one, choked with tears. Matt looked up to see his mother. Her eyes were red, and she looked like she hadn't slept in a week. When she saw him, she stopped and teetered, as if she wasn't sure it was really him.

"Hey, Mom."

She ran forward then. Ran and threw her arms around him. Jake said, "Watch the hammer!" and she only hugged Matt tighter, saying, "I don't care. I don't care at all."

Matt felt a hand on his shoulder. He looked over to see his father. His mother let go and his father gave him a fierce hug. Then he pulled back and said, "You did it, Matt."

Matt nodded, mute.

"You did it," his dad said again. "We knew you would, and if you thought, for one second, we doubted that, then we have a few things to work on." Another hug. "Now, let's get you home."

LAURIE

Laurie stepped through the portal, last as she had to be. She'd had a moment of fear that the portal wouldn't open, that her god-gifts would vanish with the monsters. She'd had a fear that her mom would be furious, that Fen would be rejected, that Matt's family wouldn't want him home, but as she looked around, her fears vanished.

Her father was hugging Fen tightly, and her mother and Jordie were already wrapped around her so tightly that she thought she might wince in pain. Of course, that would mean admitting that she was beaten up a bit.

"You did it," Dad said, pulling Fen toward them so there was a giant Brekke hug. "I'm so proud of you two!"

"How did you stop the world from ending?" Jordie asked.

Laurie and Fen exchanged a glance.

"There was a battle. We won," Fen offered after a moment. He was doing his normal Fen-softens-details thing that he'd always done around her mom.

No one spoke, and Laurie realized that she and Fen were both a bit bruised and bleeding in several places.

"We're okay," she blurted out as she saw her mom cataloging her injuries. "Aunt Helen was there. We couldn't have done it without her and the Raiders and the other descendants. Matt fought the serpent. Oh, and the Valkyries and some of the descendants were with him."

"Yeah, without help, I'm not sure what we would've done when the jötnar...I mean..." Fen looked at Laurie and gulped.

Laurie reached and squeezed Fen's hand, silently telling him that she was okay with his slipup. "There were some monsters, but we won. The world is safe, and we're home. We're not injured, just a little scratched up."

Her parents still said nothing. It was an odd, tense silence, and her mom looked like she might cry. Then Jordie asked, "Who's Aunt Helen?"

"Um, Loki's daughter. She rules Hel, the um, afterworld," Laurie said quietly.

"Oh." Her mom blinked. "Right . . . as in *really* his daughter? How did you even—do I want to know?"

"Probably not," Fen answered.

Laurie smiled at her mom and added, "We did it, Mom. Everything's okay now."

"And I'm so proud of you," her mother said. "*Both* of you."

"Let's go home," Dad added.

Although Laurie knew he meant all of them, Fen obviously didn't. He nodded and looked away. "See you later, then," he said quietly.

"You too, Fen," Mom said. "You could both use something to eat, and a shower, and a good night's rest."

"Shower first. You both stink," Jordie piped in.

Fen stared at them, surprised that Laurie's mom and brother seemed happy to see *him*, too. No one but Laurie had ever been proud of him before Ragnarök. He stared at them, half expecting a laugh at his gullibility in believing them. They didn't laugh, though. They smiled at him.

EPILOGUE

Matt lay in bed, staring at the ceiling, listening to his alarm blaring. His door opened. Jake pushed his head in. "Hey, you going to turn that off, kid? Or wait until you wake the whole neighborhood?"

Josh pushed in behind Jake. "Wakey-wakey, Matt. Mom made you something special for the first day back at school. Rakfisk and whey. Breakfast of champions."

Matt groaned.

Josh laughed. "Just kidding. She made waffles. You can stay in bed for a few more minutes, okay? Give us time to eat them all."

Matt shook his head as they retreated, closing the door. He yawned, stretched, and rolled out of bed.

It was good to be home.

In a home in Blackwell, Laurie curled up in bed, not quite ready to get out of the soft, warm cocoon of blankets. After so many nights in a sleeping bag on the cold ground, it felt incredible to be in her bed. There were no monsters coming in the door, no mara with their nightmares, no trolls shaking the floor, no jötnar. What *was* there was the smell of breakfast cooking and a bark of her father's laughter.

"Get up, sleepy bones," her mother said as she sat down beside Laurie. "Your dad, Jordie, and Fen are driving me crazy."

"Glare at them; it works."

"Nope. I'm outnumbered," her mother added. "Come to the kitchen and help me."

Fen couldn't smother his grin as he watched his cousin come into the kitchen. A few days ago, he was afraid that neither of them would survive. The odds of stopping the end of the world had been . . . bad. Every adult he knew—except the villainous ones—thought that kids had no business running around fighting monsters, and while Fen wouldn't have admitted it out loud, he had sort of agreed with them.

Fate—or the Norns, actually—hadn't cared one bit about his opinion, though. Honestly, for most of his life, no one had.

Now he was the alpha of a pack of *wulfenkind*, ones he was going to try to convince to go to school and try to plan better futures. Maybe then, if some other lunatic came along talking about ending the world, they might not be so quick to listen.

"Fen? Laurie?" Laurie's father looked at them both. "I have a proposal for you. The three of us were talking while you were away...fighting. I'm not going to roam anymore. I have permission to stay in Blackwell because of what you kids did."

Fen and Laurie exchanged tense looks, but he noticed her little brother grinning widely.

"I talked to Eddy," Laurie's father continued. "He's willing to terminate his parental rights if you agree to let us adopt you, Fen. Would that be okay?"

"Say yes, so you get to be my brother," Jordie blurted.

Laurie reached out and squeezed his hand. "You're already my brother. Always have been."

Then Fen looked at Laurie's mother. His aunt had never really liked him, and although he'd stayed with plenty of relatives who didn't like him, this felt different. She'd be his *mom* if he said yes.

"Give me a chance?" she asked. "I misjudged you."

Fen nodded. "Okay."

Both Laurie and Jordie launched themselves at him, and his new parents smiled and joined the giant group hug. He wasn't usually a hugger, but this was sort of an exceptional moment. He had a family, a real family who *wanted* him. He could hug them.

Laurie and Fen walked to school in a sort of comfortable silence that meant even more to her after everything that had happened. They were almost there when he glanced at her and asked, "Do you think your mom minds?"

"No." She bumped him with her shoulder. "She'd have stopped him before we knew about it if she disagreed."

Fen nodded, and they walked a little farther before he said, "Baldwin sent me a message. He's trying to convince his parents to move here."

Laurie laughed. "If anyone can do it, it'd be him." She looked at her feet, not really wanting to tell Fen that she'd heard from Owen, but not seeing any way to avoid it. They'd learn to get along, or they wouldn't. There was no way she was choosing between them—but if she did, they all knew Fen would win.

"So did Cyclops boy call yet?"

"Fen!" She blushed and looked away. She'd never had a boy like her before. "Don't call him that."

"I could call him other things," Fen growled.

Laurie met his eyes. "You might be an alpha now, but you're not the boss of me. You don't have any more right to pick my...friends than before."

"Oh come on, Laurie, he was willing to let Matt die and didn't tell you I was going to end up with the Raiders." Fen's voice was growly like the wolf he was sometimes. "I don't like him."

She sighed and admitted, "But I do."

Fen bumped her with his whole side. "Yeah, well, I'm *really* your brother now, and it's not just me he'll need to prove himself to. I'll be telling Unc—I mean, *Dad* and our little brother all about your *boyfriend*."

"Of course you will," Laurie muttered. They might have saved the world together, but Fen was still Fen—overprotective and surly. "Well, maybe I should tell them about the crazy stunts you pulled when we were fighting."

Fen laughed. "Like you sending flaming arrows at a frost giant? Or opening a portal to Hel?"

Laurie sighed. "How about we don't tell them any of it, *including* anything about Owen."

For a moment, Fen said nothing. "Fine, but you tell the Cyclops that I'll be keeping both my eyes on him, and I have a pack of wolves ready to release if he even makes you think about being sad."

She hugged him. "I love you, too."

Then she made a note to try to get Matt or Baldwin to talk some sense into Fen. It felt kind of wonderful to only have to think about her small problems instead of the world ending or monsters attacking. Of course, there was no guarantee that the monsters wouldn't come again, but right now, the only crises she was expecting were Fen's attitude and the upcoming math test she was woefully unprepared to take.

Even the pending apocalypse couldn't keep school closed for long. Nor, apparently, did saving the world from that apocalypse earn him a few extra days off.

Matt's phone buzzed as he walked. It was a new phone, courtesy of his parents, who had also bought him the iPad he'd been putting aside money for. Apparently, saving the world did come with a few perks, though he still hadn't been able to talk Mom into the dirt bike. Defeating an eighty-foot dragon was all well and good, but it didn't compare to the dangers of off-road biking. He'd keep working on it. He'd learned a few things about strategy over the last couple of weeks.

He'd also learned a few things about his family, and the mistakes they'd all made. He wasn't going to dwell on that—he just wanted to move on—but they'd talked a lot, him and his parents. They'd talked about Granddad, too, and Matt was still working through that, how he felt. There was grief and there was anger and there was confusion, and maybe someday he'd figure it all out, but that wasn't happening anytime soon.

He'd gotten an e-mail from Astrid that morning, letting

him know she was fine. He wasn't sure how to respond to that. That was another thing Matt was still working out. Astrid had ultimately done the right thing, but he couldn't forget that she'd killed Baldwin.

Luckily, the text was from someone he could easily respond to. Reyna was reminding him that Ray had invited him to Deadwood for a historical festival next month. Matt had a feeling the invitation didn't really come from Ray, but he wasn't questioning it. It was easier to explain to his parents that Ray invited him, and they'd agreed that a weekend away with his new friend seemed like a fine idea. They wanted to meet the twins' parents. Not exactly what Matt had in mind, but how bad could it be? Maybe he shouldn't ask that. The last time he did, his "serpent" turned out to be a fire-breathing, poison-spitting dragon.

Matt chuckled to himself and texted Reyna back, telling her what his parents had said. They were still texting as Matt stopped on the corner. Kids passed and waved and called hello. A couple of his distant cousins stopped, as if wanting to walk to school with the "champion," and Matt chatted, but he stayed where he was. Then he saw who he was waiting for. Laurie and Fen. Laurie was weighed down by her book bag, and Fen was trudging along, trying to look as if he was being dragged every step of the way.

Matt sent a final text to Reyna, called "Hey!" and ran to catch up with Laurie and Fen.

MORTAL HEROES.
IMMORTAL ADVENTURES.

K. L. ARMSTRONG & M. A. MARR

LOKI'S WOLVES

"Norse mythology brought to life...ideal for Percy Jackson fans."
—*Kirkus Reviews*

THE BLACKWELL PAGES

K. L. ARMSTRONG & M. A. MARR

ODIN'S RAVENS

When Thor is in the family, the pressure to save the world hits you like a hammer.

THE BLACKWELL PAGES

K. L. ARMSTRONG & M. A. MARR

THOR'S SERPENTS

Norse gods. Mythical monsters. Epic adventure.

THE BLACKWELL PAGES

Fantasy, adventure, and Norse mythology collide in this heart-pounding series from two *New York Times* bestselling authors.